CHARLIE MAC

By Maria McDonald

A KILDARE woman has delved into her own family history for a new book telling a true tale of love across the sectarian divide in Ireland a century ago.

Maria McDonald, who lives in Newbridge, County Kildare, has written the true story of her great-grandfather, "Charlie Mac," a Protestant from East Belfast, who married Mary Jane, a Catholic from rural Co Down. Charlie's life began with the hope of the Home Rule era in the last quarter of the 19th Century, and was ended abruptly by sectarian murderers, just as partition and the creation of a new southern state became a reality in 1922.

This book began with the writer researching her family history and grew into a family memoir. But the story also has resonance for her own immediate family experience, as her own parents, Ernie and Mary McMullen, felt obliged to leave their native Belfast in September 1976, as the day-to-day reality of the Troubles descended into a vortex of sectarian violence.

The McMullens built a new life in Kildare, becoming immersed in sport and social activities in their adopted home town of Newbridge. But they maintained contact with family north of the border up to the present day and Maria remained acutely aware of their family story.

The author has subtitled her book "A story of ordinary people who lived in extraordinary times." The self-published book – "Charlie Mac" – offers a chunk of Ireland's recent history in an engaging tale of ordinary people facing the realities of the troubled times in which they lived. It takes Irish history out of the textbooks and into the kitchens and workplaces of everyday life.

Dedicated to my Dad

Ernie McMullen the 2nd

Contents

Chapter 1 February 1922

Charlie sipped his tea, the only sound the tick-tock of the mantel clock and the hiss of the fire. The peace and quiet was shattered by a cacophony of noise on the street outside. With a deafening bang the front door burst off its hinges, scattering glass and splinters into the room. Hobnail boots crunched the remnants into the polished linoleum and the shouting reached a crescendo.

"Fenian lover"

"Traitor."

Gunshots reverberated around the house, ricocheting off the walls and pinging as they hit furniture and flesh. The sulphur hung in the air and the acrid taste burned in the throats of gunmen and victim alike. Mary-Jane froze, her hands over her ears. Ernie ran out of the scullery into the front room just in time to see the two gunmen charging out into the street over the remnants of the front door shouting incoherently. Ernie started to run after them, but his mother's screams stopped him, "Charlie..."

Silence descended as Charlie slumped in his chair as if in slow motion. Mary-Jane winced as she felt the impact of his cup when it hit the hearth and shattered, great goblets of dark tea dancing over the floor. They could hear Mamie tearing down the stairs, but Ernie turned and caught her, directing her outside, "Run, get help." Mamie ran, without looking left or right, through the ruins of the front door and out into the street screaming. Alice from next door came running towards her while young Jimmy from the other side of the street ran to get an ambulance.

Mary-Jane felt like her world was invaded by a thick fog, she watched Mamie run out through what was left of the front door, she watched Ernie run to his father's aid calling out his name, but Mary-Jane stood motionless with her hands over her ears. She felt like she was screaming but no sound came out. All she could hear was a rushing sound in her head like the waves of the sea breaking on the shore in her native county Down as Charlie, her beloved Charlie, gasped for breath, his blood dripping onto the floor. The sounds of her neighbours running and screaming all seemed to be miles away as she watched Ernie trying to find his father's pulse.

Charlie's large, workman's hands flailing as Ernie tried to lift his father out of his chair. Alice ran into the room and Mary-Jane heard her gasp of shock.

"Ah Mary-Jane love, what have they done," she exclaimed as she wrapped her arms around her friend. Mary-Jane remained rooted to the spot. Unfeeling, unthinking, unable to take in what was unfolding before her. Ernie nursed his dad in his arms as he waited and prayed for help. Charlie was unconscious, his head nodded against his son's broad shoulders, his arms flopped by his side and the blood poured from his body.

Many years later, when Mary-Jane recounted the event to her grandchildren, she said she had a premonition that something was different that day. The day started normally. Every household on their street followed the same Saturday routine, the women scrubbed their homes while the men finished out the working week with a half day's work and then a hot bath in front of the fire on their return home in preparation for the Sabbath. Most of the people on Sherwood Street left their houses every Sunday morning to attend church services on the Shankill Road. Mary-Jane and her children parted company with their neighbours at the bottom of their street and went towards Ballymacarrett to St. Matthew's Catholic Church.

That fateful Saturday Charlie was ill and unable to go to work. By mid-afternoon Charlie dozed in his armchair on the left-hand side of the fire, Mary-Jane peeked around the door at him, a worried frown on her face as she noted his colour and beads of sweat on his forehead. Ever since the flu epidemic a few years ago, she worried when any of her brood sneezed let alone showed symptoms like Charlie had. The Spanish flu had killed more people than the Great War. Alice's daughter had succumbed to the flu, while Mary-Jane's eldest son James had been injured in France during the Great War. Mary-Jane counted her blessings that at least she still had her son, but poor Alice grieved every day for her daughter.

Mary-Jane had brewed a fresh cup of tea and brought it into Charlie along with a plate containing a piece of fresh soda, warm from the griddle with creamy butter melting and sliding off the side of the bread forming a buttery puddle. Charlie had straightened up in his armchair,

"Thanks love, that looks delicious," Charlie sank his teeth into the warm bread and sipped the strong tea, "lovely Mary-Jane, sit with me and have a cuppa."

"Give me a minute Charlie, I've more sodas on the griddle, when they're done I'll make myself a cup and come back into sit with you."

At that Mary-Jane went back to the scullery to see to her bread and to put on the kettle for more hot water for young Ernie's bath. He was due in shortly. Seconds after Ernie walked in the back door, Mary-Jane heard the ruckus at the front of the house. She grabbed Ernie's arm and tried to push him back out, terror etched into her face.

"There's someone hammering at the front door. Run, Ernie, get out of here."

The crash of the front door coming off its hinges in pieces stopped them both. Mary-Jane felt her heart miss a beat then jumped as the crack of each shot jangled her nerve endings. Ernie pushed past her and ran to the front room. She followed her son, her heart beating in her throat. The other noises receded into the background as she saw her beloved Charlie slump in his chair. She remembered she had screamed out his name. She remembered Alice wrapping her in her arms. She remembered Alice leading her out of the house to the waiting ambulance and she remembered the thought that struck her. They had lived in Sherwood Street for nearly thirty years. They had raised their family side by side in those narrow, terraced streets with their neighbours. But when Charlie was shot, only Alice from next door came to their aid.

The other neighbours gathered outside in the street, their voices lowered, their expressions cowered, for they knew that to sympathise could mean the same treatment for them. They all agreed that Charlie was a good sort, a hard worker and a family man, that Mary-Jane was a great wife and mother and the best neighbour anyone could wish for but then came the 'but'. Charlie had married a Catholic woman and his children were Catholic. It was silently acknowledged that the McMullens had no place in Sherwood Street. As Mary-Jane followed Charlie's limp body out of their home she never looked back, she couldn't. She couldn't look at Charlie's blood on the chair and on the floor. The crowd parted to allow them access to the ambulance and she could hear the whispers.

"They were shouting Fenian lover,"

"I heard the shooting, God bless us, what's to become of us all."

Several women reached out and patted Mary-Jane sympathetically on the arm as she passed, but Mary-Jane could not look anywhere but in front of her at her beloved Charlie, her mind in turmoil, wondering how their lives had come to this point.

CHAPTER 2 CHARLIE FROM BELFAST 1893

Charlie crept into the house under cover of darkness. He eased the bedroom door open gently, groaning as it creaked. He crept into the room on all fours hoping not to wake anyone especially his father whose gentle snoring could be heard through the ceiling.

He slid into bed, lay on his back with his hands behind his head, and smiled broadly in the darkness, for Charlie was in love. He had met Mary-Jane only a few weeks ago and just couldn't keep away. He finally drifted off to sleep thinking of her smile and the way it lit up her face, her sweetheart mouth and soft lips.

Charlie woke early the next morning and stoked the fire ready for his mother to prepare breakfast. He usually met his uncle and his cousin Michael at the end of the street to go into work together at the corporation yard. The families were close, meeting up in each other's homes on Saturday nights for a game of cards, a bottle of stout and debates, when the family would put the world to rights. The McMullens took pride in their city and Charlie enjoyed listening to the older relatives discussing the good old days.

Their last discussion was over an article his Da had read in the newspaper

"It says Belfast is likely to pass Dublin out as the largest city in Ireland," Thomas said.

"Sure, we all know Belfast is far superior to Dublin." Gerard said, as everyone nodded in agreement, "Sure look at Harland and Wolff, there's no industry like that around Dublin. Look at the linen mills, sure Belfast linen is famous the world over."

Charlie listened and thought that the prosperity brought its own problems. He had heard the men in work talk about a housing shortage and large-scale poverty and he said as much to Thomas.

'Sure, of course, there are problems, but I tell you now, compared to years ago, we are lucky to live in such a prosperous city. Long may it last."

"Yea but Da, think how prosperous this city could be if we didn't have this violence. As far back as I can remember there are people killed every summer around the 12th July marches. Why do the Orange Order persist with them and why do the Fenians hate them so much. The Battle of the Boyne was over two hundred years ago. Surely it's time to come to some sort of compromise."

"Och it's not just that son. It's this Home Rule campaign. The nationalists want Home Rule. Think about it. Self-government for Ireland. No more dictates issued by London. We would have our own representation in our own parliament. Not just a few voices shouting to be heard against every other part of the British Empire. But the Unionists don't want it, they think that Home Rule would put them at a disadvantage and could possibly lead to Ireland breaking away altogether from the empire. And they are entitled to their opinion son, don't get me wrong. But you're right, no one should die over it."

Charlie nodded in agreement. Most of his workmates and neighbours were firmly in the no camp, thinking that Home Rule meant Rome Rule. Charlie was brought up in a Protestant neighbourhood, a mixture of Presbyterian and Anglican. In his neighbourhood, there was a real fear that the 'Fenians' would be granted Home Rule and the country would end up ruled by the Catholic Church. So, every summer violence would erupt, bricks and stones and all sorts of debris were scattered the length and breadth of the city streets. Then the inevitable onset of colder, darker days put an end to the mayhem for another year.

Charlie and Michael skipped through the door at the depot just as the clock struck the hour. "You two cut it fine, join your team straight away, you are doing road repairs this week, more trouble last night and the stupid buggers have pulled up half the cobbles we put down last week," Philip barked, shaking his head at the sheer nonsense of it. "Do they think we have nothing better to do than repair what they wreck only for them to wreck it again, that road will never be finished at this rate."

Most of the men mumbled their agreement, with others offering loud opinions as to what the authorities should do to prevent the trouble to anyone who would listen. The murmur of voices rose as the men separated into their teams for the day ahead. Charlie and Michael were on the same team. Six men, all of them older and all of them knew the McMullen family well. Charlie's exuberant mood wasn't lost on them.

"Has to be a female," remarked Mark, "only a girl can put that smile on a young man's face at this hour of the morning."

All the men laughed, and Charlie felt his face burning up as the good-natured ribbing continued.

"Come on lad, give us a name." They all took turns at winding Charlie up and kept it up for the rest of the day. Charlie said nothing, just smiled enigmatically.

The team quickly loaded the cart with materials and made their way downtown all the while chatting back and forth. The August weather was fine and dry. They made good time and got straight into the backbreaking job of gathering all the loose cobbles that had been pulled up during the rioting, gradually starting the job of laying them all again. By the end of the day, every man felt the ache in his back and shoulders that only hard, manual labour can inflict, and they were all quite happy to knock off and head home.

"Good night lads, good days work today, same again tomorrow," shouted Mark, the foreman, "And you, Charlie, leave that poor lass alone tonight and get some sleep," which started a barrage of teasing from the others. Charlie waved off their comments and left taking it all in the spirit intended and laughingly refusing to comment or reply.

He parted with Michael at the corner as he turned into his street and walked into Maggie, herself on her way home from work. Like most of her peers, Maggie worked in one of the linen mills. "Hard day sis?" Charlie asked as she linked her arm through his.

"The usual. Did you hear John Pettigrew and Sarah got engaged? There'll soon be no single women left in that mill. I'm beginning to think Granny's right that I'm going to be left on the shelf at the ripe old age of nineteen."

Charlie laughed out loud, "Don't mind Granny, you just haven't met anyone good enough for you yet, your day will come."

Maggie and Charlie could both turn heads. They looked like twins, both dark and tall and both with open sunny smiles which infected everyone around them. The two of them linked arms and strolled home in the rare August sunshine hailing their neighbours as they passed.

3 MARY-JANE MOVES TO BELFAST 1893

Mary-Jane had been apprehensive at first about moving to Belfast but now she was enjoying life in the big city. Annalong was such a small village where everybody knew everyone's business. Belfast was huge in comparison and still growing rapidly. Her aunt had recommended the lodgings in Rosetta Park in Belfast to Mary-Jane and reassured Mary and James that their daughter would be safe there. Sitting serenely on a long tree lined avenue, it was a large house, spotlessly clean and ran with military precision by its owner. A formidable woman, Mrs Best had been widowed at a young age and never had children nor did she appear to have any family or, so it seemed to her boarders, mainly female, who came to the city in search of work in the linen mills. She interviewed her potential boarders and was careful about who she allowed into her home. Mrs Best provided clean comfortable rooms, breakfast and an evening meal of a standard that many top hotels could not match in terms of quality.

Mary-Jane had the utmost respect for Mrs Best. She enjoyed living there and enjoyed the company of the other women. Mrs Best herself presided over the evening dinner table. She facilitated conversation over their evening and a wide range of subjects was discussed. Mary-Jane felt that she learned more during those dinners than she did during all her years at school. The women who boarded there came from all walks of life and each brought different experiences to the table.

"Now ladies, we have a new dinner companion this evening, may I introduce Mary-Jane O'Brien." Mary-Jane nodded at her companions.

"How do you do? I'm Agnes." A slight dark-haired girl sitting beside her offered her hand. "Hello, I'm Kate, I'm from Ballinderry, you'll find Agnes is not much of a talker but the rest of us make up for that," she laughed, and a ripple of laughter twirled around the table.

"Kate is the chatterbox, no-one else gets a word in. I'm Louisa, by the way, and nearly as much of a chatterbox as Kate," Louisa nodded to Mary-Jane.

One by one the girls introduced themselves, Emma, Betty, Cecelia, Jean, all eager to make her feel welcome. Mary-Jane quickly settled into her new accommodation and become friends with all her co-lodgers, but her best friend was a co-worker at the mill. Mary-Jane had met Emily on her first day at the Mill. It was Emily's first day as well and they literally bumped into each other on the pavement outside the gates. Emily's father had escorted her part of the way to work, parting at the corner of the street. Emily had turned back to wave an acknowledgement to her father's 'good luck' and walked backwards into Mary-Jane, who was staring apprehensively at the mill gates. They both collided, and both exclaimed "sorry, sorry, my fault" at the exact same time, then both started to laugh and chatter like old friends. Emily was a Belfast native and when she realised that Mary-Jane was from outside the city she quickly took her under her wing.

"You will get used to us city folk soon enough, Mary-Jane. You were lucky finding work here. It is one of the better mills."

"Have you worked here long," Mary-Jane asked her new friend.

Emily laughed, "I'm starting today. But my Ma and my sisters all worked here at some stage or another and sure I know most of the women working here. If you are going to work in the mills this is one of the better ones. The pay is good, the hours are regular, and they treat us right."

On Saturdays work finished at 2 pm and didn't start again until 7 am the following Monday. Once a month after work on Saturday afternoon Mary-Jane took the train to Newcastle and headed home to visit her family. She brought treats for her brothers and spent Saturday night playing with them and catching up with her sisters and her parents. Sunday mornings she attended mass with the family and then after Sunday lunch she would start the commute back to the city, spending Sunday evening preparing for the week ahead. She missed her family and really looked forward to those monthly visits.

Emily was always asking her to go out with her circle of friends. Mary-Jane refused at first but eventually, she became bored spending so many Saturday nights alone and decided it was time to widen her horizons. Emily suggested a dance that was being held in the local church hall the last Saturday of the month. It was well supervised, and Mrs Best had encouraged her lodgers to attend.

"Your friend is quite right Mary-Jane, you need to meet more people your own age and with Emily with you to introduce you to others you will surely have some fun," Mrs Best had gently scolded. Mrs Best had met Emily on several occasions and had told Mary-Jane that she thought Emily was "a good sort, from a good family, with a really pleasant disposition," and she actively encouraged Mary-Jane to get to know Emily's circle of friends. Emily was delighted when Mary-Jane said she would go to the dance and shared the news with her sisters Susie and Mabel and her brother Michael.

The following Saturday Emily and Mary-Jane literally ran out of the mill when the whistle sounded at 2 pm. Mrs Best had hot water ready for Mary-Jane as soon as she got in so that she could bath and wash her hair. She spent all afternoon getting herself ready for the dance. Mrs Best had thoughtfully pressed Mary-Jane's best dress, a beautiful creation, in a pale green coloured fabric, designed by her sister Bridget. It had a sweetheart neckline with a fitted bodice which flared out to a full skirt finished with an extra frill around the hem that rippled around her ankles as she moved. She brushed her hair until it shone and piled it high on her head, held in place with some silver pins and matching green ribbons. Seven o'clock finally arrived and Mary-Jane started down the stairs to greet Emily when she arrived to meet her.

"You look like a picture Mary-Jane," Mrs Best exclaimed, "You will be the belle of the ball. Your sister Bridget is seriously talented. That dress is beautiful." Embarrassed by the attention, Mary-Jane blushed but was saved by the arrival of Emily and Michael.

"You look wonderful Emily, very handsome," Mrs Best complimented Emily. "I trust you will look after these two young ladies and ensure they have a lovely evening?" Mrs Best enquired of Michael.

"But of course, Mrs Best," Michael replied, "I am honoured to escort these two beautiful women to the dance and will guard them with my life." He crooked both arms and offered one to each woman. They laughingly accepted as Mrs Best watched with a soft smile on her face and a friendly wave as they turned onto the street "Have fun ladies, see you later."

On arrival at the church hall, they stood in the foyer to remove their outer clothing. Emily and Mary-Jane were standing with the entrance behind them when they heard Charlie shout a greeting,

"Hello Michael, got here before you, Hello Emily, what about you?"

Emily turned to greet Charlie with a ready smile. Charlie was their cousin and the similarities between Michael and Charlie were obvious. Both were handsome men, tall with dark hair and eyes that sparkled with mischief.

"Hello Charlie, Mary-Jane, meet Charlie, I've told you about him."

Formal introductions completed Charlie lifted Mary-Janes hand to his lips and kissed it gently, "Enchanted, Mary-Jane, so good to meet you."

He held onto Mary-Jane's hand and she had to gently tug her hand out of his,

"I am very well Charlie, nice to meet you," she replied. Emily noted the spark between them. Michael noticed it as well and was slightly nonplussed.

"Mary-Jane, allow me to escort you inside," he deftly took Mary-Jane's arm and gently guided her through into the dance hall.

Mary-Jane had the time of her life. She never left the dance floor. She danced with either Michael or Charlie all night making mental notes to thank her father for the impromptu dance lessons he had given her and her sisters when they were younger. She had wonderful memories of her whole family dancing under the stars on warm summer evenings. The sound of music still automatically made her break into a smile and tap her feet in time to the music. That night was no exception and her smile was infectious. Both men appeared to be vying for her attention and she was immensely flattered. During one short break for refreshments, Emily and her sisters teased her, comparing the two young men to puppies vying for their master's attention. Mary-Jane blushed before admitting to having the time of her life. All too soon the music stopped, the night was over, and it was time for home. Mary-Jane faced a dilemma. Both Michael and Charlie offered to walk her home and she did not want to make a choice between them. Michael made the decision for her.

"I promised Mrs Best that I would look after you. It would be remiss of me not to escort you home. You, Charlie, are of course welcome to join us."

They all agreed and set off together and before long were in Rosetta Park, "Good night gentlemen," Mary-Jane said, "thank you so much for a wonderful evening, I really enjoyed it."

At that, she turned and ran up the steps to the front door.

"Goodnight gentlemen, goodnight Emily," Mary-Jane waved from the doorstep before disappearing inside.

Mary-Jane found it hard to get to sleep. She was so happy. She had so much fun. She loved to dance, and Charlie was a great dancer. Not that Michael was a bad dancer, he was a lovely young man but there was something about Charlie. She pictured his face and his sparkly mischievous eyes, and then she pictured his lips and wondered what they would feel like on hers. Stop, she thought, what would your mother think? Eventually, she fell asleep dreaming of Charlie, of dancing with Charlie, of walking with Charlie and kissing with Charlie.

The next day Mrs Best was keen to know all the details and Mary-Jane felt her cheeks flush as she talked about her dance partners.

"Tell me more about this Charlie," Mrs Best said.

Mary-Jane told her everything she knew, happy to talk about him. Later that day Mary-Jane was in her room preparing her clothes for the week ahead when Mrs Best knocked on her door.

"Your young man is here Mary-Jane."

Mary-Jane opened the door, surprised "whatever do you mean?"

Mrs Best closed the door behind her and sat down.

"Your young man, Charlie McMullen is downstairs in my parlour. He introduced himself then he asked me, in lieu of your father of course, for my permission to call on you. I must say I am very impressed. He is a perfect gentleman," Mrs Best told Mary-Jane.

Mary-Jane was dumbfounded. "I presume I was correct in giving him permission Mary-Jane, I can withdraw that permission if you prefer," Mary-noted a hint of puzzlement in Mrs Best's voice.

"Oh no, Mrs Best, that is fine, perfectly fine," replied Mary-Jane.

She checked her reflection in her dressing table mirror and tried to subdue the delight evident in her eyes. Both ladies retreated downstairs to the parlour and Charlie rose from his seat when they entered the room.

Mary-Jane hung back for a minute trying to regain her composure. The sight of Charlie had thrown her off kilter and she felt her heart miss a beat. She was aware of her flushed cheeks and shallow breathing and certainly did not want him to notice anything amiss. Charlie looked so handsome. His face lit up when he saw her,

"Hello Mary-Jane,"

"Hello Charlie, good to see you."

With that Charlie was at her side with his hand on her elbow guiding her to a seat. She was delighted she had decided to wear the cream lace dress today to Mass. She knew the colour complimented her and she looked good in it. Charlie seemed to think so, she could tell from the admiring glances he kept sneaking.

"Can I get you some tea Charlie?" enquired Mrs Best,

"That would be lovely Mrs Best," replied Charlie.

Mrs Best rang the little bell on the side table and her maid Agatha appeared in the doorway. Mrs Best gave her instructions to which she nodded and curtsied politely, then left the room only to reappear some twenty minutes later with a silver tray laden with fine china. They had tea and a selection of Mrs Bests' delicious cakes in the parlour and talked about the dance the previous night. Charlie told Mary-Jane about his family and their home in Knockbreda and Mary-Jane told Charlie about her family, her sisters, her brothers and their affliction and her family home in Annalong. All under the watchful eye of Mrs Best. Before long it was time for Charlie to leave and they arranged to meet again the following Saturday evening. Mary-Jane retired to bed that evening with a lightness in her step and hopeful anticipation for the days ahead

CHAPTER 4 THE O'BRIENS OF ANNALONG

Mary O'Brien stood at her front gate looking up towards Slieve Donard, waiting on her husband James returning from work. The light was just beginning to fade on what had been a bright spring day. The light from the fire spilt out from the window into the yard, casting shadows that leapt and danced in tune with the flames on the fire. Now in her mid-forties, Mary was still a fine-looking woman. Her figure was fuller now than it was in her youth, but she was still in good shape thanks in no small way to the sheer hard work and effort it took to look after her family and manage their small-holding almost single-handedly. Her dark auburn hair was tied up loosely at the base of her neck and she had just pulled her shawl over her shoulders allowing the cool sea air to tease her hair and wipe some strands loose. She still wore her apron, stained now from her efforts over the stove preparing the family's evening meal.

The Mourne Mountains soared high above their home, dark, imposing and majestic. Their local village, Annalong was just eight miles down the coast from Newcastle. Granite from the Mournes was much in demand and they earned a good living from it. With six mouths to feed in addition to themselves and a small farm, well, a smallholding really, they would not have survived without the quarry work. They wanted a better way of life for their children and the extra income made a big difference. The O'Brien's small-holding was too small and rocky to feed a family of eight but large enough for Mary to keep chickens for eggs and for eating, some dairy cows for milk for the family and some sheep on the upper slopes.

Mary was an excellent cook and she had passed on her skills to her daughters. But Mary didn't only teach her daughters to cook, she taught them skills she felt they needed to become good wives and mothers; she taught them respect for their elders and she taught them how to care for those who cannot care for themselves. Mary sighed as she thought about her sons. All the girls treated their brothers with the utmost respect. They understood their brother's disability and loved them more because of it. The girls were finished school now and all were employed. The boys, of course, had no trade and never would have. They never learned to read or write.

Their poor little minds could not absorb knowledge and they existed in their own happy little world without ambitions or worries. The O'Brien name would die with her husband James when the time came. That fact weighed heavily on James and Mary at times. Although Mary knew that the girls would never abandon their brothers and there would always be someone to look after them when their parents were gone to their maker, she still worried about the burden they were placing on their offspring. Not that the girls ever considered their brothers a burden.

Mary worried about the boys but, she reminded herself, at least they were able to look after themselves up to a point and were able to complete menial tasks around the farm. Sure, only for them she would never manage. They may have the minds of children locked in adult bodies, but they were happy souls and they shared that happiness with the rest of the family. All she needed now was to get the girls married and set up in life. The two oldest were now in their twenties and it was time they were settled and no longer their father's responsibility.

The O'Briens made a decent living, enough to allow the odd day trip into Newcastle. The Belfast and County Down Railway operated a regular rail service from Belfast to Newcastle bringing thousands of holidaymakers out of the city and into the picturesque seaside resort. On a good summers day, the main promenade was thronged with people taking the sea air. Children frolicked on the beach, paddled in the sea, built sand castles, and played ball while their parents chattered and enjoyed a rare few hours of pure relaxation. It was one such day towards the end of the July holiday season when the O'Briens decided to travel to Newcastle on a rare family day out. Mary-Jane was taking the train from Belfast and Susan had the afternoon off and was meeting them at the train station. The weather for the few weeks previous had been miserable even by Irish standards with drizzly rain every day, the type of rain that seeps into your pores and wets you through to the bone. They were all relieved to see the sun make a welcome return and it was a glorious day, the sun sizzled in a deep blue sky without a suggestion of a cloud on the horizon.

James and Mary settled the boys into the cart and made good time into Newcastle. There were hugs and kisses and screams of delight when they all met up with Mary-Jane and Susan. The boys were delighted to see their older sisters and were extremely vocal in letting them know they were missed. When they all eventually settled down they sat on the seawall and exchanged news. Mary-Jane was full of stories about her life in the big city and the boys were fascinated when she told them all about the train journey to Newcastle. Susan regaled them all with stories from the big house and life as a lady's maid. Bridget showed her sisters her latest creation, the beautiful dress she was wearing, and both begged her to design them new dresses for the winter. An hour later Mary and her daughters were still talking and laughing but the two boys were getting bored.

"Stop! I have some errands to run," said Mary, "and your brothers want to go on the swing-boats."

So, they split up, with the girls heading for a walk down the promenade. They arranged to meet back at the cart in two hours to sample the picnic lunch Mary had prepared earlier in the day.

"Great," thought Mary, "that gives me time to pick up some little extras for the picnic," ticking off in her head what she had packed; fresh milk, bread still warm from the oven, her own butter and cheese from her store cupboard along with the last of the pickles and apples from the orchard. She had promised her two lads a go on the swing-boats, so before she would look around the shops she and James would bring them to the amusements on the main promenade and spend an hour there. She could leave James with them then to ramble along the length of the promenade while she made her purchases.

The girls all loved Newcastle and loved to walk the length of the promenade especially on a beautiful sunny summer's day. They set off with their father's dire warnings about not talking to strangers washing completely over them. Mary-Jane was 22, a beauty with long strawberry blonde hair, green eyes and a quick and ready smile. Susan was just 11 months younger and many mistook them for twins. They both had lots of male admirers and lots of offers and were enjoying the attention despite the grave warnings from their mother that they were getting on and needed to settle down. Their Grandmother was in agreement with their mother "Before you know it you will be too old and will be left on the shelf." Bridget and Maggie were 19 and 17 and idolised their older sisters. Bridget was the fairest of the sisters with light brown hair and pale skin while Maggie's auburn mane and freckled skin matched perfectly with her green eyes. Together the O'Brien sisters created quite a spectacle on the Newcastle promenade attracting admiring glances from the many young men who loitered along the promenade sipping lemonades. The girls headed straight for the promenade where they parted company with their mother and walked its length chattering, enjoying the sunshine and flirting with the many admirers. It was a perfect summer's day; the sun was beating down on the sand from a clear blue sky and the faint breeze from the water kept everyone from overheating. Mary O'Brien enjoyed the spectacle walking along in a world of her own. She was startled into laughter when the girls swooped on her as she left the greengrocers. They each took a package from her to lighten her load and they chattered happily all the way back to meet the boys.

As they approached Mary noticed James watching their return, a look of sheer pride on his face. "The beautiful O'Brien women," he said as he bowed a welcome to his wife and daughters.

"Our daughters are the belles of the county," Mary said.

"Yes, but they take their good looks after their mother," James said, "For she is a fine-looking woman." Mary blushed as her daughters laughed. James kissed his wife lightly on the cheek and took her basket from her.

"Now what about some of that food?" he asked.

The boys, Will and Jimmy, were noisy and boisterous, both wanting their mother's attention so that they could tell her about the fun they'd had in the swing-boats. Mary and the girls set out the picnic and before long they were all feasting on soda bread, eggs, cheese, apples and preserves washed down with lemonade. The long walk and the sea air had given everyone an appetite and silence reigned for a short time while they ate their fill.

But all too soon the time had come to pack up and head home. James and Mary had to get back before darkness closed in and the boys were starting to get tired. They would sleep in the cart on the way home with Bridget and Maggie beside them to hold their hands and soothe them, all the excitement of the day trip had worn them out and they were starting to get fractious. Susan had some more time to spare and was going to wait with Mary-Jane on the last train back to the city before returning to the big house. James and Mary issued their usual warnings to their two eldest daughters and then James ushered the remainder of his family onto the cart and they set off on their journey home. Will and Jimmy waved at Mary-Jane and Susan who stood waving back until the cart moved out of sight around the coastline.

It was a long and uneventful journey home. Mary had a great voice and she sang for part of the journey, with the boys taking turns joining in. When they paused for breath, James sang, his rich baritone voice carrying forward on the gentle sea breeze into the path ahead. Mary loved to hear him sing and felt the warmth of his voice wash over her like waters in a warm bath. She looked around her at her family and thanked God for her blessings. When they arrived home she quickly lit the fire that she had set before they left and lit the lamps. The house was cosy in minutes. Bridget and Maggie quickly and deftly dealt with the aftermath of the picnic while Mary set to work on the evening meal. James fed the donkey and put away the cart. He had to milk the cows before supper and he called Will and Jimmy to help. They were wound up after their day out and even though they had slept on the way home they were tired. Nonetheless, they had their chores to complete so wordlessly they all set about their tasks and before long dinner was ready. Normally mealtimes were noisy affairs with each of them chatting about their day but not that evening. They were all tired but happy after the exertions of the day and ready for sleep. After the children retired Mary and James sat at the hearth, in the light of the fire, reflecting on the day.

"Mary-Jane seems to have settled into the city quite well. Although I'm not sure about this Charlie calling on her," mused Mary,

"Mary-Jane is right, it's early days yet. He has only called on her twice and both times Mrs Best was present," replied James, "and Susan seems to be enjoying life in the big house judging by the stories she was telling us today. Isn't it great to see them both happy, although I would be happier if they both settled down."

"Och sure I know, love, but they will. Give it time," said Mary, "Sure you remember wee Sean, Tom Maddens lad, he is always asking after our Mary-Jane, I'd rather she was seeing him than a stranger from Belfast, and as for Susan, did you notice how often she mentioned the footman."

"aye I did," said James, "she actually blushed when I asked her if he was a handsome young man and if he would make a good husband."

"All in good time James, all in good time, they are enjoying their lives at the minute so let them be for now. If marriage is meant for them it will come to them, all in good time."

CHAPTER 5
THE MCMULLENS OF TEUTONIC STREET 1893

Margaret watched as Thomas stoked the fire sending embers exploding into the darkness and falling back down like a miniature meteorite shower. His eyes were creased with a black frown under grey bushy eyebrows as he wondered aloud where Charlie had got too.

"That lad should have been back. He has his work to go to in the morning, Maggie do you know where he went tonight?" he queried his daughter. Maggie was just about to go upstairs to bed and hesitated for only a second.

"No Da, he didn't say, goodnight," and swiftly took the stairs two at a time before her Da could ask any more questions.

Her mother Margaret just smiled, "goodnight, Maggie." She had no doubt that Charlie had told Maggie exactly where he was going and who he was going to see but had sworn her to secrecy. Charlie and Maggie were very close and not only in age, "No doubt she knows well where he is," thought Margaret but decided not to share that with Thomas for the moment. Turning her attention to her husband, "He's young, Thomas, he will be back for work, don't fret." The light from the dying embers of the fire shed a warm glow over the room and threw deep shadows into the corners. The only other light was from a candle on the table beside Margaret where she sat darning socks, her eyes straining in the poor light.

"Now, finished for tonight," she turned and smiled at Thomas. Tall and thin as a rake with a shock of silver grey hair, Thomas was the love of her life. Twenty-three years of marriage and nine children later Maggie still felt a warm glow when she looked at him. But not tonight, his frown emphasised the lines around his eyes and tiredness dulled the sparkle normally present in his dark eyes. "Probably some girl has taken his eye, I will ask around, the neighbours are bound to know who she is. Let's get to bed Thomas, leave the door on the latch for Charlie, I'm sure he will be home shortly." Thomas shrugged and agreed before stubbing out the candle and following his wife upstairs.

Their room was at the top of the stairs, more of a box room really but big enough to accommodate their small double and a bassinet for the baby, a constant piece of necessary furniture in their room for the last twenty years. Their eldest boy Charlie, was the first to inhabit the bassinet, followed ten months later by Maggie. Their four daughters were in the back bedroom sharing one large double bed sleeping two up two down, while the four boys were downstairs in the room off the scullery. Tom, the baby and she swore her last one at that, was gone two but Maggie was reluctant to move him down to the boy's room where her older sons Charlie, Randal, Ernie and John already shared a bed.

"Time enough," she mused "sure the older ones will be getting married and out from under our feet shortly and there will be plenty of room for baby Thomas then." She dampened the wick and lay down beside her husband who was already snoring gently beside her, the exhaustion of a long day's physical labour, sending him off to sleep as soon as his head hit the pillow. Margaret heard Charlie creep into the house shortly afterwards and closed her eyes breathing out a sigh of relief to have all her offspring at home in their beds.

The following morning Margaret thought she was the first to rise so was surprised to see her firstborn raking the fire and setting it for the breakfast when she came into the front room. "Morning ma, going to be another fine day," he greeted her with a wink. Margaret started the porridge while Charlie got himself ready for work. The rest of the family started making an appearance one by one and by the time Margaret had the porridge ready they were all at the table. Charlie had a quick bite to eat while his Mam wrapped up some soda bread and butter to take with him for his lunch that day. "Bye love, see you this evening," she called as Charlie headed out the door whistling as he marched down the street to work, meeting up with his uncle Gerard and cousin Michael near the junction on the main road. Margaret bustled around, organising her brood for their day before sitting with a cup of tea and her thoughts. Her eldest son always brought a smile to Margaret's face. He was so full of life and energy; always had been since the day he was born. Bold as brass of course, but not in a bad way. The dark eyes he had inherited from his father twinkled with sheer delight and devilment from the moment he rose until he put his head down at night. He had been a happy child that had grown into a happy, cheerful young man, who embraced life to the fullest and raised the spirits of everyone around him. Tall and lithe like his father, Charlie was handsome in a rugged sort of way, with sallow skin, shiny black hair and eyes framed with long dark lashes that any woman would die for. A yelp from baby Thomas shifted Margaret out of her reverie and she smiled at her youngest as she lifted him up to change him.

Her day's chores kept her busy and before she knew it was time to prepare the evening meal. Thomas sat at the table after washing his hands in the scullery,

Randal and Ernie rushed to do the same, squabbling over who got to wash up first. Annie and Lily set the table for the family while John played with Tommy in the corner out of harm's way. Dinner was always a boisterous affair in the McMullen household. As the youngsters started to work, more money was coming into the house which eased the pressure of feeding such a large family. Although they weren't alone when it came to family size. Nearly every family in their neighbourhood had large families. The McMullens counted themselves as fortunate that their own brood was healthy and happy. With Charlie, Maggie and Randal working and now with Ernie ready to start in Eastwood's scrapyard, life was on the up and looking around, Margaret counted her blessings and thanked the Lord for her good fortune.

CHAPTER 6 THE COURTSHIP

On her next visit home Mary-Jane was all talk about her young man. Mary and James were keen for details.

"What does he do Mary-Jane?" Mary asked her daughter.

Mary-Jane had anticipated their anxiety and was prepared for their questions for even though she knew they trusted her judgment she also knew they worried about her living away from home and away from their influence. They were grateful to hear of Mrs Best's careful supervision.

"I will write a letter to Mrs Best offering our thanks for her kindness James," Mary said and immediately penned a thank you note which she sealed and gave to Mary-Jane to bring back to Belfast with her. They invited Charlie to Annalong to meet them and on the next monthly visit, Charlie accompanied Mary-Jane to Annalong to meet her family. Charlie came prepared with presents, Belfast linen for Mary and James, chocolate for her sisters and best of all a bag of marbles for her brothers. Will and Jimmy were overjoyed and immediately hugged Charlie with such abandon that James had to tell them to put Charlie down. Their joyous approval broke the ice and they all sat down to dinner talking happily.

After that Charlie accompanied Mary-Jane on every monthly visit. Her brothers now treated him as one of the family and he shared their room at the rear of the house, Jimmy gave up his bed for him and slept on a blanket on the floor during Charlie's visits.

"They are great Mary-Jane, they are so much fun to be around."

Mary-Jane brought Charlie for long walks along the seashore or into the foothills of the Mournes. She watched his face as he took in the dramatic scenery.

"I can see why you love going home Mary-Jane. It's a lovely spot." Mary-Jane laughed, Charlie had never been outside of Belfast before but now he was starting to think of Annalong as his home away from home.

Some evenings Charlie would accompany James to the local for a pint. Charlie had been taken aback the first time James had asked him to join him, but Mary-Jane had signalled to him to go and he had enjoyed it.

"It was great, I got to meet all the locals, they were all so welcoming. All full of questions about the city," Charlie told Mary-Jane on his return. On one such evening in early Spring, Charlie and James went down to the local for a pint after the chores of the day were finished. Mary O'Brien was surprised to see Charlie make his way back an hour later and called Mary -Jane. Charlie called to her from the gate.

"Hello, it is a lovely evening out there. Will you join me for a walk?"

Mary-Jane accepted his invitation and donned her coat and hat.

"Won't be long Mam" Mary-Jane called out to her mother as she closed the door behind her.

The salty sea air was refreshing after the heat of the fire. Dusk was fast approaching and the lights from the harbour cast shadows on the quayside. It was low tide and the waves lapped gently against the harbour wall.

Mary-Jane inhaled deeply, "Taste that sea air, Charlie, isn't it just lovely."

Charlie was silent. He stood staring out to sea and Mary-Jane was puzzled. She took his hand, "What is it Charlie, is something wrong?"

Charlie took a deep breath and got down on one knee, "Mary-Jane, will you marry me?" Mary-Jane beamed, "Oh, yes, Charlie, yes."

Charlie whooped and took Mary-Jane in his arms, spinning her around before kissing her on the lips. "You have just made me the happiest man alive." They strolled back to the house arm in arm to tell Mary-Jane's mother the news. "I have already spoken to your father. I asked him for your hand on the way to the pub. He said yes but he was still going for his pint. I couldn't. I had to get back... had to ask you. I love you Mary-Jane." Charlie said as Mary-Jane silenced him with a kiss.

CHAPTER 7 MOTHER'S WORRIES

Mary O'Brien was extremely worried.

"What are we to do?" she asked James. "I know you like Charlie, he is a nice man, I like him myself but let's face it, he is not Catholic. Think about all the problems they are going to have to deal with."

In Mary's eyes, the main problem was religion, the second problem was that he was a Belfast man and they would settle in in the city.

"Mary, a mixed marriage isn't ideal, but Charlie makes Mary-Jane happy. They love each other. They are both strong characters and I have no doubt that if anyone can make a mixed marriage work then they can," James said, "As for the fact that they would live in Belfast, we always knew that the children would more than likely move from Annalong, it's only a small village and the opportunities are in Belfast, especially for the young."

But Mary wasn't convinced. She had so many dreams for her beautiful daughter and marrying a Protestant from East Belfast was not one of those dreams.

"I knew it, James, the first time I saw the two of them together, I knew it," Mary wrung her hands seeing her plans for her daughter's future were in danger. "That Charlie is just too easy on the eye."

Charlie being from the big city added a certain attraction to her daughter, Mary understood that, but why couldn't Mary-Jane feel the same attraction to the local youths, "to Sean, he had been so sweet on her, a hard-worker, and a Catholic," she grumbled. It's not that she had a problem with Protestants, after all, the entire village was predominantly Protestant, she had friends who were Protestants, but mixed marriages bring their unique set of problems. Added to that was the fact that they would live in the city, in Belfast amongst his kind. City living was very different from the village life that Mary-Jane had grown up with. Your religion did not seem to matter as much in country life. People just co-existed and got on with life in Annalong but in Belfast it was different.

"Maybe something to do with living in such close proximity to each other," pondered Mary, "but religious differences seem to be so much more important to city folk." And East Belfast was not only Protestant but Unionist with most of the people totally against the concept of Home Rule for Ireland. The notion of Home Rule was first tentatively raised in the public arena before Mary-Jane had even been born, and since then there had been riots and murders and massive civil unrest particularly in Belfast. Mrs O'Brien feared for her daughter's safety in the big city.

CHAPTER 8 MOTHER'S OBJECTIONS

Charlie's mother Margaret was staunchly Protestant and was vehemently opposed to the wedding.

"Mixed marriages are a bad idea and could only lead to trouble within both families," she said, "I absolutely forbid it, Charlie, you cannot marry this girl."

Charlie told Mary-Jane of his mother's initial objections and Mary-Jane was horrified but Charlie wasn't worried.

"Don't worry my love, we will sort something out, I'm going home now to talk to my mother, she will come around when I make her understand that this will make me happy."

Charlie left her with a smile and wave. Whistling down the street, secure in his own mind that his mother loved him and wanted him to be happy therefore she would agree to his marriage in a Catholic Church because marrying Mary-Jane would make him happy. It seemed simple to Charlie but he hadn't factored in his mother's faith in her church, it simply had not occurred to him that she had such a strong Anglican streak, "more like Presbyterian," he thought.

That night Charlie answered his mother back in anger for the first time in his life. His father stood up out of his chair and ordered him to apologise to his mother, Charlie was immediately chastened and apologised, "I am so sorry ma, really sorry that I have offended you, but please, I do not understand why you are so against me marrying Mary-Jane, I love her, why can't you understand that?"

Margaret looked at her eldest son, her bright-eyed boy, with a heavy heart.

"Oh Charlie, of course I understand, and don't get me wrong Mary-Jane is a lovely girl, but she is wrong for you. She is a Roman Catholic, and I know you say that is not important, but it is. It is very important. Do you realise that they will expect you to convert to the Catholic faith? Do you? Do you realise that they will insist that your children must be brought up in the Catholic faith? Do you? Have you thought this through Charlie?"

Charlie stepped forward and took his mother's hand, "Of course we have Ma, but don't you see, it's not important to us, we love each other and that's all that matters."

Margaret snatched her hand away and jumped to her feet, "How can you say that Charlie, we brought you up to be a good God-fearing young man, how can you deny your upbringing." Turning to Thomas she implored him, "Where did we go wrong with him?"

"Now, now Margaret," Thomas moved to console his wife, he could see how upset she was and realised this argument was getting out of hand. "Why don't we all just put this whole matter aside for tonight and think about it, we can talk again tomorrow night. Charlie, you think on what your mother has said tonight, you might not agree with her now, but her views are valid, and you need to consider them. Your mother and I only want the best for you and at times you might not always agree with what we think is best. You are an adult now. We brought you up to make your own decisions but think on, think about what your mother has said and then weigh it up, consider carefully and we will talk again tomorrow."

At that Thomas led Margaret, who was now weeping silently, out of the parlour and upstairs. Charlie looked on, in horror at the anguish in his mother's eyes, unable to fathom what had just happened. He sank down into the settee with his head between his hands in utter despair. He just could not understand why his mother had reacted so strongly against his marrying Mary-Jane, he had not anticipated such strong objections and was totally dumbfounded and without any idea of how to talk his mother around.

The following evening, Charlie met Mary-Jane after work and walked her home to Rosetta Park. They sat in the parlour while he relayed what had transpired the night before between him and his parents, his voice shook slightly as he told her about the look of sheer anguish in his mother's eyes, "I don't understand them Mary-Jane, and what's more, I don't think I want to, I love you, I want to marry you, we can make a life together, we will make a life together with or without their blessing."

Mary-Jane shook her head, "No, Charlie, no, you have always been so close to your parents, I will not come between you and them, it would not be right, talk to them again or maybe we should talk to them together."

"Ok Mary-Jane, I'll go home now, and I'll meet you after work tomorrow. Good night my love." With that Charlie set out on the walk home and as Mary-Jane watched him from her window she noted that his jaunty walk and whistle had been replaced by the hunched shoulders and slow pace of a dejected man.

Charlie was surprised when he got home the following evening to find his father home from work slightly earlier than usual. "I wanted to have a word with your mother before you got home," Thomas told Charlie. "I agree with your mother, well, to a certain degree anyway that mixed marriages are difficult. But I have to say I don't think those difficulties are insurmountable and from what I have seen of Mary-Jane, she is a lovely girl and I think she would make you a good wife."

Charlie was delighted to hear his father's words, but Margaret spoke up, "I can't go along with this. It is so wrong. You cannot marry her. Mixed marriages do not work."

Thomas looked at his wife "Margaret, let's face it, in your eyes, there isn't a woman alive that would be good enough for your Charlie. Mary-Jane is a Christian and our son wants to marry her, that's what's important."

But Margaret was adamant. Charlie argued with her and Thomas tried to reason with her, but to no avail. She threatened to boycott the wedding if they went ahead with it. So, Charlie threatened to elope and live in sin with Mary-Jane. The prospect of her son living in sin with a Catholic was even worse than the prospect of him marrying a Catholic so eventually after much cajoling and reasoning from her husband, she gave in and grudgingly gave her blessing for the wedding.

CHAPTER 9 WEDDING PLANS

With both families now on board, Charlie and Mary-Jane started planning their wedding. Of course, that quickly became mired in controversy. Mary-Jane's mother wanted them to marry in the local Catholic Church in Annalong and have a small reception at home, Charlie's mother said she couldn't set foot in a Catholic Church and she suggested they marry in the Church of Ireland in Knockbreda, a suggestion which Mary-Jane's mother dismissed saying the bride must be married in her own parish.

"Look Mary-Jane, at the end of the day, it's up to you. You decide what you want, and I will back you. You are the bride, it's your day," Charlie paced the parlour floor.

"Thank you, Charlie, but it's your day too, having said that, at this stage, I am wondering if we would be better of just eloping and not telling any of them?" Mary-Jane replied.

Charlie laughed at Mary-Jane's outburst, "Don't think so Mary-Jane, your mother would be horrified."

"I know, I know, but I can't help feeling that they are being unreasonable and spectacularly unsupportive. How are we going keep everyone happy!"

Mary-Jane sat on the sofa dejected. Mrs Best noticed the difference in the composure of the happy couple straight away as they sat in her parlour.

"Why the long faces? Two days ago, you were the picture of happiness, newly engaged, planning a wedding and now you look like you have to plan a funeral," she enquired of them.

"Oh, Mrs Best, it's our parents," said Mary-Jane, "or rather our mothers, are making planning a wedding impossible and we don't know what to do."

"Do tell," said Mrs Best, and made herself comfortable on the settee while Mary-Jane and Charlie poured out their tale of woe. "Why, my dears, it seems quite simple to me. Myself and my late husband faced a somewhat similar dilemma. Although it was quite some years ago and I had hoped that, at this stage, when we are heading towards the turn of the century, that times had changed for the better but obviously some things never change. It is important to remember that you will never be able to please everyone so if as you say, the religion is not important to you, then don't get married in any Church, have a civil ceremony, then neither Mother can complain."

Mary-Jane and Charlie looked at each other in astonishment, such a simple solution and the idea had never occurred to either of them.

"Oh, thank you so much, Mrs Best, that makes perfect sense." So, Mary-Jane went home to Annalong that weekend to tell her parents her compromise and get their agreement while Charlie spent the weekend with his mother talking her around. In the end, they all agreed that a low-key affair would probably be best, so they opted for the civil ceremony with separate church blessings afterwards which both sets of parents could attend in their own Churches on different weekends. On Monday they set the date.

Then came the wedding luncheon, Mrs Best suggested that she host a wedding party in Rosetta Park as her wedding gift to the young couple. When Mrs Best told Mary-Jane of her plans, Mary-Jane had been delighted but when she told her father of Mrs Best intentions on her monthly visit home, he had been far from pleased.

"I won't have it Mary-Jane." James O'Brien rarely raised his voice but on this occasion, he shouted, his voice hurt and angry, a dark red colour spreading from his neck up to his hairline, as he banged his fist on the table, "You are my eldest daughter and it is my duty to pay for your wedding."

Mary -Jane was stunned into silence. Her father had never raised his voice to her before and she had no idea what to say to him. Dinner was a quiet affair that evening, James glanced over at his eldest daughter every so often, then bent down to his plate again shielding his eyes from view. Mary-Jane ate quietly, her eyes red and her skin blotchy from crying. She felt her father glance at her without lifting her head and felt his anguish radiate out from him as if it was physical. She ate little, then rose from the table clearing her plate and those of her brothers without uttering a word.

Mary broke the ice, "stop it, the both of ye, I will not tolerate that kind of silence in this family, you talk to each other and you sort this out." She whipped her apron off and tossed it on the table before stalking out of the house leaving her husband and eldest daughter in stunned silence.

"Ah lass, your Ma is right, not talking to each other is not going to solve anything. Your Ma suggested that we should speak with Mrs Best and accept her offer and I think we should, but on one condition, and I mean this, I will pay for all expenses, she provides the venue and let that be the end of it."

Mary-Jane threw her arms around her Da, "Ah thank you Da, thank you, I'll talk to Mrs Best when I get back and maybe you and Ma could come up to Belfast next weekend and we could sort out the details."

"Ok Mary-Jane, now go get your Ma."

The following day Mary-Jane travelled back to Belfast and spoke to Mrs Best the moment she arrived back in Rosetta Park. Mrs Best listened carefully to Mary-Jane noting the shake in her voice when she mentioned her father's objections.

"Now, now Mary-Jane, that will not be a problem, I would be delighted to meet with your parents next weekend and have no doubt that we can organise your wedding party between us. After all, we all want the same thing, to give you and Charlie a lovely wedding day." Mary-Jane breathed a sigh of relief knowing that once Mrs Best set her mind to it, any problems or objections over their upcoming nuptials would be dealt with to everyone's satisfaction.

The following week Mary and James O'Brien travelled to Belfast and called on Mrs Best. Mary-Jane watched with delight as Mrs Best charmed her parents. James soon found himself agreeing to everything she suggested whilst believing that the suggestions had been his. Her logic was indisputable. She smoothed over the difficulties both mothers had with the mixed marriage and before James had a chance to air any of his grievances she had asked him if he would consider allowing her to facilitate his lovely family by putting on a wedding luncheon for his daughter and her beau, provided of course he was willing to supply the foods and drinks and even asking if he would have any objection to her baking a cake as her input for the wedding feast. Mary-Jane was astounded. Very quickly a compromise was reached whereby the O'Briens supplied the bread, cheese, preserves and cooked meats while Mrs Best supplied cakes and of course the venue. Mrs Best assured Mrs O'Brien that she would put out her best china and table linen and that the luncheon would be a fitting meal for the young bride and groom. Mary looked around, her nodding her head in approval to Mary-Jane. "It is a beautiful house and that dining room, why it must be one of the nicest rooms I have ever seen." James and Mary said their goodbyes to Mary-Jane with a spring in their step.

"Do you know Mary-Jane, I always had the highest regard for Mrs Best and now after speaking with her at length about your upcoming nuptials, I really consider Mrs Best a true friend and a worthy role model for you," Mary O'Brien told her daughter.

James agreed, "Yes, that Mrs Best is a fine woman, you have made a great friend there." Mary-Jane stood at the top step of the imposing house waving as her father waved back enthusiastically and smiled as her mother tucked her arm through her husbands as they strode out to the train station to make their way home.

CHAPTER 10   THE NEWLYWEDS OF 1895

Charlie looked across at his bride and matched her beaming smile. Mary-Jane looked radiant. Her sister Bridget had designed her wedding dress, an elegant ivory dress with a high neck and fitted bodice over a long skirt with a short train. The lace underskirt peaked out from under the skirt when she moved. She wore a long veil, which her mother had lent her as her something old, the same veil that she herself had worn when she had married James. Her something new was her beautiful dress, something borrowed was a silver chain lent to her by Susan, something blue was a garter, a present from Maggie. Her father walked her down the short aisle to the top of the registry office and handed her soft white hand to Charlie after a vigorous handshake and slapping his shoulder in a manly fashion. Susan stepped forward and lifted the veil from over her sister's face. Mary-Jane's luscious strawberry blond hair was tied back and held in place with silver hairpins emphasising her fine cheekbones and perfectly shaped lips. She looked like the picture of happiness which radiated out from her, infecting everyone present. Charlie beamed at his bride, looking resplendent in his new suit and hat, they were a handsome couple, well-matched and openly happy despite the reservations of their prospective families.

Both mothers had made their reservations about the marriage perfectly clear. Charlie and Mary-Jane were very aware that their marriage would be frowned upon, particularly in Belfast, but they reasoned that a new, and surely modern 20th century was now just five years off with Charlie certain that times were changing and mostly for the better. Belfast got its city status only seven years earlier and was rapidly expanding into one of the major industrial cities of the British Empire. Charlie felt extremely lucky to be permanently employed by the City Council, okay it was hard physical labour, but he was young and fit and enjoyed the work. There was also the added benefit of a preferential treatment on the housing list and he had just been assigned their home, a newly built two-up two-down in Sherwood Street, in East Belfast.

Charlie signed the marriage register and passed the pen over to his new wife who, for the very last time, signed her name as Mary-Jane O'Brien.

"Congratulations Mrs McMullen," whispered her sister Susan as she signed the register as the witness. "I wish you long life and happiness."

Randal added his signature and winked at his brother, "All over for you now, Charlie, old married man now."

Charlie playfully punched his brother's arm and grinned at Susan. Charlie's father Thomas shook his son's hand in congratulations and kissed his new daughter in law Mary-Jane softly on her blushing cheek. Mary-Jane's sister, Susan shed a happy tear and hugged her sister tightly, only releasing her to allow their father James to hug his daughter. Both mothers watched stony-faced while their offspring made their vows, both women of the opinion that their child was making the worst mistake of their lives and both convinced "it would all end in tears." Bridget and Maggie had waited at the back of the registry office with Will and Jimmy until the ceremony was over. The second it ended Will bounded up to Charlie and shook his hand so vigorously that Charlie's whole body shook. Mary-Jane started to laugh and within minutes the whole wedding party were laughing, even the two mothers. The laughter broke the atmosphere and it was a light-hearted entourage that spilled out onto the city street.

They all left the Belfast city registry office together and walked the short distance to Rosetta Street where Mrs Best had kindly insisted on putting on the wedding luncheon for the happy couple.

"Good morning Mr and Mrs McMullen," she warmly welcomed the newly- weds. "Congratulations to you both, I am so happy for you."

She air kissed the new Mr & Mrs McMullen then turned her attention to her other guests,

"Everyone, come in and welcome."

Mrs Best radiated goodwill to all her guests as they filed past her through her ornate front door and followed her directions through into the dining room. A sumptuous feast was spread out before her assorted guests and Mary was openly astounded at the sight of the large table laid out to accommodate the wedding party.

"Why, Mrs Best, this looks quite wonderful, thank you so much."

"Not at all Mrs O'Brien, I think between us we have done our loved ones proud." And they had, fresh salmon supplied by the O'Briens and steamed to perfection by Mrs Best. The O'Briens best lamb raised on the lower slopes of Mount Donard, delicately roasted with butter and rosemary by Mrs Best, thinly sliced and served on a silver platter accompanied by an assortment of cheeses, vegetables and breads all laid out on the buffet table. The table was set with the finest silver cutlery and crystal glasses and of course Belfast linen. The centrepiece was the beautiful wedding cake iced to perfection by Mrs Best herself.

The wedding party took their places and conversation and laughter soon flowed, thanks in no small part to Mrs Best and her considerable social skills. The

McMullens and the O'Briens were soon chatting like old friends. Margaret McMullen chatted with Will and Jimmy and praised Bridget's dressmaking skills. Mary O'Brien chatted to Randal and Ernie and praised the good manners and pleasant demeanour of Charlie's younger siblings. Charlie's uncle Gerard was there and his cousins Michael and Emily, who was also Mary-Janes best friend. The other young ladies who lived in Rosetta Park also attended, Agnes sat quietly, Kate and Louisa chattered to Michael while Emily and Cecelia chatted to Maggie looking for hints and tips on upgrading their wardrobes. Susan engaged Betty and Jean in conversation enthralling them with stories about being in service in a large household.

After they had eaten their fill, James stood and tapped his glass,

"Ladies, Gentlemen please, if I may say a few words."

He hesitated as his face turned red from the neck up.

"Thank you for joining us today to celebrate my daughter's marriage."

A polite round of applause turned riotous when Jimmy and Will joined in and everyone laughed at their antics.

"I know some of us had our objections...worries really, but I think you will agree that Mary-Jane and Charlie have shown us that there is always a compromise, always a way to work through objections and we all know that a successful marriage is a series of compromises."

"Here, here," Thomas lifted his glass to James.

His voice breaking with a mixture of nerves and emotion James continued,

"I know you will join me in wishing Mary-Jane and Charlie the very best future, long life and happiness. Please raise your glasses, to the Bride and Groom."

At that everyone raised their glasses and toasted the bride and groom. James sat but not before asking Charlie to say a few words. Charlie stood up and positioned himself behind Mary-Jane who was sitting at the table. He laid his hand on her left shoulder and spoke,

"Thank you, family and friends, thank you all for being here with us today. I am the happiest man alive," a cheer arose from Will and Jimmy which caused more cheers and laughter from the rest of the guests, he continued in a voice shuddering with emotion, "I thank you all for being here to witness our marriage and I promise to make this woman the happiest woman in Ireland."

Randal and Michael stood up and cheered while everyone clapped their approval. Margaret McMullen wiped a tear from her eye with her lace handkerchief while Thomas beamed with pride at this son. James stood up and offered his hand to Charlie, "Well said son, well said," as the others formed a queue behind him to shake Charlie's hand and Mary-Jane's, whose eyes were bright with unshed happy tears.

Before long it was time to leave. Mary-Jane retired upstairs to her old room with her sisters to change out of her wedding dress and into the beautiful day dress and coat her sister Brigid had designed and made for her. In a beautiful soft pink fabric, the bodice was fitted with a skirt which showed just enough leg to be extremely fashionable without upsetting the older family members by its boldness. The matching coat was of a darker fabric and finished with fur trim on the collar and cuffs. Mary-Jane twirled in the middle of the room admiring how the outfit accentuated her figure before thanking Bridget profusely. Bridget, Maggie and Susan hugged their sister tightly before they made their way downstairs to their waiting families.

Goodbyes were extended and offers of visits and meetings made their way throughout the wedding party. Mary and James O'Brien watched their daughter descend the staircase and Mary heard the short intake of breath from James as he caught sight of her. She was radiant. Mary hugged her daughter to her while James shook Charlie's hand,

"Look after my daughter Charlie,"

James said gruffly before kissing his daughter on the cheek and quickly turning to the door before anyone could see how emotional he felt. Mary quickly followed before she too shed a tear, then laughed as Will and Jimmy both hugged their sister with such force that Charlie had to intervene to save his wife being squeezed to extinction by her brothers. Michael was waiting to escort the O'Briens to the train station and waited until they boarded their train back to Annalong, County Down. Thomas and Margaret said their goodbyes to Charlie,

"Mary-Jane was a beautiful bride," Thomas said, "and she is from a good family, lovely people."

Charlie thanked his father and hugged his mother. She hugged him close "Charlie, you know I still have my doubts about mixed marriage, but I've been thinking. That Mrs Best is a knowledgeable woman. Smart, educated, and if she thinks you and Mary-Jane have a chance of making their marriage work then maybe I should just stop worrying. Mary-Jane is such a lovely girl."

Thomas patted his wives hand in agreement.

"Exactly, Margaret, congratulations son."

Thomas and Margaret set off home to Teutonic Street, arm in arm, with Thomas quite happy with how the day had went and Margaret subdued but happy enough with the day's events, their children following behind them.

The newly-weds thanked Mrs Best profusely.

"Mrs Best, I cannot thank you enough for everything you have done for us. My mother enjoyed herself despite her reservations and your cake recipes will be copied in my mother's house" Charlie noted, "Now allow us to help you tidy up."

"I would not hear of it, Charlie, the ladies here have all offered to help put the house back to normal and we shall have that done in no time at all. Go, time for you and your beautiful bride to start your married life and I have no doubt that you will be very happy." Mrs Best sent them on their way to start their married life in their new home in Sherwood Street.

When they reached the front door, Charlie produced the key then turned to Mary-Jane, scooping her up in his arms he carried his new bride over the threshold and into their new lives together as man and wife. Charlie had spent the previous week getting the house ready so that they could start their married life in their new home. He had bought a new bed and Mrs Best had kindly supplied bed linen. He had organised for his friend Michael to set the fire so that he could light the fire as soon as they arrived to make their home cosy and warm. The men he worked with had organised a table and two chairs and best of all two comfortable armchairs for either side of the fire. Mary O'Brien had sent up pots and pans and Margaret McMullen had provided some crockery so that they could start their married life with some home comforts. Charlie lit the fire quickly while Mary-Jane lit some candles. She smiled over at her Charlie, the candles sending dancing shadows into every corner of the room. The candlelight shone off Mary-Jane's red tresses and sparkled in her eyes.

"Hello Mrs McMullen," Charlie smiled as he brought his wife in closer to him, "I love you."

Mary-Jane lifted her face to him and he kissed her gently before lifting her into his arms and carrying her upstairs to their new marital bed.

Charlie and Mary-Jane settled into married life quickly. Charlie worked long hours with the new City Council, but Charlie was a grafter. Hard physical labour suited him, he loved the work, enjoyed the male companionship of his workmates and the rough and tumble that went with the work. Every evening when the day was done he especially loved going home to his new wife. As he turned the corner onto his street he could see the light glowing from behind the bright curtains she had insisted on hanging in the parlour, the smoke bellowing from the chimney and when he opened his front door the delectable sight of Mary-Jane smiling at him welcoming him home. Of course, there was also the delicious smell of food cooking in the range. For Mary-Jane was a great cook, she could make the most delicious dinners from the bare essentials and always had his dinner ready for him the minute he opened the door. Mary-Jane spent her days cleaning their home and cooking and getting ready for the arrival of their first child. They were both so excited and scared and delighted and anxious and so very, very, happy.

CHAPTER 11　　　SWEET BABY JAMES

James Thomas McMullen was born one cold and snowy night in October 1896. Mary-Jane's sister, Susan had travelled up from Annalong a few days earlier to stay with her to help her with the birth of her first child. Susan had married that summer leaving her job in service and moved in with her new husband Robert in Annalong. Her mother had been delighted to see one of her daughters settled so close to her and Susan was happy helping her husband in their smallholding near the sea and making a home for them both and please God for their future children. Winter came early that year and the snow was thick on the ground that night. The birth was long and arduous but finally, just before dawn, James made a raucous arrival into the world letting the whole street know he had arrived and was hungry.

The moment she laid eyes on her son, Mary-Jane knew she was smitten. He was bald and red and bawling and the most beautiful baby she had ever seen. Exhaustion took over from elation after such a long, difficult birth but Mary-Jane was reluctant to relinquish hold of her new baby son.

Susan implored her, "Come on Mary-Jane, let me take him and settle him down so you can rest, get your strength back. You're going to need it to look after him in the days and weeks ahead. I'm only going to be here a few more days to help you so take your rest while you can."

Charlie nodded his head in agreement, "Susan is right Mary-Jane, you need rest, sure myself and Susan will watch over him, you sleep, and I promise you I will wake you when he wakes."

Complete exhaustion overtook Mary-Jane as she acquiesced, "Okay but call me when he wakes, promise me." Susan shook her head smiling gently at her sister, "Of course I will, now get some sleep," and at that Susan lifted the sleeping infant from Mary-Jane's arms and put him into his crib.

Charlie was over the moon. A son. His son. And a bouncer of a baby boy at that. Charles felt as if his heart would burst with pride at the sight of his newly born son. They had already decided that if their first child was a boy he would be named James Thomas, James after his Grandfather James O'Brien and Thomas after his other Grandfather Thomas McMullen.

"James Thomas," thought Charles, "yes, it suits him, and his Grandfathers will be pleased, and hopefully the birth of the first grandchild on both sides of the family will mend some bridges."

Divisions had arisen with both sides of their family when Charlie and Mary-Jane announced that they were expecting a baby. Religious differences once again came to the fore with both mothers becoming increasingly entrenched in their separate viewpoint. The issue of religion was unimportant to Charlie. While he had been brought up with Church of Ireland teachings he didn't see much difference between the teachings of his church and the Roman Catholic teachings that Mary-Jane had been brought up with. He had no problem allowing their children to be baptised in the Catholic faith. His mother had other ideas and tried to reason with him but Charlie's main purpose in life was to please his wife and his mother soon realised she was fighting a losing battle and eventually stopped speaking to her son.

CHAPTER 12
THE FIRST MCMULLEN GRANDCHILD

The day James was born Charlie sent a telegram to both sets of parents informing them of the birth of their first grandchild. His father Thomas called in to see them the following day, to wish them well and meet his first grandchild. He excused his wife's absence by saying she was under the weather. Mary-Jane glanced over at her husband, but Charlie never missed a beat, shaking his father's hand before presenting his newborn son to him. Thomas was delighted when he heard his grandson was to carry his name.

"Come lad, let's go wet the baby's head."

Thomas kissed his daughter in law on her cheek and cap in hand headed out the door.

"Won't be long love," Charlie whispered in his wife's ear before following his father out the front door and down the street. The days passed, and Charlie waited on his mother's visit, but she never arrived. He was hurt at first at his mothers' intractability but that hurt turned to anger as the days turned into weeks without his mother visiting her grandchild.

CHAPTER 13
A WELCOME FROM THE O'BRIENS

James O'Brien was at work when the telegraph arrived. Mary held it in her hand turning over again and again, reluctant to open it, afraid of bad news. Her youngest daughter Maggie arrived to visit her mother a short time later and found her mother sitting in her armchair deep in thought.

"What's wrong Ma?" she dropped her shawl on the table and rushed to her mother's side, alarmed to find her mother just sitting still at this time of day and not moving around the kitchen or the farm working as was her wont. Mary handed Maggie the telegram, who ripped it open immediately then squealed with delight when she read the news of her sister's safe delivery of a baby son.

"Ma, Mary-Jane had her baby, a boy, and they are calling him James Thomas, ah ma that is wonderful news," Maggie danced around the kitchen. The boys who had been outside in the vegetable patch heard her shouts and came in to join the celebration. Maggie, Will and Jimmy danced around the kitchen while Mary just sat still, letting the idea that she had a grandson seep slowly into her consciousness. Mary had not seen her daughter since the day of Susan's wedding in the summer, reluctant as she was to visit her in Belfast.

"We will go up to visit her tomorrow Ma, go and see baby James, oh I can't wait to see him and Mary-Jane of course" Maggie hugged her mother.

"I don't think so Maggie, I don't think I can, I have too much to do around here," Mary replied.

"But Ma, you have to see your grandson, Bridget would stay here with the boys, she could work on her dress making here and supervise the boys, I am sure she would be happy to, and you and Dad can travel up," retorted Maggie. "They are so happy together ma, you really should go visit and then you might feel better about Mary-Jane living in Belfast with a Protestant," she told her mother.

She had said as much to her mother on countless occasions before as had Susan and Bridget and they always got the same reply, "No, Maggie, I know you mean well but mark my words, it will end in tears, not that I want that for our Mary-Jane, God no, she deserves the best, but marrying a Protestant, I just hope and pray I am wrong."

But now with the birth of baby James, they were all hoping her mother's attitude would soften. Her first grandchild.

"But ma, they are bringing up James as a Catholic, and they are so happy, you would see that if you could see them in their home," Maggie cajoled her mother, "And Susan is already up there helping Mary-Jane with the baby."

It took all of Maggie's powers of persuasion to get her mother to go and see her grandson, but she was so glad she made the effort. The moment Mrs O'Brien set eyes on her grandchild her heart melted, and she became the doting granny. Throwing her arms around Mary-Jane she hugged her daughter tightly, "My beautiful daughter has a son," she thanked God for his safe delivery and her daughter's joy. Lifting baby James out of his bassinet she cradled him in her arms completely overcome by the emotion she felt looking at her first grandchild. "Such a beautiful child, Mary-Jane," she whispered. Baby James gurgled in her arms and opened his eyes to stare at this Grandmother. Mary and James O'Brien nearly missed their train back to Down they were so enthralled with their new grandson.

On her return to her home later that night Mary O'Brien sat in her favourite chair in front of the fire and started to crochet a christening gown, with her husband smiling at her from his armchair.

"I am so glad that you have made peace with Mary-Jane, my love, it was so hard to see you so upset. We are so blessed with a happy, healthy grandson and look at Mary-Jane and Charlie, did you see how happy they are? Did you notice how gentle he was with her? How attentive?"

"I know, I know, you can feel the love in that house," his wife agreed, "I have wasted so many months and I am going to make up for that now. So what if he is a Protestant, let's face it there is not much difference between Catholic and Protestant. I will never stop worrying about her living in the city in a mixed marriage for there are people who have no tolerance for that but at least now that we have made our peace with her she knows that she can come home anytime with her husband and son if times go bad in the city. At least I hope she knows that they are all welcome here."

"Of course she knows Mary, and so does Charlie, for I said as much to him today, so stop fretting and start working on that christening gown," replied James, leaning back into this armchair and lighting his pipe, amusement dancing in his eyes.

CHAPTER 14   THE CHRISTENING

Charlie called to his childhood home to tell his family about the christening.

"Baby Thomas will be christened in St. Matthew's Church on Bryson Street. We have asked Mary-Jane's sister Susan to be God-mother. She is delighted. Susan has been great Ma, she's been a great help to Mary-Jane. We'll miss her when she goes home."

Margaret barely nodded, her lips set in a firm line. "I won't be attending any christening in a Catholic Church."

Charlie's face froze. "But Ma, James is my son. I want you there to see him christened. Your grandson." Margaret turned on her heel and left the room. Charlie turned to his father and pleaded with him to help talk Margaret around.

"Leave it with me son," Thomas walked his son to the door and waved goodbye.

Thomas talked to Margaret to try and get her to attend the Christening, but Margaret would not budge. She folded her arms in front of her and her mouth in a straight line.

"No Thomas, our grandson James, christened into the Catholic faith. No, I could not bring myself to go into that Church."

Thomas was torn. He loved his son, but he loved his wife and felt it was his duty to support her, but he also felt she was wrong in not acknowledging her only grandchild. Eventually, Thomas gave his wife an ultimatum.

"Mary-Jane is your daughter in law, Charlie's wife and she has given him a fine son, your grandson. Yes, he will be christened into the Catholic faith and, truth be told, I don't see a lot of difference between Catholic and Church of Ireland, we both believe in the same God, the same Jesus Christ. So, make peace with this Margaret, because if you don't you are going to lose your son, our son and I don't want that." But Margaret refused to relent. "Stop being so stubborn Margaret, you still haven't laid eyes on your only grandchild. What does it matter if he is to be baptised Catholic as long as he is baptised."

But Margaret stuck to her guns and in the end, Thomas went to St. Matthew's to see his grandchild christened into the Catholic faith. He hugged his lovely daughter-in-law and kissed baby James Thomas on his perfect little rosy cheek. He shook hands with Mary and James O'Brien and congratulated them on their first grandchild. He patted his son on the shoulder saying, "Well done son" and throughout it all he made excuses for his wife, pleading a sudden onset of influenza, which prevented her from attending.

When he returned home that evening he told Margaret where he had been. Margaret was furious.

"How dare you, Thomas, how could you," she screamed at him, "how could you let me down like that, pretend I was sick, go there, into that Fenian hole, how could you?"

"Enough," said Thomas as he banged his fist on the table. Sickened by his wife's venom, he raised his voice for the first time towards her, anger choking his throat and chest,

"How dare you ignore our only grandchild, ignore our son's wife. How dare you put me in the position you put me in today. It is you that has let yourself down, has let me down, has let your family down, over what? Over what, Margaret? Are your religious beliefs really worth destroying this family?"

He slammed the front door on his way out and walked down to the pub. "Better to cool off with a pint," he thought, as he marched down the road disappearing into the foggy night.

Margaret stared after the slammed door, shocked into silence. Thomas had never walked out on her before. Suddenly it felt like vindication to her, she knew who was to blame for all her problems, that Fenian of course, she no longer got to see her adored eldest son, her husband had walked out on her tonight, all because of that Fenian. That Fenian her beloved eldest son had married. That Fenian he loved and now had a child with. Her head spun with it all. Thoughts racing each other around, her anger slowly dissipating and being replaced with utter dejection. Tears started to roll slowly down her cheeks. What a mess, she thought, "maybe you are the problem Margaret, maybe if you tried to see your son's point of view and not just your own you wouldn't be sitting here in this state. Maybe it's not all the fault of that Fenian. Maybe Thomas was right after all. I have let my family down, my Charlie," and with that Margaret wept sorely, heartbroken. Thomas returned home some hours later to find her asleep on the settee, worn out by her crying, her apron soaked with her tears. His heart melted when he saw the state of her but the memory of the venomous words she had used before he left sprang into his mind and he quickly lost all sympathy for her. He left her there and climbed the stairs to bed, on his own, for the first time in their 24 years of marriage, he slept in their marriage bed alone.

CHAPTER 15   SPRING IN ANNALONG

The first few months of motherhood were tough for Mary-Jane. Her sister had stayed with them to help her over the first few days which meant Mary-Jane had time to bond with her new baby. Her milk had taken some time to come in and in the first few days, she found it painful to feed him. With Susan there to run the house, Mary-Jane could concentrate on her baby and not worry about the normal day-to-day chores that had kept her totally occupied before James was born. But all too soon Susan had to return to Annalong. Her husband was missing her, and Susan had discovered that she was pregnant and could not wait to tell her husband and her parents. Mary-Jane was apprehensive about being on her own with her new baby, but she was also delighted for her sister and insisted that she return to her own life, thanking her profusely for being so helpful and attentive and assuring her that she could manage easily.

James was a hungry baby and most of her time seemed to be taken up with feeding him. When he slept, she slept, and her home started to look slightly neglected. She didn't have the same time to fuss around the house and there were days when she felt guilty about the lack of preparation she put into Charlie's meals. Not that Charlie objected. He was completely and utterly enthralled by his son. He kissed his forehead every morning before he left for work and the first thing he did when he came home in the evening was to smile at the sight of him. Before long baby James was smiling back at his Da from the crib. Charlie was totally smitten and every evening after dinner he sat with his son in the crook of his arm and Mary-Jane in the other armchair and they relaxed and talked and counted their blessings. As James was weaned he became easier for Mary-Jane to manage. He quickly grew into a happy, contented baby and both mother and child fell into an easy routine. The aroma of freshly baked bread and delicious stew once again wafted out the door and down the street to greet Charlie on his way home.

The days and months flew by. Mary-Jane couldn't believe how big James had grown by the spring. He was a happy, placid baby, always smiling and content. Everyone loved him, even her mother had come around and was besotted with her grandson. So much so that Mary-Jane and James were travelling to Annalong to spend Easter with her family and she was so looking forward to it. She loved living in Belfast, loved the hustle and bustle of the big city but she had to admit there were times when she missed the slower pace of life and the peace and quiet that existed in Annalong. It was a beautiful part of the country, nestled at the foot of the Mourne Mountains looking out to sea, the air was fresh and clear, and she eagerly anticipated bringing her son out for walks along the coast and into the surrounding countryside. It would be a welcome change. Charlie was working so he was going to travel down with her on Easter Saturday evening, stay for dinner on Easter Sunday then travel back for work the next day. Mary-Jane was staying for a whole week.

She was looking forward to seeing her siblings again as well. She hadn't seen Susan since the week James had been born. Susan had given birth only two days earlier to a baby boy, Sean, a cousin for James, and Mary-Jane could not wait to see him. Bridget and Margaret had travelled up to Belfast to see baby James for his christening, but she hadn't seen them since and she hadn't seen Will and Jimmy since Christmas when her parents had brought them to Belfast to visit. Mary-Jane hummed quietly to herself while packing her bags, while baby James lay on a blanket on the floor beside her cooing and gurgling his delight with the little silver rattle he was shaking, a gift from his Godmother Susan. Mary-Jane smiled contentedly at her son before turning back to the task in hand. She packed treats for the boys, marbles and chocolate, baby clothes for Susan and some fine linen for her mother. Her fingers lingered over the fine cloth. She had saved for months to buy the linen for her mother and had enjoyed her trip into the city centre to Anderson and McAuleys where she picked a simple design but one she knew her mother would love. Alice had accompanied Mary-Jane on her shopping trip with James tucked up warmly in his pram. She had really enjoyed her trip into town and had spent longer than she should have, admiring the linens and lace and the fine silverware. She had picked up some ribbon and dress trimming for Bridget and was looking forward to telling her sister all about the large range of trimmings and fabrics the shop now stocked, items she knew Bridget would like. They had spent so long in the store that they were late returning home to start the evening meal. Not that Charlie minded, Mary-Jane smiled to herself remembering Charlie's reaction when his tea wasn't quite ready. "great my love, more time for me to play with James," and he lifted his little son tenderly and bounced him on his knee while James giggled so contagiously that they all laughed until their sides ached. When she had finished packing their case Mary-Jane hugged baby James to her, "oh you are going to love it James, the air, the sea and wait until Will and Jimmy see how big you have got." She spun around while baby James gurgled and laughed up into his mother's face. Baby James features were so like his fathers, dark eyes, sallow skin and a shock of black hair, surprising in a baby so young. Mary-Jane was so looking forward to her trip, spending time with her sisters but also spending some time with her brothers Will and Jimmy as well. Their simple outlook on life was refreshing and had a calming influence on the whole family. They found fun and laughter in every task from feeding the chickens to harvesting apples.

It was a happy family that locked up their home in Sherwood Street on Easter Saturday as Charlie and Mary-Jane made their way to the train station to catch the last train to Newcastle. Mary-Jane's father was picking them up in Newcastle to bring them on the last leg of their journey to Annalong. Six months old James smiled angelically at the other train passengers causing the ladies to stop and comment on what a handsome child he was and how pleasant his demeanour. The men patted him on the head pronouncing him a fine fellow indeed. Charlie and Mary-Jane were delighted with the attention their son received and not a little relieved that James stayed placid and smiling for the whole journey. James sat on his mother's lap staring out the window at the passing landscape, fascinated by the continually changing view of cityscape rapidly changing to green fields and then the sea. James was waiting for them as they alighted from the train. He shook Charlie's hand before talking James into his arms pronouncing him a fine child, he handed James back to Mary-Jane.

"You have done us proud, love, now let's get moving so we can get you home before nightfall."

They finally arrived in Annalong just after dusk on Saturday evening. Mary-Jane could see the glow from the fire through the curtains on the front window like a welcoming beacon calling her home. The spring evening scents and the salt in the air, the mountains towering above them, and the fresh clean air all assaulted her senses. She felt her heart miss a beat as they pulled into the yard and her mother came out the door to greet them. She threw herself into her mother's arms hugging her tightly,

"I have missed you so much," she whispered in her mother's ear, before turning to lift her baby James from Charlie and hand him over to her mother.

"Oh, he is such a bonny wain and he has got so big. Come on inside now and we'll get you all settled."

Mary O'Brien hustled her family indoors where a huge fire burned in the hearth. A gigantic pot was hung over the fire with a mouth-watering aroma wafting through the whole room. Mary O'Brien's soup was famous throughout the county. Her recipe was coveted by all her neighbours, but she kept it close to her chest not even divulging it to her daughters. A delicious concoction of carrots, turnip, potatoes and herbs her soup never failed to satisfy the most discerning pallets or indeed the hungriest. The soup was accompanied by freshly baked soda bread, companionable conversation, and much laughter. Even baby James joined in the conversation, babbling as babies do to anyone who would listen.

On Easter Sunday morning they all rose early and set off to Mass. Mass on Easter Sunday was a celebratory mass full of imagery and joy. Mary-Jane was delighted when Charlie told her how struck he was by the upbeat nature of the service and the similarity to the Anglican services he had attended as a child. He didn't attend his local Church of Ireland anymore, he had told Mary-Jane that he didn't see the point, but he was happy to accompany Mary-Jane and James along the route to St. Matthew's Catholic Church before heading to the park on a Sunday morning. He rejoined them when mass was over and walked home with them. Mary-Jane knew that it would never occur to him to go in to mass with them in Belfast but here in Annalong it was different. Charlie had told her that he felt it would have been disrespectful to his in-laws not to go with them and he didn't see any harm in it, after all, they were all Christians.

"If only my mother felt the same way," he said to her as they walked up the steps of the church, Mary-Jane touched his arm in support and Charlie smiled at her as they entered the church. Charlie went to the left side along with the men while Mary-Jane went to the right with her mother and sisters, and baby James, as was the custom. The woman donned their mantillas to cover their hair whilst the men removed their caps to uncover their heads and the only sound was the muffled whispers of neighbours greeting each other. Mary-Jane wore a black lace mantilla, a gift from her mother, who wore a similar one. Her younger sisters wore white lace mantillas as did all of the young women and girls in the congregation. The smell of ancient oak and wax polish mingled with candles and incense in the dim interior while the alter burst with the colour of vibrant daffodils. The choir began to sing the opening hymn, and all bowed their heads in prayer. After mass had ended, the family met up outside the church door and then set off to the sea front greeting friends and neighbours along the way. James attracted the most attention particularly from the women who all pronounced him a bonny wain and destined to be a heartbreaker. Charlie and Mary-Jane positively beamed with pride with the attention their precious son was getting and dawdled along enjoying the rare spring sunshine and the interaction with the O'Brien's neighbours. Stopping at the village shop they bought the Sunday newspaper and from there they set off for Susan's home, a stone's throw from the seafront.

Susan had been unable to attend mass on Easter morning. Her new son Sean was less than one week old, so she had stayed home with her baby while Robert had attended with his family. She couldn't wait for Mary-Jane to see little Sean. She missed her sister and was so looking forward to comparing notes on childbirth and getting tips from her sister on settling her new son. The whole O'Brien family arrived en masse together with Mary-Jane, Charlie and baby James. Mary O'Brien busied herself in the kitchen making tea for her brood, whilst exchanging smiles with James who looked fit to burst with pride at the sight of his two grandsons.

Mary-Jane produced her bag of clothing for Sean which baby James had outgrown. "I kept this for you especially, Susan," Mary-Jane said as she handed Susan a parcel wrapped in delicate tissue paper. Susan unwrapped it carefully to reveal the beautiful crochet christening gown their mother had lovingly made for baby James. "We will make it a family heirloom," Susan squealed with delight and hugged her older sister. Everyone admired the delicate workmanship of the robe before Susan carefully wrapped it again in the tissue paper and put it away. After tea was drunk and many tips were exchanged they put their coats back on and made their way back to the O'Brien smallholding for a late lunch.

The bracing sea air set them all up for the sumptuous feast Mary had prepared. Easter Sunday dinner was always special after the fasting of Lent. A leg of lamb kept from lamb raised on their own smallholding roasted slowly over the fire and basted with her own special blend of oils and herbs: spring vegetables and new potatoes grown and carefully tended by the boys. The wooden table was scrubbed until it was nearly white, lovingly covered by the linen tablecloth Mary-Jane had given her mother and set with the best plates and cups to accommodate the whole family. James sat on his mother's knee and ate off her plate. Mary looked around her table and beamed at her family with a sense of contentment. Mary-Jane mirrored her view, "This is what it's all about," she thought, "family sitting around a table, talking and laughing and eating." She looked up and caught the eye of her husband and he smiled, and she knew that he was thinking the exact same thing. Family meant everything, to each of them. Mary O'Brien said grace before meals and gave thanks for her family and for their two new grandsons. Mary-Jane and Charlie echoed their thanks.

Later that day, Charlie set off on his trip back to Belfast, leaving Mary-Jane and baby James to stay for the week. Mary-Jane was looking forward to spending time with her parents and her siblings, but she also knew that she was going to miss Charlie and she knew he wasn't looking forward to spending the week alone. Mary-Jane had a suggestion for him, "You could go to your mother. She would jump at the opportunity to give you your dinner every evening after work, especially if she knew you were alone." Charlie said no, he wasn't going to tell his mother that his wife and son were in Annalong for the week. He felt it would be a betrayal of them as his mother still had not seen or acknowledged baby James. "Her loss," he said, "such a bonny child and his own Grandmother still hasn't seen him."

The week went by in a flash for Mary-Jane. The weather was unseasonably dry and fine enabling her to walk over to Susan every day with baby James in his carriage. She enjoyed fussing over Susan and making her sleep while her baby slept, helping her with chores and trying in some small way to repay her sister for her help when she gave birth to baby James. Susan was recovering well, and baby Sean was doing great. Robert's family were always popping in to help. Sean was the first grandchild in his family as well and Robert's mother was delighted to help the new family in any way she could. Every day she brought fresh baked bread and tales from the village, and before she left she set the fire and prepared the evening meal, "just till ya get on your feet, Susan, no need to mention it to Robert, sure what would men know about wains." She laughed as she set off for home again. Mary-Jane was glad to see her sister so loved and looked after.

Will and Jimmy adored baby James, they took turns to make funny faces and strike poses to make James laugh, which he did unreservedly. While they entertained baby James Mary-Jane helped her mother cook the evening meal then when everyone got home they all sat together to eat and discuss the day and their plans for the following day. Mary-Jane caught up on the local village gossip, who married, who had died and who had babies. Laughter filled the house and James bloomed with all the attention.

CHAPTER 16   CHARLIE HOME ALONE

In Belfast thoughts of his mother lay heavily on Charlie's mind and by Wednesday he had decided he was going to call into his parent's home that evening after work and try to reason with her again. He had always been close to his mother and he thought that maybe if he spoke to her again she would come around. After all, she had attended the wedding, it had taken a lot of persuasion from both him and his Dad, but she had attended. Surely, she realised that they would have children, and he knew that if she laid eyes on James even once she would be smitten like every other woman who set eyes on him. That smiley disposition never failed to charm women and men alike.

He knew his Da was fine with everything, he had even turned up at the christening and made excuses for Ma. Charlie had known he was lying but he didn't want to upset Mary-Jane, so he didn't challenge it. Mary-Jane hadn't commented on the fact that Margaret had never visited them to see James nor had she ever suggested that they go as a family to visit Margaret, so Charles had felt it wiser to just say nothing. So, after work that evening he walked up the back alley to his parent's house and opened the back door into the scullery, "Hello, anyone home?" he shouted.

Kendal bolted down the scullery with his hand stuck out in front for a welcoming handshake, "Charlie, great to see ya. Look Ma, it's our Charlie," he shouted behind him.

Margaret startled and straightened up from where she was leaning over the fire stirring the stew pot. She made a move as if to run towards Charlie but visibly stopped herself. Cleaning her hands on her already well soiled apron she asked in as cool a voice as she could muster, "Oh, come in Charlie, what brings you to our table?"

"Nothing Ma, just called in to see you," Charlie said, suddenly nervous about how to broach the real reason for his visit. His two younger sisters Lily and Emily ran to meet him, "Welcome home Charlie," they both greeted him.

Charlie's father Thomas remained seated at the head of the table taking in the situation, "Welcome Charlie, stay and have a bite," Susan set a place for him at the table and Lily ran to get another plate which she brought to their mother, so she could dish up a plate of stew for Charlie.

Margaret put the full plate in front of Charlie, "Enjoy son" she tapped Charlie's shoulder and returned to the fire.

"So, Da, how is work going for you?"

And the talk around the table settled on the mundane whilst Margaret kept a watchful eye as she moved in and out of the scullery, gradually clearing away the empty plates and washing up, clearing the remnants of the meal away until nothing else was left to be done.

"Sit Margaret, sit with us," Thomas called, and Margaret sat at the table beside her husband without a word.

"Well Charles, how is James?" enquired Thomas,

"Great Da, great, Mary-Jane is staying at her parent's house for a week so that all his Annalong family can get to know him. Mary-Jane thought the sea air would be good for him after the really smoggy winter we have just had. It was lovely there when I was leaving them on Sunday evening, I would have liked to have stayed with them but couldn't afford time off from work, so I can't wait to go back and collect them next Saturday," Charlie replied, "You should have seen him on the train Ma, he was a picture, good as gold, smiling at everyone and taking in every minute."

Margaret stood up from the table, "Excuse me, I have darning to do. Lily, Emily upstairs now," she stated in a terse voice and with that, she left the room and went upstairs. Lily and Emily hugged Charlie quickly and followed their mother.

Charlie looked after her retreating figure despairingly.

"I'm sorry, son, I have tried everything I can think of. I have argued again and again but I cannot seem to get through to her," Thomas sighed resignedly.

"It's not your fault Da, I know you have tried. I suppose it could be worse she could have stopped you from seeing us, or Randall and Maggie. At least I still have you three. I will call in to see the girls whenever I can but as for Ma, well, least said soonest mended."

Charlie shook his head then stood up to leave. Shaking his father's hand, he wished him good luck and left for his own home in Sherwood Street.

He got through the rest of the week as best he could. He had never learned to cook or clean, so he found it quite difficult, but he struggled through with a lot of help from his next-door neighbour Alice. The morning he left to collect Mary-Jane and baby James Alice came in and gave the house a thorough clean so that all would be spick and span for Mary-Jane's return. He really didn't know what they would do without a neighbour like Alice. She was so good to them and such a great friend to Mary-Jane. Mary-Jane still saw Emily from time to time, but she was busy working and was stepping out with a young man from the other side of the city, so her visits were becoming less and less frequent. While Mary-Jane missed her company, baby James took up so much of her time and energy she didn't really have time to brood over it.

Charlie couldn't wait to see his wife and son. He had never been apart from them before and made a silent pledge that he would never be separated from them again. So, with a spring in his step he set off on Saturday afternoon to travel to Annalong. His father-in-law collected him from the station and regaled him with stories about baby James on his way back to Annalong. Mary-Jane with baby James in her arms moved quickly down the path to meet him when he arrived. He enveloped them both in a massive hug then stood back to look at them.

"I swear Mary-Jane, you are even more beautiful," he planted a kiss on her check then held out his arms to his son, who jumped into this Da's arms. They walked up the path in unison with baby James in Charlie's left arm and his right arm planted firmly around his wife's narrow waist.

"Good to see ya," Mary welcomed her son-in-law with a smile. As always in the O'Brien home a delicious smell of home cooking wafted out the door greeting all who entered. Dinner was ready and they all sat around the scrubbed table eating and talking with baby James babbling away on his father's knee.

The following morning followed the same pattern as the previous Sunday with all of the family attending mass in the village. The local villagers gossiped that, "Charlie the prod who married the eldest O'Brien girl," had the cheek to attend a Catholic mass again. The O'Briens ignored the gossip and spoke to their friends who once again fussed over baby James. Then they all walked the short distance over to Susan to say goodbye. The two sisters clung to each other before parting, swearing to meet up again, with Susan promising to travel to Belfast during the summer.

The O'Briens then all retired to their home in Annalong where Mary had dinner prepared and simmering during their absence. Dinner was served quickly and eaten quietly. Mary O'Brien dreaded the moment Mary-Jane and baby James would leave. She ordered her family around like a sergeant major in a barracks. Plates were cleared, washed and put away. Bags were packed and suddenly it was time for Mary-Jane to leave.

"Right, go now, you don't want to miss your train and I have work to do."

She quickly hugged her daughter, kissed her grandson on his little forehead and retreated out to feed the chickens so that no one could see the tears pouring silently down her cheeks. Will and Jimmy took their cue from their mother and said quick goodbyes and followed their mother out to the chicken coop. Bridget and Maggie helped Mary-Jane out to the waiting carriage with her bags and baby James, they all hugged a tearful goodbye with promises to visit during the summer, before James set off to bring them to the station. When they were safely ensconced on the train Charlie turned to Mary-Jane "Well did you enjoy your week my love."

"I did Charlie, it was great, but I missed you and I missed our home."

"Not as much as we missed you my love."

Charlie kissed his wife on her cheek and his precious son on his forehead where he slept curled up in his mother's arms. They all nodded off to the rhythmic sound of the train only waking when they arrived in Belfast. They hurried through the streets in the twilight to their home, where the neighbours had lit a fire and closed the curtains ready for their arrival home. The glow from the fire radiated out to the street through the window. Mary-Jane felt her heart leap at the sight and hurried the final 100 yards, anxious to return to her little home. Charlie unlocked the front door and stepped aside to allow his wife and child to enter. The heat from the fire greeted them and within minutes Mary-Jane had baby James settled on a blanket on the floor and the kettle boiled for some tea. They sat in their armchairs either side of the fire admiring their baby son as he played with his rattle. They were both stunned when he rolled over onto his tummy and laughed at his own actions. Both laughed out loud startling James whose little face scrunched up and a huge tear formed,

"Ah James its fine, do that again, that was fun,"

Mary-Jane soothed her son before he could cry. James smiled at his mother as she turned him over.

"Won't be long till he is crawling, getting under your feet and into all sorts of mischief," Charlie quipped, "time for another?"

Mary-Jane danced away from her husband's arms, "Not in front of the child, Charlie," she scolded with a smile.

CHAPTER 17   GORGEOUS BABY GEORGE

The following Autumn Mary-Jane discovered she was pregnant again. Charlie and Mary-Jane were delighted and started planning for their new arrival due the following spring. Baby James started walking shortly after his first birthday and kept Mary-Jane, and her growing bump, on her toes. He was a loveable toddler, constantly smiling with an affectionate and pleasant nature. When his little brother was born on a bright and frosty March day James climbed into bed beside his mother and kissed little George on his soft downy cheek where he lay in the crook of his mother's arm. After a while, Charlie lifted James and carried him into the kitchen and left his wife and newborn to rest. Mary-Jane's younger sister Maggie was in the kitchen preparing dinner and immediately gathered James into her arms and started to sing to him. Neighbours called to congratulate them on the new baby and copious amounts of tea and soda bread were consumed. Maggie had arrived from Annalong the previous week and was going to stay with Mary-Jane for a few weeks to help her with the new baby. Maggie had married her childhood sweetheart the previous December and was hoping and praying for children. She loved her little nephews Sean and James and was only too delighted to help Mary-Jane get over the birth of her second son.

All the O'Briens travelled up from Annalong to congratulate the new parents. A heavily pregnant Susan travelled up with Robert and their son Sean who was thoroughly enjoying the attention from his aunts. Mary-Jane and Charlie had asked a delighted Maggie to be Godmother, so she brought Thomas to St. Matthew's Church to be christened when he was just 8 days old. By that time Mary-Jane was up and about, nearly recovered from the birth and happy to see her family. She cooked lunch for everyone on Maggie's return from the church with her new-born son.

As Mary cradled new-born George in her arms she nudged Maggie, "Where is Charlie's mother?"

"Mr McMullen mentioned she was ill and couldn't make it Mam,"

Maggie whispered in her ear before scurrying away to the kitchen to help serve lunch. Mary-Jane had confided in her mother the previous spring when she had stayed in Annalong for the week after Easter, that Charlie's mother had never called to visit and had never seen James. Mary had been horrified. "How could any woman refuse to see their own grandchild, and James is such a sweet child. He is the spit of his Da, maybe more of your personality Mary-Jane, but the spit of Charlie," Mary said.

On baby George's christening day when Mary inevitably asked about the absence of Margaret at the christening, Mary-Jane changed the subject anxious that attention would not be drawn to her absence. Charlie hadn't said much about it, but Mary-Jane was conscious that he was upset over his mother's intransigence. Despite Margaret's absence, it was a happy day, full of family love and laughter. As she left to return to Annalong that evening Mary hugged her daughter to her.

"We are so glad to see you and your little family so happy and contented."

The weeks flew by for Mary-Jane. Rearing her two boys while maintaining her home and looking after her husband, filled her days and she fell into bed each night exhausted but so happy and at peace with the world. Outside of her front door she knew there was unrest and sectarian violence, but she refused to let it intrude on her little family. Before long summer was over, the leaves on the trees in the park were turning golden and the nights were drawing in. Every day Mary-Jane brought the babies to the park for a walk in the open air. It was a bit of a trek to get there but she felt it was important for the babies to experience the open air, to feel grass under their toes rather than the hard city surface that surrounded their home. The city landscape that surrounded their everyday life sometimes made her feel somewhat suffocated and at times she longed for the fresh sea air of Annalong and the beauty of the Mournes, but she also loved the hustle and bustle of city life and Charlie's work was in Belfast, so she made Belfast her home. Her daily walks to the park during the summer months and the occasional trips to visit her family reminded her of how lucky she was to have the best of both worlds. After all, she had neighbours who had never been outside of Belfast, even on a day trip. Alice Russell, her next-door neighbour and newly found friend, had never been outside Belfast and had no inclination to even consider a trip outside the city. Alice had four children, the eldest girl Emma and three boys, the youngest was a year older than James. They had got chatting when both were out in their backyards hanging out lines of nappies and praying for some drying. Alice had been 'born and bred' in Belfast and was fascinated by Mary-Jane's country accent. Mary-Jane, in turn, was bowled over by her new friend's Belfast twang and her in-depth knowledge of the entire neighbourhood. Her husband Willy worked in the shipyards and both women worked to the same timetable when it came to putting dinner on the table before their husbands returned home from work. Despite their different backgrounds, the women had a lot in common and it was Alice who introduced Mary-Jane to the best butcher, the best greengrocer and the best local shops as well as the closest parks. When the weather was fine the two women were regularly seen pushing their offspring in their prams to the park and several hours later rushing home again in a bid to get fires lit and dinner on for their menfolk. But the summer was coming to an end and the evenings were drawing in so their walks to the park would shortly be curtailed, well for the winter months at least.

"We have so much to look forward to," Mary-Jane told Charlie that night over dinner. The children were already asleep, and a sense of calm and tranquillity transcended the chaos that a toddler and a baby can cause during their waking hours. Charlie had just been promoted and the extra few bob that brought in really helped with the growing expenses of their little family. Mary-Jane was a good housekeeper and made the most of their budget even allowing for some savings for their future. They were both looking forward to Christmas that year as they were planning to spend the day in Annalong with Mary-Jane's family. Charlie damped down the fire and they made their way upstairs. Mary-Jane looked in on her babies, pulled the blankets over James where he had kicked them off and tucked in George where he lay in his cot sucking his thumb and looking angelic. As they tiptoed out of the babies' room, Charlie looked over her shoulder smiling fondly at his son's peaceful slumber. He kissed Mary-Jane's cheek and they both got into bed and slept soundly.

The next morning Mary-Jane woke earlier than usual. She sat straight up in bed stricken with a sense of dread and fear. She felt as if a cold hand had clasped her heart and she did not know why, but she knew somehow that something was seriously wrong. She jumped out of the bed and ran to the babies' room and knew straight away that George was dead. He lay, where she had left him just hours earlier, but he was no longer sucking his thumb, his skin was pale and cold, and his little body was totally lifeless. She tried to call Charlie, but no sound came out. She tenderly lifted her little baby and wrapped him up in his blankets and hugged him close to her, but he was so cold. She felt Charlie's presence in the doorway and looked up to see him looking at George in disbelief. They both hugged him and rocked him and prayed for him to come back to them, but it was no good.

Charlie went next door to fetch Alice and within minutes the whole street had arrived. Alice's mother took George out of Mary-Jane's arms and brought him out to the doctor while Alice tried to comfort Mary-Jane. The community took over and cared for the McMullen family as best they could over the next few days. George had been baptised, so he had a Christian burial but Mary-Jane and Charlie barely functioned, allowing their friends and family to organise the burial. Mary-Jane's family travelled up to Belfast the evening after George had died. Mary and James O'Brien were heartbroken at the death of their grandchild and even more heartbroken to see their daughter in so much pain. Mary-Jane felt a deep physical pain in her heart that made her want to lie down and die along with her baby. She heard herself talking to people, accepting their sympathies and their advice but that person they were talking to was not her but some stranger who had inhabited her body and was stopping her from being with her baby George. Her home was full of well-meaning neighbours, but she wondered how they could possibly understand her devastation. She felt that no one understood how she felt, even her parents, none of her siblings had died, they did not know the pain of losing a child. They could not understand the guilt she felt, the constant dread, the fear that she had somehow done something wrong, that she had caused her son's death.

In the midst of the subdued chatter Charlie heard a quiet knock on the open door and turned saying, "come in, it's open," and there to his surprise was his mother, Margaret along with his father. Charlie was stunned. His mother had never even seen George, or James for that matter, yet here she was. Her hands shook as she placed them on her son's arms.

'Charlie, I am so sorry for your loss. We lost a baby son, many years ago, me and your Dad have never forgotten him. I am so sorry that you and Mary-Jane have to go through this pain'.

Mary-Jane was standing just inside the hall door and heard the exchange through the fog in her head. She stepped forward and looked into her mother-in-law's eyes.

Margaret held out her hand, "I am so sorry for your loss Mary-Jane, no mother should have to bury their child," with that Mary-Jane started to cry and no-one could console her. Not Margaret, not her mother, not Susan, not Alice, not even Charlie. Eventually, it was James who managed to stem the flow of tears. Susan had taken him next door to play with Alice's children and brought him back home to put him to bed. James saw his mother and heard her distress, and toddled over to her, climbed up on her knee and hugged her as tightly as a two-year-old can. He made not a sound, but tears streamed down his cheeks. The feel of her son's arms and his hot tears eventually registered with Mary-Jane and she hugged her boy, telling him everything was going to be all right and kissed him on his tear-soaked cheeks. She lifted him and brought up to his bedroom. Someone had removed George's crib and only James's little bed remained. Mary-Jane exhaled in shock at the realisation that George was gone but James was still with her and he needed her more than ever. She tucked James into bed and lay down beside him to sing him a lullaby. Maggie was watching from the door and turned and left them in peace. She checked back ten minutes later to see her sister in an exhausted sleep with her sons' arms around her neck as if he was trying to comfort her. She pulled a blanket over Mary-Jane and returned downstairs.

The following weeks and months became increasingly difficult for Mary-Jane. The death of her baby had left a huge pain in her heart. Even James tugging at her skirt for attention would not shift the pain. There was a little voice in the back of her head scolding her and telling her not to ignore James, that he needed her too, but all she could think of was George and how cold he was. The physical pain in her chest seemed to be getting heavier and heavier and she had no energy to dress herself let alone dress her toddler. Maggie had stayed with her for a month but eventually, she had to return home. Maggie was four months pregnant with her first child and would have stayed longer with her sister, but her husband was worried about her and the effect of looking after her grief-stricken sister and her family would have on their baby. Everyone was agreed that Mary-Jane needed to get on with her life and that she needed to consider James, but no-one could advise on how exactly she should go about that.

Each day Mary-Jane rose and started her daily routine but inside she felt dead and heavy and full of pain. Charlie tried to help but he could see that the spark in her eyes was gone and he did not know how to rekindle it. Alice called in every day and pushed Mary-Jane into going out to the shops for supplies and reminding her of the meals she liked to cook for her family. Margaret called every other day, helping with James and with the general household chores. Margaret told Mary-Jane that she regretted not being part of his first two years of life and she regretted bitterly never having seen George, "but that is my cross to bear," and she vowed to help Charlie's family in any way she could. Margaret told Thomas that spending so much time with Charlie and Mary-Jane now in their sorrow made her realise how loving a family they were, and she prayed every day for God's grace to help them get through this pain.

It was the following spring before Mary-Jane found that the everyday chores became easier and the pain in her heart started to lessen. James was the one who pulled her back from the brink and into life again. He was such an intuitive child, able to gauge his mother's emotions, knowing when to hug her and when to leave her alone. Sometimes Mary-Jane just looked at him in wonder before hugging him so tightly he would cry out. She loved James so much and she was so afraid that God would take him too and leave her totally bereft. Mary-Jane prayed every night for her baby, grateful that he had been baptised and praying that he was safe in heaven, she prayed for James that he would stay safe and healthy and for herself and Charlie, that somehow this pain would ease.

With the passage of time, things got easier. Charlie was relieved to come home from work in the evening and occasionally find her humming. She even smiled now and again and gradually hope started to return to the family. Mary-Jane and Alice returned to the park, not as often as before but as often as Mary-Jane felt up to it,

CHAPTER 18   NEW LIFE: NEW HOPE

Mary-Jane was quite shocked when she discovered she was pregnant again. It took her some time to get used to the idea of another baby and she held off on telling Charlie until she visited a doctor and spoke to him at length. She worried about carrying the baby, she worried about the baby dying like George had. She knew she could not go through that pain again and she worried how Charlie was going to feel about another baby. She had gone to skin and bone after George had died, but now with the pregnancy, she started to gain weight again. When Charlie commented one evening on how she was starting to look better, 'with a bit of meat on your bones,' she knew she couldn't put off telling him any longer.

"I'm having another baby Charlie," she said, and she patted her belly as if to comfort the child growing inside her, "I'm four months gone."

She studied his face for his reaction and was relieved when he beamed at her, his smile lifting her battered spirit.

"Delighted, my love, delighted," he said as he hugged her to him tightly, "Wonderful news."

They both went about their normal day to day activities for the next week, each worrying in their own little cocoon and shielding the other until one evening Charlie arrived home from work early to find Mary-Jane crying softly over the fire. He dropped his lunch pail in fright and ran to her side,

"What's wrong my love, what's happened?"

Fear caused his voice to tremble as he took her in his arms, ignoring James who was sitting on the floor playing quietly by himself.

"Nothing, love, nothing, I just feel a bit emotional at the minute," Mary-Jane leapt to her feet wiping her tears with her apron and lifting the pot lid to check on the dinner.

"Come on Mary-Jane tell me what's wrong, love, let me help you."

Mary-Jane could not hold back her tears and she wept loudly while Charlie held her until she was spent. Through her tears, Mary-Jane managed to tell Charlie about how scared she was,

"I worry so much Charlie. Every morning I worry that I will find James dead in his cot. Every day, I worry that something will happen to this baby growing inside me. I can't find any joy in anything. Not in playing with James, not in looking after our home. I'm just so scared, all the time." Charlie sat and held her as they talked and talked, first about James, about the new baby and then about George. Mary-Jane wasn't surprised to hear Charlie tell her that he felt the same way.

"I'm scared, Mary-Jane, of course I am. But I'm more worried about you. It will be fine, you know. Just talk to me. I will always listen to you, love. I understand, honestly, I do. George was my son too."

Mary-Jane hugged Charlie to her.

"Oh Charlie, I'm just so scared. Why did our baby have to die, why our gorgeous little George," and she sobbed into his shoulder as he held her tightly to him.

"Hush now love, hush. George is gone but we have to think of James and the baby inside you. We have to look forward, not back."

He pulled her away from him and held her by her upper arms. Looking into her tear-soaked eyes, "We will never forget George, but we have to look forward. For James and for the child you're carrying."

Mary-Jane nodded as Charlie wiped away her tears. Talking to each other and realising that they both felt the same way helped them both to come to terms with their feelings and put their fears to one side. They both swore that they would never again bottle up their fears and would help each other through whatever life threw at them.

As the months passed and Mary-jane got bigger she started to relax and took her condition as a good omen for the future. James was fascinated by his mother's big belly and by the movement he could feel when he sat on his mother's knee. Every evening after dinner James sat on his mother's lap and put his little ear gently on her bump, laughing out loud with excitement when he felt a kick from the growing baby inside her. His laughter set Charlie and Mary-Jane laughing too and for the first time in months, a sense of happiness returned to the McMullen family. Charlie tucked James into bed at night and read him a story from his story book that his grandma Margaret had bought him while Mary-Jane got on with her knitting. Mary-Jane loved to see her husband so attentive to James, to hear his voice so gentle and kind and James hanging on every word. Her knitting needles clicked furiously every evening and the pile of baby clothes grew, leaving her with a sense of contentment and achievement. She was finally looking forward to this new life.

James turned three in October and just six weeks later Susannah was born. She was a beauty just like her mother. Mary-Jane teased Charlie that he took one look at her and fell in love. By the time Susannah was a year old, she had a full head of red curls and a temper to match. She ruled the household with her tiny fists and laughter once again filled their home and their hearts. Within two years the family expanded again with the birth of baby Charlie followed closely by Mary Bridget. James immediately named her Mamie and the name stuck with her until adulthood. With four children under the age of seven Mary-Jane did not get time to brood over little George but he was always there in the back of her mind. Every so often a smile or a sound from Charlie or Mamie would trigger an instant flashback to George and in that split second, she could smell him and feel him and when that second was over all that was left of that warmth was a cold pain in her heart which made her catch her breath and threatened to totally engulf her until she exhaled. James seemed to understand when these flashbacks hit her, somehow recognising the pain, visible in her eyes and in the way she held herself. When he saw those signs, he took her hand and smiled, a smile that pulled her back into their lives.

James had started school and was doing well. He remained a placid child with a bright friendly personality and he made new friends easily. Mary-Jane fed and dressed her brood every morning and they all escorted James to the school gates. Susannah cried when James started school. She couldn't understand why her brother was allowed to go to school and she had to stay home with the babies. In her little brain she and James were the same age, so it made no sense to her that he was allowed to go to school and she wasn't. The first few mornings when they left James at the school gate she stamped her feet and demanded that she go in as well. She cried the whole way home which started her younger brother and sister crying in sympathy. By the time she got home Mary-Jane was fit to be tied. After three mornings of bad-tempered foot stamping and incessant crying by all three Mary-Jane was at the end of her tether. It was her mother in law Margaret who came up with a plan. She sat Susannah down and explained to her that her ma needed her to help with the babies, she explained to Susannah that she was a big girl and that she was needed more at home than in school. She told her that next year when Charlie and Mamie were bigger, her ma would be able to look after them on her own and then Susannah could go to school. At first, Susannah was incredulous but as she listened to her granny the idea gradually seeped in and slowly Susannah started to smile. Minutes later Susannah was falling over herself trying to help Mary-Jane feed and change the babies. The next morning a totally cooperative Susannah helped Mary-Jane, dressed herself and helped to get the babies ready for the walk to the school. "Me staying home to help Ma, I go to school next year when Ma can look after the babies by herself," she told James with a smug air. Mary-Jane smiled to herself and thanked Susannah for her help. She admired her daughter's strong spirit. Susannah liked to be in charge, but she also liked to be useful, to be needed. She was going to be a formidable woman. Mary-Jane felt a debt of gratitude to Margaret for her advice. "Thank you so much Mrs McMullen, I never would have thought of that." Margaret smiled at her daughter in law, "not at all Mary-Jane, Emily was just the same when Annie started school."

Margaret had become such an intricate member of their little family and Mary-Jane was grateful that she was in her children's lives. She realised that Margaret bitterly regretted never having seen little George before he died. In the days after baby George's funeral they had talked while Margaret and Mary-Jane had both wept, "I know I cannot make up the years I have missed but please let me try. Let me see my grandson." Charlie and Mary-Jane had opened their arms to her and had never held it against her, involving her in her grandchildren's lives at every opportunity. Margaret called into Mary-Jane every other day and once a week she offered to babysit while Mary-Jane went to the shops. She brought them out to meet her neighbours and boasted about what lovely children they were.

"James favours his Da's looks but not his character, he's a placid child, pleasant and easy going. Susannah favours her mother's looks, but she definitely inherited her father's personality, just look at the devilment in those eyes and sure her sunny smile could light up a room. The two youngest, Charlie and Mamie are too young yet to judge who they're like, but I reckon they both have the look of her Charlie about them, don't they?" Margaret told her neighbour, Mrs Smith.

Once Susannah had settled down and devoted herself to helping her ma, the mornings became easier for Mary-Jane. After dropping James at school in the mornings Mary-Jane strolled back home with the baby, little Charlie perched on top of the pram and Susannah walking alongside her. If the weather was fine, she would go to the park for a little while before going to the shops to buy provisions for the daily meals and then home to do their chores. Her daily routine kept her extremely busy and fulfilled. She loved working around the house making the daily chores into a game with Susannah. She taught her little daughter how to cook and keep house in the same way that her mother had taught her. Susannah lapped up the attention from her ma, aping her actions and doting on her younger brother and sister. On Wednesdays, Mrs McMullen called and minded the children for a few hours while Mary-Jane went into the city with Alice from next door. Susannah kissed her mother goodbye and helped her granny mind the babies. Alice and Mary-Jane both looked forward to these weekly trips into town. Mary-Jane acknowledged that while she loved her little house and her young family, sometimes, just sometimes, an hour without them in adult company was good for her mind and soul. Alice had four children as well but her youngest was a year older than James and her eldest girl Emma was in her teens and able to look after her younger siblings. Alice and Mary-Jane talked over the back wall on a daily basis and brought their children to the park as often as they could. The children played together while the two women chatted. They could talk about everything and often enjoyed a healthy debate particularly when it came to politics. With both women from different backgrounds, the prospect of Home Rule for the island of Ireland was a hot political topic, Alice was firmly against it and Mary-Jane firmly in favour. The two argued out the pros and cons and always agreed to disagree. Their friendship was too important to them both to fall out over it. They both believed that at the end of the day the decision would not be taken by them but by the men in power and they would have to live with whatever situation they found themselves in.

CHAPTER 19   LIFE ON THE RAILWAY 1905

It was late spring of 1905 when Mary-Jane announced she was pregnant again.

"At least when this baby is born Susannah will be at school as well, it should be due a few weeks before Christmas, so Charlie and Mamie will be well reared," she told Charlie that evening over dinner.

Charlie kissed his wife and hugged her tight. "Great news my love." Charlie was quiet for a while and Mary-Jane realised he was mulling over something in his head.

Worried in case he was unhappy about the new baby, Mary-Jane touched him gently on his shoulder, her eyes anxious as she searched his face for clues.

"What is it Charlie? Are you worried about another mouth to feed?"

Charlie jumped out of his reverie, "Lord no, Mary-Jane, it's something different entirely. There's something I've been thinking about for the last few months..." and he went on to tell her what was troubling him. Belfast Corporation had taken over the Belfast Street Tramways Company earlier that year, they were in the process of electrifying the lines so that they could modernise and expand.

"Yes, I heard that although do they really need to modernise?" Mary-Jane asked.

"Well, they do. The old horse-drawn carriages were slow and expensive to run so they are gradually being replaced," Charlie hesitated.

Sensing his trepidation Mary-Jane said, "Go on, what has all that got to do with us."

Charlie went on to explain that the corporation was recruiting amongst their current employees and offering full training for tram drivers, and Charlie had been considering applying.

"It's clean work, in out of the weather, no mucky overalls and boots and to top it all the money is good, better than what I'm on now," Charlie hesitantly explained to Mary-Jane.

"Why wouldn't you apply, what are you waiting for. Go into the office in the morning, apply before all the places are gone!" Mary-Jane scolded him.

Charlie laughed and hugged his wife before spinning her around the room much to the surprise and delight of the children. Susannah grabbed James and spun him around mimicking her parents with both children squealing with delight.

The following morning Charlie went into work early and headed for the office with Mary-Jane's voice ringing in his ears.

"Go down to the office first thing and apply before all the places are filled."

Mary-Jane was on tender-hooks waiting on Charlie to arrive home that evening.

"Well?" she asked the second he stepped through the door.

"I made the application first thing. I went into the manager, Mr. McClelland and he couldn't have been more helpful. Told me that it was men of my calibre they need on the trams," Charlie beamed, "The application is gone in and he as good as told me I have it."

Mary-Jane gave a whoop of delight and they danced around the kitchen, much to the delight of their children who joined in the fun.

The transfer came through quicker than they had expected and by the following month, Charlie had been transferred into the tramways section. He came home every evening full of stories about the training, his excitement spread to the rest of the family. When training finished, and he brought his first tram down Royal Avenue in the city, Mary-Jane was there with the children to cheer him on. He was just so happy in his work. Margaret told Mary-Jane that Charlie had never shied from hard work and had always been happy with his lot in life, but Mary-Jane knew that this new job fulfilled a need in him that he didn't know he had. She thought he looked smart in his uniform and took great care to have it pressed to perfection every day. He left the house whistling every morning with a spring in his step and returned each evening with a smile. His pay packet at the end of the week reflected the extra responsibility and life was good.

William Ernest was born in early December and was christened in the run-up to the Christmas activities in St. Matthew's church. All of his siblings had been christened there and his brother George had been buried there. Charlie was still Church of Ireland and while he rarely attended Church, he was quite happy for Mary-Jane to attend and to bring their children up in the Catholic faith. Her neighbours never commented directly to her face, but she knew that their family was the subject of gossip from time to time. Most of her neighbours were more concerned with putting food on the table and getting on with their day to day lives but every so often Mary-Jane heard the muttered comments as she passed by with the children on her way to mass or in the mornings when she was bringing them to school. The majority of her neighbours were Protestant and proud of it, a lot of them were members of the Orange Lodge, an organisation which was vehemently anti-Catholic. Alice had told her all about The Ballymacarrett Orange Hall. According to Alice, it had only recently been completed, the free hold of the building had been bought out and presented to the Orangemen of the district as a gift from the local MP for East Belfast, Mr G.W. Wolff. As part owner of the shipyard Harland & Wolff and owner of Belfast Ropeworks, he was also the chief employer in the area and a popular figure. The two women sat on a park bench supervising their children as they talked, "He's a member of the Conservative and Unionist party, totally against Home Rule and a strong supporter of Edward Carson. He's German-born but worked in Manchester before he ended up here in the shipyards," Alice told Mary-Jane.

"But is he not retired from the shipyard now he is in Westminster?" Mary-Jane asked her friend.

"Yes, that's right, Willy was telling me they call him Teutonic in Westminster after one of his ships."

Mary-Jane knew that Mr. Wolff was highly regarded by their neighbours and that most of them had voted for him. She had heard the talk in the shops and on the street. Her neighbours knew she was Catholic but rarely brought it up in front of her. If a group of neighbours were chatting and the subject of Home Rule came up, they changed the subject if Mary-Jane was within earshot. They also gossiped about her when she not around, she had heard their whispers when they thought she couldn't hear them, but she ignored them believing that if she didn't comment they would grow tired of gossiping about her. She never mentioned any of this to Charlie in case he would get angry or hurt on her behalf or insist on tackling the women concerned. She didn't want Charlie sticking up for her in public, thinking it was better to say nothing. Let sleeping dogs lie, was a favourite saying of her mothers and Mary-Jane decided that was the best course of action. She would never dream of telling her mother any of this because she knew that Mary worried about her and the children living in the city and she also worried about the fact that theirs was a mixed marriage. Mary-Jane had no wish to add to her mother's worries by telling her of incidental stuff that was of no real importance, at least not to Mary-Jane and Charlie anyway.

CHAPTER 20
GENERAL STRIKE AND COMRADESHIP 1907

Charlie arrived home from work late that July evening. He burst in through the door and swooped on young Ernie, who at nineteen months, was finally walking, although somewhat unsteadily. The poor child got such a fright he screamed in terror. His little face screwed up and his bottom lip trembled. Charlie hugged him tightly, "it's okay Ernie, it's just your Da." At that, he hoisted Ernie up on his shoulder and used his other arm to draw Mary-Jane in close to his chest. He danced them both around the kitchen with the other children joining in.

"It's days like these that make me proud to be a Belfast man, my love," and he planted a kiss firmly on her cheek.

Mary-Jane laughed and spun back to the stove. "It's great to see people pulling together Charlie isn't it?" Mary-Jane had witnessed herself the rally at the City Hall earlier that day. Normally she packed up her herself and her children and headed to the relative peace of Annalong around the time of the 12th July marches. The Orange Order held marches every year on the 12th July to celebrate the Protestant King William of Orange defeating the Catholic King James 11 in 1690 at the Battle of the Boyne. Every year those marches sparked sectarian violence in the northern portion of Ireland but this year, for the first time ever, both Unionist and Nationalist flute bands marched down the Shankill Road towards a rally at City Hall were upwards of 200,000 people attended, Protestant and Catholic united, rallying together towards a common goal. The whole city was energised, with workers from all parts of the city united in their struggle for a better way of life, a better standard of living, a future for themselves and their families.

While Charlie was extremely happy in his work for Belfast Corporation Tramways, most of his friends and neighbours were not so lucky. They were mostly unskilled workers in the shipyards and engineering works, with long hours and no fixed contracts. Unless you were a skilled worker, hours could be erratic at times and many found it difficult to keep the rent paid and food on the table. There was general unrest in the city and talks of unionising the docks to improve working conditions for the majority of the more than 9000 men employed there. Earlier that year Charlie's next-door neighbour, Willy, had told him about a meeting he had attended where he heard James Larkin speak to hundreds of men about joining the National Union of Dock Labourers. Larkin was from Liverpool, but he was charged with organising the Union in Belfast docks.

"Inspirational he was Charlie, inspirational. I've joined the Union and I'm talking to other lads to get them to join as well for if we stand united surely we can fight for a better life," Willy told Charlie.

"Aye he was some speaker," John agreed. John was a packer and had already been a member of the Union for some time. "And everything he said was plain common sense. We need to stand together and if we do, everyone will benefit."

The strike had started in April and had spread rapidly. Everyone Charlie and Mary-Jane knew supported the strike.

"At least we have some sort of income while the strike is on," Alice told Mary-Jane, "The strike pay from the Union may not be much but its constant and it will be all worth it when we win, and Willy gets better pay and working hours."

All their friends and neighbours had attended the rally that day at City Hall. Thousands of people thronged the city centre, all marching for the chance of a better life. For the first time that most people could remember Protestant and Catholic were united in a common goal. Even the Royal Irish Constabulary supported the strikers, refusing to escort blackleg drivers brought in from the mainland to replace the striking carters. This mutiny by the Royal Irish Constabulary led to British troops being deployed on the streets in Belfast. But once that happened things took a dramatic turn for the worst from the striker's point of view.

Mary-Jane was at her usual place in the scullery preparing dinner when Charlie came home with the news. She knew by his face the moment he walked in the door that something was wrong.

"The British army shot dead innocent people in west Belfast, Catholics," Charlie told her with a worried expression, "God knows where this will lead, there's all sorts of talk being bandied about and the old sectarian views are coming out again."

True enough the press stoked the sectarian aspect to the shootings, once again pitting Catholic against Protestant. Then to make matters even worse the Union realised they could not afford to pay these striking dockers for much longer and within weeks the strike was broken, and normal life resumed. Sectarianism was rife once again but working conditions gradually improved as employers realised that they did not want a repeat of summer 1907.

That small change was all that was needed for Willy and Alice and their neighbours.

"When you constantly live on or below the breadline then just a small improvement can make a major difference in your life," Alice told Mary-Jane. And that's how it was in Belfast. Steady work rather than infrequent hours meant the world of difference to most families. But sectarianism got steadily worse. The unification of workers regardless of religion witnessed in the lead up to and the duration of the strike was gone forever.

Life for Charlie and Mary-Jane continued as normal. Their priorities lay in raising their children as best they could. They took frequent trips to Annalong to visit Mary-Jane's parents. Mary-Jane wanted her children to breathe in the fresh sea air and to feel the might of the Mournes so any time there was a hint of violence in Belfast she packed the children off to her mother in Annalong. Every summer Charlie booked his annual holiday to coincide with the "12th week." During the run-up to the loyalist parades on the 12th July, Sherwood Street, along with most of the city, was festooned with banners and Union Jack flags. Gone were the days of 1907 when Catholic bands marched in the Orangeman's parade down the Shankill and into the city, instead, anti Home Rule rhetoric and anti-Catholic sentiment abounded. Charlie knew of plenty of others working on the trams and for the corporation who did the same as his family, packed up their loved ones and travelled to visit relatives outside of the city, anywhere to get away from the city, Protestant and Catholic alike. Charlie considered himself lucky that his family had the luxury of knowing that if ever things got too bad in the city they were always so welcome in Annalong. At the end of their holiday, Charlie and Mary-Jane left the older two children with their grandparents to finish out the summer in Annalong. Their grandad put them on a train in Newcastle and Charlie picked them up in the city, at the end of August, just in time for them to return to school.

The children loved their time in Annalong. They helped Will and Jimmy with the crops and feeding the chickens. Their grandad taught them how to catch fish and how to clean them out. James loved to fish as did his cousin Sean. Their grandad took great pleasure in bringing the two boys down to the harbour and showing them the best places to fish in safety. The County Down coastline is magnificent but could be extremely dangerous particularly for children. Their grandad showed them several good fishing spots and gave them a stern warning that those spots were the only places they were allowed to go fishing on their own. On the days they caught fish their Granny cooked their catch for dinner that night along with the vegetables picked from the plot. Susannah preferred to stay with her granny helping her in the vegetable plot or in the house or with her aunt Bridget who had a dressmaker and mending shop in the village. Bridget taught Susannah how to hem and sew which Susannah picked up quickly as well as developing an eye for design that Bridget actively encouraged. Charlie, Mamie and Ernie loved to help Will and Jimmy with the chickens and collecting eggs became a favourite game with each child vying to find the most eggs which they collected in little baskets. Their granny always praised each one of them in turn and rewarded the winner with an extra dollop of her home-made blackcurrant preserve on their scone. All the children enjoyed a sense of freedom in Annalong that they couldn't have in Belfast. Mary and James loved to have them stay and on fine days planned day trips to Newcastle to visit Maggie and her three boys. Picnics on the beach with all their grandchildren were the highlight of the summer for Mary and James. Their happiest days were the ones when the whole family, daughters and husbands and the grandchildren descended on Newcastle for picnics on the beach. If the weather was fine Mary and James played with the children dancing in and out of the waves as they lapped gently on the golden sand, while their mothers strolled arm in arm down the promenade enjoying the warmth of the sun and relaxed in the knowledge that their children were safe and loved with their grandparents.

CHAPTER 21. THE GREAT SHIPBUILDERS

Rumours raced around the city about a new contract landed by the shipbuilders Harland & Wolff to build three new luxury passenger liners and early in 1909 work commenced on the first of the liners, the Olympic, followed three months later by the Titanic and then the Britannic. Alice was overjoyed when her husband Willy found work in the shipyard.

"It's at least three year's steady work, Mary-Jane, Willy is so happy. These ships are so large they have brought in engineers from Scotland to build a new gantry and new slipways for the project," Alice was bubbling over with excitement.

"Here Alice, a cup of tea and some cake to celebrate, it really is a great start to the new year," Mary-Jane handed her friend a large cup of tea and a huge slab of fruitcake. The two women sat companionly together at the kitchen table munching on their cake. Mary-Jane was delighted for her friend. Life had been tough this last few years and the prospect of steady employment for the next few years was a Godsend. Up and down the streets of Belfast men and women were talking about the new ships. Families who had suffered after the strike were once again hopeful of steady employment, tentative plans for the future were made and everyone was positive for the near future at least.

By the end of the year the ships gantries were clearly visible rising above the cityscape. The prosperity generated by the shipyard filtered down into all walks of life in the city.

"Yes indeed, Belfast is buzzing," Charlie told Mary-Jane as he told her about his day. He still loved his job with the tram company and Mary-Jane was happy for him. His good humour was infectious, as he told her about his regular passengers, how they knew him by name, bidding him the time of day as they boarded and disembarked. Mary-Jane had no doubts that Charlie was a favourite with his work colleagues as well, he was so cheerful and considerate. A good sort, the type of man you could depend on and once again she counted her blessings.

Willy called in to seek Mary-Jane's support. Willy worked long hours in the shipyard and arrived home at night exhausted but content.

"It's all worth it, Mary-Jane, when I hand over my pay packet to Alice at the end of the week. You know yourself we have been struggling for so long now. I've watched Alice make meals from nothing but potatoes and mutton bones, stretching out the few shillings I could earn for so many years."

Mary-Jane and Charlie nodded their agreement. "I always tell Alice to spend it as she sees fit. She's no spendthrift, my Alice," said Willy. Mary-Jane knew what Willy was thinking. Alice had been without money for so long, she was very careful how she spent it now. She put food on the table, but she squirrelled away as much as she could every week, for a rainy day, as she put it. Willy had steady work in the shipyard for nearly a year and winter was well on its way.

"Did you see the threadbare coat Alice is wearing?" Willy asked Mary-Jane. "I said it to her, I said 'Please Alice, buy yourself a new winter coat, God knows you need it, the children are fine, they don't need anything, but you really do need a new coat.' But will she listen? No. Maybe she would listen to you, will you help me?" Willy asked, and Mary-Jane agreed without hesitation. Between Willy and Mary-Jane they finally wore her down. Alice relented and asked Mary-Jane to go with her into the city to see what was available.

The two friends so rarely had any money to spend on clothes for themselves they felt like they were on a holiday. They set off early on a Wednesday morning when the men had gone to work, and the others were in work and school and took a bus into the city centre. Anderson and McAuleys on Castle Street beckoned. Susannah had recently started working there and she came home every evening to Mary-Jane full of stories of the finery available, the gloves and scarves in silk and leather, beautiful tea dresses, fancy table linens and fine crockery. The two women took their time wandering from one department to the next. They finally found the ladies coats and Alice tried on every single one. It had been so long since she had bought herself anything she just didn't know what shape or size would suit her. Susannah spotted them going through the coats as she went out for her lunch. Susannah had a good eye for style and within minutes had found a coat that Alice loved. It was dark grey in colour with large buttons, fitted top and flared to mid-calf. It was also reduced to half price due to a small tear at the shoulder.

"I can fix that for you so that it will never be seen Alice, I know that even at half price it is more than you wanted to pay, but it will last you a lifetime, and it suits you so well," Susannah implored, "Willy would love to see you in that, you know you deserve it, come on, what do you say,"

Mary-Jane added pressure seeing that Alice was starting to waver, "okay, point taken, let me pay for it before I change my mind," Alice grinned and with that Susannah called over the shop assistant and the purchase was made quickly before Alice could change her mind. They left the shop with the coat in a large bag and giggled helplessly like two school girls all the way out of the store.

The two women travelled home on the bus laughing and joking, happy with their day out and their purchase. They sauntered up the street arm in arm before saying goodbye outside Mary-Jane's back gate. Mamie looked up as the door opened and Mary-Jane stepped into the scullery and then the front room, looking up at the clock as she did.

"Oh goodness, look at the time." Mary-Jane stripped off her coat and hat, putting them away before putting on her apron and heading to the scullery to start the tea. The younger children were in from school and Mamie had made them do any homework and then tidied up. Luckily, Mary-Jane had set the fire before she left so within minutes she had a fire going and the dinner started. She liked to have Charlie's dinner ready for him when he got home from work, not that Charlie would mind if it wasn't ready, but Mary-Jane felt it was her duty to have his dinner ready, after all, he was out working hard all day and that was her job, to make Charlie happy. She allowed herself a minute to reminisce, yes her and Charlie were happy, of course they had their ups and downs, but overall life was good. Her Charlie was still as handsome as the day she had met him seventeen years ago. He hair was still as black and shiny, well with a few grey hairs, and his smile was just as infectious, and she felt a warm glow at the thought of it. "Stop daydreaming girl and get your husband's dinner ready, it's getting late and Charlie will be home soon." Before long she could hear Charlie whistling as he came up the back alleyway and in the back door.

"Well Mary-Jane, did Alice get her coat?" he called out as he washed his hands at the kitchen sink. He planted a kiss on Mary-Janes cheek as she stepped away from the pot on the stove. "Yes, we had a great time Charlie, and our Susannah was great. I was really impressed with her, she has a great eye for clothes, obviously takes that after Bridget. She helped Alice pick out a really love coat, Alice is delighted with it."

Dinner was ready quickly and Mary-Jane was just dishing it out when Susannah arrived home from work. Dinner time was the usual boisterous affair and Mary-Jane enjoyed telling them all about her trip into the city centre.

"And thank you, Susannah you were great today, I think me and Alice would still be there if we hadn't met you, Alice is delighted with her coat."

"No problem Ma, when I'm finished dinner I will run in next door and get it off her, I have just the right shade of thread to mend that little tear and I will do that tonight, have it perfect for her."

The weeks turned into months and before long the Olympic was ready for its maiden voyage. Belfast shipyard workers were justifiably proud of the Olympic. She was a fine vessel, but the Titanic was the talk of Ulster. The largest ocean sea liner ever built.

"I tell ye, Charlie, she is an amazing sight, not just the sheer size of her, you should see the inside of her, the staircase, the glasses, the linen, just amazing," Willy couldn't stop talking about the Titanic, "They are saying in the yard that not even God could sink her."

Charlie thought that saying was asking for trouble, but he didn't want to say anything to spoil Willy's mood or the mood of everyone around them. The Titanic set sail on its maiden voyage, heading to France to pick up its first passengers, then on to Southampton for more, its last stop was in Queenstown in the South of Ireland where it picked up mainly steerage passengers before heading out to open sea for its maiden voyage to New York. It seemed like the whole of Ulster waved the Titanic off from the shipyard, the crowds were incredible with everyone involved in her patting each other on the back and revelling in a job well done.

When the reports filtered through to Belfast that the Titanic had hit an iceberg and sank with the loss of over fifteen hundred lives, the shock engulfed the city with many unable to understand how this could have happened. This beautiful ship, this unsinkable ship, had foundered on its maiden voyage. Willy was still working in the shipyard and he was first to break the news to Alice and Mary-Jane. Charlie heard about it from his passengers. It was the only topic of conversation for weeks afterwards. It seemed like the whole city was in mourning. The air of optimism that had prevailed throughout the city for the last few years disappeared and a general air of sorrow took its place. Prayer services were held in churches across the country in commiseration for the dead and for the survivors. Women gossiped on the streets and in the shops with some whispering to each other that the Titanic was cursed and that those who worked in the shipyard had jinxed her by saying that even God couldn't sink her.

Charlie told Mary-Jane what he had heard in work that day.

"No Charlie, I don't believe in a vengeful God, I know it should never have been said that even God couldn't sink her but that is not the reason she sank, that is not the reason those pour souls met their maker in that freezing water," Mary-Jane blessed herself in memory of those who had died, "People just should not be talking like that, it does no one any good."

Charlie took his wife in his arms and hugged her tightly, "You are so right Mary-Jane," he whispered into her ear, "God love them, to set sail with hopes and dreams of a new life in a new country only to die like that, God bless them."

The papers for the next few days were full of reports about how the Titanic had hit the iceberg, about the people who had died, who they were, where they were from and the purpose of their journey across the ocean. Stories were told about the survivors, who they were and how they came to be on the lifeboats. Stories were told of bravery on board the ship and in the hours afterwards, and of the simple fact that there were not enough lifeboats on board to carry the number of people on board.

The papers started calling for changes in shipbuilding and in regulations, calling for legislation to make it mandatory for every ship to have enough lifeboats to carry every passenger and crew.

"And rightly so," commented Mary-Jane as Charlie finished reading the newspaper article aloud to his family over the dinner table.

"How could they have thought that design was more important than safety?" queried James.

"Well, James, I hate to say it, and I know with hindsight they know that now, but at the time do you remember they thought Titanic was unsinkable," said Susannah, "The women were talking in work today although one or two of them made the point that if women had been involved in the design and building of that ship, safety would never have taken second place and there would have been enough lifeboats on board for everyone."

Everyone nodded their agreement until James said, "Your starting to sound like one of those suffragettes. Next thing we know you will campaigning for the right to vote."

Susannah blushed, "Very funny James, although you know Vera, don't you? She worked in London for a while as a lady's maid and the lady of the house was a suffragette. Vera reckons that if more women got involved in politics then the world would be a better place."

"What nonsense Susannah, sure what would women know about politics? No, a woman's place is in the home, always was, always will be," Charlie said.

"Well, I don't know Charlie. Listen to our Susannah. Woman are educated now. Times are changing, hopefully for the better. Why wouldn't an educated young woman like our Susannah have ambition to be something other than a housewife," Mary-Jane said, smiling at Susannah's obvious surprise.

"Ma, I am impressed."

"I don't know why. I happen to have read some of the pamphlets from the Belfast Suffrage Society and a lot of what they say makes perfect sense to me."

Charlie shook out the pages of the newspaper, "Mary-Jane, how could you?"

"Don't be so old-fashioned Da," James said.

"Yes, Da, your heard Mam, times are changing."

Mary-Jane laughed at her husband's expression as she started to clear away the dirty dishes from the table. "Don't worry love, I won't make you do any housework."

CHAPTER 22   HOME RULE OR ROME RULE

Mary-Jane stood over the range praying her family would return home safely. Charlie had arrived home the night before with a cut on his head where a missile had hit him as he drove his tram back to the station. James was now working for the City Council and spent his days repairing the streets destroyed by the previous night's rioting, much as his father had done when he started working for the council. Rioting had broken out all over Belfast in opposition to the Third Home rule Bill. It looked like it was going to become law and a lot of people were unhappy about it. The Bill had been passed by the House of Commons and was due to be enacted within two years as the Government of Ireland Act 1914. Lines were drawn between unionist and nationalist with the nationalist, mainly Catholic communities in favour of Home Rule and the Unionist, mainly Protestant communities vehemently against it.

Alice explained all about the covenant to Mary-Jane. "Edward Carson and James Craig, the two unionist members of parliament, you've heard of them. They don't want Home Rule. Well, Carson has organised the Ulster Solemn League and Covenant. On 28th September 1912 he wants everyone to sign the Covenant, swearing to oppose the government introducing Home Rule. By force if necessary."

"Where will it all end Alice," Mary-Jane asked her friend as they read the reports about "The Ulster Volunteers" a militia group sworn to block Home Rule by any means necessary. On the other side, the majority of Ireland supported Home Rule with John Redmond, Member of Parliament and leader of the Irish Parliamentary Party, holding the balance of power in Westminster and using that to push through the Home Rule Bill.

Mary-Jane knew Charlie had mixed feelings about it all. Brought up in Belfast he had always known some form of sectarianism. Mary-Jane hadn't to the same extent. Life in the country areas was different. There was no physical space between communities and people had to rely on each other more, so religion did not seem to cause as much division as it did in the city. "Maybe that's why you had no fears about being in a mixed marriage," Charlie told her, but Mary-Jane was becoming increasingly more aware of the danger herself and her family could be in if the controversy continued.

"At work, the only topic of conversation is the Ulster Covenant, with every one of my workmates intending to sign it," Charlie said, "I kept my mouth shut at break today."

Mary-Jane was worried by his tone, "Why? what was said?"

"Well, Ian said that we need to show them that we will not be ruled by Rome, whoever them is, and Joe said that if this Home Rule becomes law, we will be answerable to Dublin, called them all Fenians, priest-ridden and backward, Eddie said the country would go backwards if the Fenians get their way and get their parliament in Dublin. They were all in agreement. You know Billy Hilliard, that lives down the street in number 12, he pipes up, 'Well, Ulster says no!' Not having them papists order us around. Then he told the lads to make sure they all sign it and to talk to their women as well."

Mary-Jane stirred the stew in the large pot, wondering if they should move out of the city. "Did anyone speak against signing the covenant, Charlie?"

"Yes, Ed Mahon, from number 15 and he made a good point. He said that we had home rule in this country before and there is no reason why it couldn't work again. He reckons it would give us a say in how our country is governed, that we would have our politicians protecting our viewpoint in this Dublin parliament. That's the only time I spoke. I clapped Ed on the back and told him well said. You should have heard the grumbling from the rest of them. Not one of them agreed with us. Break was over then but I got some right looks of disgust, and from men I have known for years! A few of them had the grace to look a bit sheepish, let's face it they know I'm married to a Catholic but Lord, I couldn't believe the attitude of the rest of them."

Mary-Jane knew Charlie had no intentions of signing the covenant and not just because his wife and children were Catholic. Charlie believed that Home Rule could be good for the country but the one thing he and his workmates agreed on was that civil war looked increasingly likely, with the Ulster Volunteers on one side swearing to uphold the status quo by force if necessary, and rumours that the Home Rule supporters were getting ready to defend the right to Home Rule. The irony was not lost on Charlie and Mary-Jane, those claiming to be most loyal to the crown were the ones threatening violence against that same crown if they didn't get their own way against the wishes of the majority of the people of Ireland. You could feel the tension in the air as invisible lines were drawn and people withdrew into their opposing camps.

"As I walked down this street this evening I made a mental list of which neighbours would sign the covenant. By the time I got to our door, I realised that all but one of our neighbours more than likely would sign the covenant," Charlie eyes clouded with worry as he recounted his evening. And then he smiled, and Mary-Jane felt a ray of sunshine touch her heart.

"And then I walked in this door and took in the sight of you, my love, and the waft of fresh bread and your special stew. Sure, that would give hope to any man."

He swiftly took Mary in his arms and spun her around the kitchen.

"I love you Mary-Jane."

Mary-Jane laughed and pushed him off her, "Go away Charlie McMullen, what has got into you," as she spun away from him and back to the stove. "Go wash up, dinner is just ready and call the kids as you go through."

The weeks went by until the Sunday dawned for signing the Solemn Covenant. The only subject on everyone's lips was the covenant, who had signed, rumours that some had signed it in their own blood to emphasise how strongly they felt about it. Everyone Charlie spoke to was convinced that civil war was inevitable. Mary-Jane attended Sunday mass in St. Matthew's as usual with her children but scurried home without speaking to anyone. The streets were full of people heading into the City Hall to sign. Men, women with children in tow, all making a day out of it. Mary-Jane kept her head down and her children close to her as she hurried home. It was a relief to close her door behind her and step into the sanctuary of her home. Charlie was setting the fire as she entered the front room.

"Are you okay love?" he asked as he spotted the anxious look on her face.

"Yes, fine Charlie, just worried about where this will all end. It seems like yesterday everyone was at City Hall sticking up for each other, Protestant and Catholic alike, just supporting each other for a better way of life, yet here we are five years later, and it looks like we are heading for civil war. It's hard to believe that it has come to this," Mary-Jane replied as she removed her coat and hat and put them away.

"I know love, but hopefully common sense will prevail, I wonder did Alice and Willy next door sign it?" Charlie asked.

"Of course they did Charlie, and your parents and your brothers and sisters probably signed it as well," said Mary-Jane, "Most of our neighbours pass me in the street these days with barely a nod to acknowledge I exist. Ok, I still have my friends and even though I know they don't want Home Rule we just agree to disagree on it and don't discuss it. Times have changed. Sometimes I wish we could move to Annalong and just leave all this behind us," shaking her head sadly she turned back to the scullery to prepare dinner.

"I know love," Charlie answered, wrapping his arms around her hunched shoulders, "the lads at work reckon civil war is on the cards, but if it does come to that we will get the children to your parents, they would be safer there."

Mary-Jane shook her head, "James is 16 now, a young man with a job, he won't want to be packed off to the country, he will pick a side, you know he will."

Charlie and Mary-Jane looked at each other and saw their fears mirrored in each other. At that James popped his head around the door.

"Hi Ma, what's for dinner."

Both parents turned to greet their eldest boy who was closely followed by his sister Susannah who had been upstairs putting away her outdoor clothes. She was really enjoying her work as a seamstress in Anderson & McAuleys in the city centre and was constantly working on her wardrobe. Her days with her aunt Bridget had paid off and she was extremely talented. Charlie and Ernie called out, "going out to play ma."

Mary-Jane quickly called them back, her voice strident.

"Stay indoors today lads," Charlie admonished Charlie and Ernie, "I told you earlier, today its mass then inside for the day, it's best we all stay indoors today, ok?"

The boys grumbled but did what they were told.

"Now come on, you lot, you can help me get dinner ready." Mary-Jane pulled on her apron and delegated tasks to her brood, and before long the table was set, and dinner was ready. They all sat down to eat together and before long the conversation turned to Home Rule. The younger children didn't really understand and were more interested in finishing their dinner, so they get back to playing with their marbles. Susannah listened attentively to her adored older brother and her parents discussing the impending threat of civil war.

The next few months passed quickly for Mary-Jane and Charlie. Christmas came and went while they tried to ignore the rumblings outside their front door and concentrated on their own family. Charlie's mother, Margaret, called once a week to babysit but even she was worried for her grandchildren, particularly the older two, James and Susannah. When she voiced her fears Mary-Jane agreed with her but promised her that at the first sign of trouble she would arrange for them to travel to her parent's home in Annalong. She made that promise knowing well that if or when the time came James and Susannah would refuse to go. They were both in favour of home rule and followers of John Redmond. That night after dinner, they sat around the table as usual, but once again the conversation turned to the possibility of a civil war.

James was adamant that there was no other way forward.

"Da, the Ulster Volunteers brought in guns at Larne and they are training regularly, you have seen them, you can see how well trained they are and they have sworn to resist home rule. It's rumoured that the Home Rule supporters are looking at organising along the same lines. There was talk today in work that the British army based in the main training camp in the Curragh said they would resign rather than go against the Unionists. So where does that leave us Da, if the army won't even defend the law what chance do we have?"

His father replied, "Did you hear that Edward Carson suggested leaving six counties in Ulster out of Home Rule? And he was born in Dublin, but John Redmond is adamant, that if that is the compromise, that it will be purely temporary, only until the next election."

"Let's change the subject please, you are scaring the younger ones." Mary-Jane intervened with a nod towards Charlie, Mamie and Ernie who had stopped what they were doing and were listening intently.

"Right so, that's enough for tonight, God knows what tomorrow will bring. Let's get the smaller ones to bed," said Mary-Jane, getting up from the table.

"I am not a little'un. I am thirteen and a big boy, Mamie is eleven and she is big enough to help cook dinner. Ernie is the only baby cause he is only nine," wailed Charlie.

"Sorry, Charlie, you are quite right, you are a big boy, but you still have school in the morning so up you go," replied Mary-Jane with a grin.

The months passed, and tensions grew in the city. Mary-Jane was worried sick every time one of her brood left the house, fearing for their safety. Alice sympathised with her. She had not signed the Declaration although her husband Willy had signed the Covenant, as had her sons. Like Mary-Jane, Alice feared for the future for her family. Her three sons had signed up with the Ulster Volunteers and wore the uniform and trained every week. They were opposed to Home Rule and had pledged to oppose its enactment by force if necessary. They held their next-door neighbours in high esteem but just presumed that they felt the same way, just not with the same conviction that they had.

Against his parent's wishes James, enlisted in the newly formed Irish Volunteers, whose purpose was to defend the enactment of Home Rule, which put him in direct conflict with their entire neighbourhood.

Susannah squealed with delight when he announced it over dinner.

"Well done James, I am so proud of you," she patted her brother on the back.

Mary-Jane and Charlie tried to hide their fears, but it was evident in their faces.

"I am happy to know that you have grown to be a man of principle James, but you must understand how worried me and your mother are. You are a fine young man, but you will always be our boy and it is hard for us to reconcile the two. We worry that you are putting yourself in danger, but we also respect your decision," Charlie shook his son's hand.

"Thank you Da, Ma?"

Mary-Jane hugged her son and kissed his cheek, "Just be careful son, be careful."

CHAPTER 23   THE GREAT WAR 1914

Alice came running into the house startling Mary-Jane out of her reverie at the kitchen sink. "We are at war; the papers are full of it. Neville Chamberlain announced it this morning," Alice sat heavily into the kitchen chair, putting her head in her hands. Her dull grey hair normally pulled back tightly, and secured with pins, came loose with several strands falling over her face. She pushed them back tiredly behind her ears.

"I can't believe it Mary-Jane, what are we to do."

Mary-Jane crossed the floor swiftly and engulfed her friend with her arms. "There there Alice, please God it will be over before we know it." Alice had three boys, all in the Ulster Volunteers and had been training for this day for quite a while. The two women sat in silence for several minutes contemplating what lay ahead of them. Mary-Jane could feel her heart beat frantically in her chest, even though she knew the announcement was coming, she had hoped and prayed that a solution could be found. She knew in her heart and soul that James was going to enlist. He had said as much only the week before. They were sitting around the dinner table and discussing their day as usual. The hot topic with everyone they knew was the possibility of a war on a grand scale. It seemed to be a foregone conclusion that Home Rule would be shelved until the war had concluded. James had been at training with the Irish Volunteers the night before and he told his family that they were being encouraged to sign up with the army if Britain declared war as was expected. The idea was to support the crown and their reward would be the enactment of Home Rule on the cessation of the war. James had already decided that he was going to sign up with the 14th Battalion of the Royal Irish Rifles. While most of those choosing to join the Royal Irish Rifles would be of Protestant descent and staunchly anti-home rule, James felt that serving with that unit would demonstrate to those in charge that Home Rule was the only way forward for Ireland. Charlie and Mary-Jane were both fearful, the last few years of sectarian tension in Belfast and the prospect of civil war had been bad enough but now the idea of their sons going off to fight a war as a British soldier in Europe, to defend Belgium, a country they had barely heard of and knew nothing about, was terrifying.

As expected the first Irish casualty of war was the Home Rule Act. The Act was brought into law on 18th September 1914, but its enactment was suspended for the duration of the war which they expected to be over by Christmas. With Home Rule suspended, Mr Edward Carson immediately offered the services of the Ulster Volunteers. Already trained, and uniformed, the Ulster Volunteers signed up straight away. John Redmond, the nationalist politician, called on the Irish volunteers to join the British army and support the crown which in turn would guarantee home rule for Ireland at the end of the war. In response over 100,000 Irish Volunteers signed up with Kitchener's Irish regiments and were immediately nicknamed Redmond's army. Another 100,000 Irish men joined other existing regiments in the British army, secure in the knowledge that their service during the war would guarantee Home Rule for Ireland on their return.

In September 1914 James signed up with the 14th Battalion of the Royal Irish Rifles. Mary-Jane and Charlie tried to talk him into waiting a few months.

"But why James, sure it will be over by Christmas, by the time you get through training it will be over," Mary-Jane implored him. Susannah supported James and defended him. Susannah was stepping out with James's friend Martin who had also enlisted. While she was fearful for their safety she understood perfectly.

"Do you know that they are going to war to defend Belgium from the Germans. Redmond said that Belgium is a small, Catholic country that needs us to defend it. Ma I would sign up as well if women could go to war," she told her parents, her long red wavy hair shimmering in the light of the fire as she nodded her head to emphasise her point.

"Well thank God for small mercies," retorted Mary-Jane.

"Precisely," Charlie agreed with his wife.

Mary-Jane noticed that Charlie said very little, he just shook James's hand and retreated into his favourite armchair. The smaller boys, Charlie and Ernie were all excited at the idea of their big brother wearing a uniform and going off to war.

"Will there be marching bands James? Will you have a gun? When are you going James?" questions tumbled from their mouths without waiting for James to answer.

"Steady boys, steady," James replied. "I've to go to Donegal for training first and I will be back to see you before I head off to war." Mamie said nothing, sitting at the end of the table she listened to her brothers talking about war. Mamie was tall for eleven and could have passed for older and sometimes felt much older than Charlie who was two years older than her but with half her common sense. Mamie wrapped her arms around James's waist without saying a word then retreated into the scullery to start clearing up after the evening meal. Mary-Jane realised that

Mamie had noticed her father's retreat to his armchair and her own worried expression and vowed to talk to her. Mamie was such a worrier.

The next morning Mary-Jane waved James off to work to hand in his notice.

"It's grand Ma, the supervisor told us yesterday that if any of us sign up the Company have said they will keep our jobs open until the war is over."

"That's good son, but I just wish you would wait, just a little while."

James shook his head, "No, Ma, I have to sign up. It's the best way of securing Home Rule, I have to go."

James smiled at his mother and in that second, she knew he would not be dissuaded. James set off, whistling, with Susannah accompanying him as far as the main road. That evening James couldn't contain himself.

"Ma, it was unbelievable. You could hear voices, talking, singing and laughing from two streets away. I thought there was a travelling funfair around the next corner. My mouth fell open when I saw the queue leading to the recruiting office. It snaked around two full streets. There were posters on every lamp post, recruiting posters, they said we are going to fight in defence of small nations. Isn't that something Ma?"

Susannah was anxious for information, "Did you meet Martin?" Susannah was dating Martin, a nice young man from the next street.

"Yes Susannah, myself and Martin met up in work and joined together. We are going to be in the same unit." Within a few days James, and Martin, received their notification to report to barracks for training.

Mary-Jane and Charlie hugged their son as he left their home to join his unit, Mary-Jane sobbed into Charlie's shoulder. Her first born, her baby, gone off to join the army, to learn to kill some other mother's son. Her heart broke at the thought of it, but she realised she was not alone as up and down their street the same scene was repeated on each front step as sons and fathers went off to war. At 41 Charlie was of age to enlist if he so wished, but he was not inclined to do so. Men were needed at home as well to keep the country going and anyway according to all the newspaper reports this 'Great War' would be the war to end all wars and would be over before Christmas which was less than four months away. Mary-Jane prayed that this would be the case and their precious oldest boy would never see battle.

The months flew by with no word from James until the Sunday morning before Christmas Day, when James walked in the back door in full army uniform. Mary-Jane had just returned from Sunday mass and was putting away her hat and coat. She heard the back door open and glanced at the clock, puzzled, until James stepped into the front room. Mary-Jane screamed in delight.

"Son, great to see you. It's been months, how are you, are you okay, how was training?" Mary-Jane enveloped her son with questions.

Charlie started to laugh, "Steady, love, steady, give him a chance to answer one question at a time." James laughed as he hugged his father.

"It's been great, training is over, and we head to France after Christmas," replied James, removing his coat and hat to reveal his uniform. Charlie gaped in awe at his son. Mary-Jane gasped in unison. The boy who had left only months before was now a handsome young man who held himself with dignity and honour. Mamie and Susannah arrived from upstairs after hearing the commotion and a second round of joyous screams filled the household. The younger boys sat enthralled at James in his uniform.

"James, James, so glad you are home, how long can you stay, are you okay?" question after question tumbled from Mary-Jane's lips as she hugged her eldest son to tightly he had to peel her off him to answer her questions. James sat in his mother's armchair directly across from his father and told them all about his training in Donegal. The house reverberated with questions and laughter as they all interrogated James and he regaled them with his stories of camp life. Christmas 1914 was a happy one in the McMullen household and up and down East Belfast as those units gave their soldiers final leave before their departure for France. Mary-Jane danced attendance to her son in a manner she hadn't since he was a small child. His favourite dinners were prepared, his favourite apple tarts and puddings all served up to him with a smile and a pat on the head from his mother as if she was feeding him in advance of his travels so that he could store it up in case he didn't like 'that foreign muck' as she put it.

"I'm telling you James, I heard they eat snails in France, imagine, a slimy snail, ugh it doesn't bear thinking about." James just laughed and accepted his mother's offerings telling her not to worry, that their rations would be supplied by the British army and not the locals in France.

Mary-Jane and Alice met in the back alleyway on Christmas Eve to compare notes. One of Alice's sons was in the same unit as James while the other two were already in France. She had no word from them since and waited patiently on the postman every day in the hope of receiving some communication from one of them.

"I tell ye Mary-Jane, my heart pounds every time I see the postman and then when he passes my door I am devastated cause I haven't got any word from either of them. Just one letter letting me know they are okay, that's all I need," Alice confided in Mary-Jane, "and I dread Arthur going back to his unit on Boxing Day, what am I to do with the three of them serving?"

Mary-Jane wrapped her friend in a gentle hug and the two women clung together in the back alleyway in the cold and wind with the sounds of Christmas cheer in each household filtering out in waves. Reluctantly they both returned to their households putting on their brave faces that were reserved for their families and joined in the revelries.

All too soon Boxing Day dawned and James had to leave to rejoin his unit. Mary-Jane cooked his favourite breakfast and then made up a packed lunch for him to bring with him on his trip back to the training camp. The whole family made the effort to make his leaving a joyous occasion rather than a sad one and James left Sherwood Street with his family's blessing ringing in his ears.

The house seemed incredibly quiet to Mary-Jane after he had gone. Susannah left to say her goodbyes to Martin who was also travelling back that day and Mary-Jane told her to wish him well from her and Charlie. Wee Charlie and Ernie, fascinated by the idea of war, ran up and down the back alleyway playing soldiers. Mamie was subdued but didn't want to talk when Mary-Jane asked her if she was okay, preferring to work away in the scullery, clearing up the breakfast dishes and starting to prepare dinner even though the thoughts of eating were making her nauseous. Within days the household returned to normal with the smaller ones back at school, Susannah and her father back at work and Mary-Jane back to her normal day to day chores but James was in her thoughts day and night.

Herself and Alice met for a cup of tea in each other's houses every morning waiting for the postman to arrive. Each was happy for the other when a letter arrived and each sad for the other when there were none. The weeks turned into months and the daily papers were full of horrific stories from the front. In early October 1915, Mary-Jane and Alice both received letters from their sons detailing their imminent departure for France. Both mothers worried about their son's safety and both said prayers to God that their sons would return safely.

CHAPTER 24   THE ROYAL IRISH RIFLES

James had enjoyed his military training, the comradery, the common purpose but nothing prepared him for the conditions he met in France. They had embarked in Belfast harbour and set sail for France in high spirits, ready for battle with a common enemy. They had sung and drilled and sung again during the crossing, with high hopes and a certain amount of nervousness about the unknown. His unit was dispatched to the front immediately on arrival.

The sights they met in the trenches quickly doused their high spirits. The trenches were deep, ten feet in places with sandbags lined across the top. A step was built into the side of the trench to enable the soldiers to stand up and peer through a gap in the sandbags to view 'no man's land,' the area between the allied trenches and the German trenches. When James arrived in late October 1915 the surface underfoot was treacherous. Thick mud sucked each footfall downwards as if trying to keep each boot for its own devices. In parts of the trenches, water flowed knee deep as rains soaked the surrounding ground and the latrines overflowed sending sewage and rats into the trenches. The rats were everywhere, eating the dead bodies that hadn't yet been moved and feasting on the injured before their comrades could come to their aid. The earth stank with the foul odour of blood and human waste and gunfire and death. James and his unit were shocked into silence on their arrival but didn't have time to process their reaction as gunfire rained down on them forcing them to move down the trenches to the next junction and wait there for their orders.

Movement was slow and difficult, the heavy rain making conditions underfoot more and more difficult. James and Martin stood side by side surveying their immediate surroundings with incredulity ingrained on their faces. There and then they made a pledge to look out for each other and get each other home out of this hell hole.

Their days soon fell into a pattern. They were very aware that the enemy trenches were barely sixty metres away. Each morning there was an unspoken halt to hostilities as each side had breakfast, then barely had they finished their tea when shots would ring out across no man's land and the day's hostilities would recommence. It was cold, very cold but that didn't stop the rats from feasting on anything they could find, human beings included. As the days grew colder the rain turned to sleet, then snow. James and Martin found conditions easier in the snow as their feet were no longer sucked into the mud with every step and the frozen surface was easier to move on. The months dragged on with little ground conceded and more and more of their comrades dying around them. The rain returned, and the mud grew deeper. Sometimes it seemed that the ones that died outright from a gunshot wound were the lucky ones. The wet muddy conditions lead to trench foot with soldiers losing their lower limbs from gangrene. Lice tortured the living, driving them mad with the itch and the constant pounding of guns and bombs drove them to the point of despair. Every so often parts of the trench walls would collapse from the pounding burying those sheltering there under tons of mud. James and Martin barely existed, they went about their daily duties as ordered, sleeping when they could.

There was a lot of gallows humour, of the type that only those that have served together would find funny. As one of the very few Catholics serving in the 36th Ulster Division James came in for a lot of slagging from his fellow soldiers, but he took it all in the way it was intended, which was an escape from the horrors they all found themselves in and replied to the ribbing in the same manner. When there was a lull in the proceedings each man took the opportunity to write home to their loved ones. James wrote to his parents and to his girlfriend Maria every chance he got. Those letters were treasured at home but not as much as the letters received in the trenches. Each morning at breakfast the company sergeant would do a roll call followed by calling out the names of those who had been lucky enough to receive post. The men looked forward to this every morning, praying for a letter or parcel from home. The letters were eagerly received and read and re-read for weeks on end until the next letter was received. Contact from home was the only thing that kept the men putting one foot in front of the other and getting through each day in the hellhole of the trenches.

Some days when there had been continuous shelling and lots of injuries, James thought he would go mad if he heard one more shell. The constant noise of the shelling, the screams of the injured and the shouting and expletives from the living all merged together in a crescendo that he reckoned was about as close to hell as the living could get. There were days when he considered putting his head up over the sandbags so that he could be shot in the head and wouldn't have to listen to the noise anymore or live in fear of when his turn to go over the top to attack the enemy was going to come or even if the rats would eat him alive at night as he slept. He knew he wasn't alone, looking around at the faces of his comrades he could see his fears reflected back at him in their eyes when they spoke. That common fear held

CHAPTER 25   LETTERS HOME

With the arrival of every letter Mary-Jane thanked God and his blessed mother for the safety of her son and implored them to look over him for the duration of the war.

"So much for it being over by Christmas," Mary-Jane said to Charlie, "It's now seen two Christmas mornings and not a sign of it ending and our James in the middle of it." She blessed herself and turned to see to the fire. The papers listed the dead every day and every day Charlie checked the lists before going home from work. Mary-Jane listened out for his arrival every evening in a way she hadn't since they were newly-weds. She watched out the top bedroom window and knew from his gait that their son was not on the list today. Alice was devastated when her eldest was reported missing in action at the Battle of Gallipoli, but she prayed daily that he had been captured and was somewhere behind enemy lines and would be returned to her someday. She prayed with Mary-Jane every day for the safe return of their boys, figuring that Protestant and Catholic they prayed to the same God and maybe God in his mercy would listen to them.

Some of their neighbours were not so lucky, Mary-Jane had lost count of the number of households she had visited offering her sympathy to a demented mother and bringing bread and tarts to feed the grieving family. Husbands and fathers never to return to this warren of streets leaving wives alone and children fatherless. Willy Hughes from the bottom of the street died in Gallipoli, leaving a young widow and a new baby son that he had never laid eyes on. Emily Malone lost her husband in the Boer War and didn't want her sons to go off to fight, she tried reasoning with them, but they were adamant, they believed the recruiting posters, they believed Lord Kitchener and Sir Edward Carson so off they went to war against her wishes only to die in a field in Flanders only months later.

"How can our God be so cruel, how can one person be expected to bear such pain," she touched Alice's arm as Alice and Mary-Jane left her home after offering their sympathies to their neighbour. Mary-Jane could not sleep that night, she tossed and turned thinking of James in a trench somewhere in France, hoping and praying for his safe return.

CHAPTER 26   THE BATTLES OF 1916.

News of the rebellion was slow to filter through to Belfast. Mary-Jane couldn't believe it. How could this have happened?

"All those Irish men over in Europe wearing a British uniform fighting for small nations and what happens, some lunatics try to overthrow the British government in Ireland," Mary-Jane shook her head in disbelief.

"I know," Alice replied, "Willy is going mad, how dare they, how dare they distract government attention from what our boys are going through in Europe."

The newspapers were full of it. There had been an uprising in Dublin at Easter. Most of the city lay in ruins, the rebel leaders had been arrested and an uneasy peace had been restored. Mary-Jane and Charlie had never been to Dublin, but they had heard stories of beautiful buildings and a gentle way of life but had also heard stories of horrific poverty on a scale unheard of in Belfast. Civil unrest in Dublin was recent, with a general strike only the year before the war led by Jim Larkin, the same union leader who had led the Belfast general strike in 1907. Jim Larkin had led the workers of Dublin in a strike for better conditions but were locked out by the employers who brought in blackleg labour from the British mainland and other parts of Ireland. The strike was defeated with union members blacklisted and unable to find work anywhere. The only option for some was to join the British army so at least they could provide for their families. Others felt that no Irish person would prosper under British rule and became militant joining The Irish Republican Brotherhood. The rising took place on Easter Monday and the city now lay in ruins.

The newspapers reported that the people of Dublin did not support the rebels. They had sons and husbands fighting with British regiments. Thousands of men and boys had joined up to fight in the belief that when they returned their reward would be the enactment of Home Rule for Ireland and a lot of people were of the opinion that the rising put Home Rule for Ireland in jeopardy.

At the dinner table that evening Mary-Jane and Charlie were discussing the letter they had received that day from James. The letter had been written some two months earlier and James was in high spirits. He wrote to his parents that he was doing well, the food was good, and the conditions were not too bad. Mary-Jane was convinced he wasn't being truthful with them as she had heard that from other wives and mothers that the conditions in the trenches were dreadful.

"Why would he lie to us Charlie?" she shook her head.

"He just doesn't want us to worry Mary-Jane, he is trying to protect you," Charlie tried to reassure his wife.

"Sure, he is bound to know that there are a lot of men from this area in the same unit and they are writing home as well, there is no need for him to hide anything," Mary-Jane retorted, "I am going to write back and tell him I know how bad things are and to be truthful in future. Should I tell him about the uprising in Dublin, do you think, although I'm sure he will hear about it anyway."

"You have to tell him, sure, you can't complain that he isn't telling you the truth about where he is and not tell him something as important as that," Charlie replied.

"Wish I was in Dublin Da, I would love to be part of that, making history they are," wee Charlie piped up.

Mary-Jane and Charlie both stopped and stared at their son in horror but before they could say a word Susannah interjected, "Charlie how could you, and your brother over in France, wearing the British uniform, fighting for small nations, sure, this uprising will only set back the cause of Home Rule."

"Aw Susannah, do you actually believe we would ever achieve Home Rule? Sure, Carson wants the northern counties to be treated differently, those boys will never allow Home Rule to happen. The boys in Dublin were right, hit them when they are occupied elsewhere. Don't forget we are a small nation, at least we would be if we got freedom from the British," Charlie retorted.

Charlie was tall for his age and looked older than he was. He was due to leave school the following summer and his father had put in a word for him in the Corporation hoping to get him an apprenticeship. Charlie and Mary-Jane still treated him as a young boy and both were amazed at his outburst.

"Charlie love, you are too young to understand, just remember your brother is away fighting for the liberation of small nations, that's why he is in France. Have you no respect?" Mary-Jane said.

"Aw Ma, course I have respect for James, he is doing what he believes to be right, but I think James and thousands more like him were duped into signing up the British army and someday they will understand that," wee Charlie replied.

Susannah couldn't stay quiet, "Well I think you are disrespecting all those men who did the right thing and went off to war. What happened in Dublin was disgraceful and totally against the wishes of Redmond's army."

Her cheeks were red with rage and her eyes flashed danger at her younger brother. She spun on her heel and walked out of the room and upstairs with a flounce.

There was an uneasy truce within the family for a few days until the news filtered through about the execution of the rebellion leaders in Kilmainham prison. The executions went on and on and when the news filtered through that James Connolly, the trade unionist and socialist, who had been shot during the rising and was seriously injured, had to be tied to a chair so that he could face the firing squad, public opinion first in Dublin then throughout the country started to change. Martial law had been imposed and thousands were arrested. Men were shipped to England and Wales and held in camps accused of rebel activities. Charlie read the report from the paper aloud to his family that evening. One of the leaders of the rising Countess Markievicz had been sentenced to death but her sentence was commuted to life imprisonment in an English prison. Mary-Jane was fascinated, a woman leading a rebellion, who would have thought such a thing. Susannah was enthralled and also rather horrified. She was still convinced that the rebellion had damaged the Home Rule campaign.

Wee Charlie argued with her. "They were never going to allow Home Rule, the only way Ireland can rule itself is by taking Ireland back from the British."

Charlie and Mary-Jane exchanged glances as they listened to their children debate the issues. Mary-Jane thought that things had been bad enough before the outbreak of war when they lived in fear of civil war but now it was looking like they would have to endure war at home and abroad and she feared for her family.

The following July started off with fine, sunny weather which brought people out into the streets and parks. Mary-Jane and Alice had been to the local park for a walk before heading up to prepare the evening meal for the family. Everyone they met were talking about the latest news from France, the Battle of the Somme. The 36th Ulster Division were there, and both prayed for their boys. Alice had received a telegram the month previously that her son who had been reported missing at Gallipoli was a prisoner of war.

"I feel bad saying it Mary-Jane, cause I know there are so many other sons over there, two of them my own, but at least I know he is safe if he is a prisoner of war, at least I know he will be coming home." Alice had told Mary-Jane when she burst in the back door brandishing the telegram, beaming from ear to ear. Both women had celebrated over a cup of tea before resuming their household duties. As they returned from their walk in the park they exchanged the latest news they had received from their sons with other wives and mothers who also had loved ones at the front.

When she had finished organising the dinner Mary-Jane went out to the back alleyway to sit on the step and enjoy the evening sunshine as she waited for Charlie to return from work. Susannah and wee Charlie would also be home shortly, and Mamie and Ernie joined her in the back alleyway, Mamie on the step beside her, so earnest and anxious to be grown up, while Ernie and his pals played marlies.

Mary-Jane was so busy laughing with Mamie at the younger boys playing that she didn't see Charlie at first when he turned the corner into the alley.

She felt his shadow over her and jumped, "Charlie, I didn't see you coming," she laughed, but the laughter died in her throat when she saw the expression on Charlie's face.

"Charlie, what is it, is it James, tell me Charlie," Mary-Jane implored Charlie with her apron up to her face and a tightness in her chest.

"We don't know anything yet Mary-Jane, but James is on the injured list, he was injured at the Battle of the Somme, but we don't know yet how badly," Charlie wrapped his arms around Mary-Jane and held her as she tried to digest this information. A scream had formed at the back of her throat, but she would not let it out. She was conscious of Mamie, dear sweet anxious Mamie still sitting on the step, her face turned up to her parents with an expression of terror on her little face. The boys had stopped laughing and playing and young Ernie came over and wrapped his arms around his mams waist.

Mary-Jane pulled herself together and hugged both her children.

"Now, first things first, no point in worrying and crying until we know what we are dealing with. Me and your Dad are going to find out exactly what has happened, and we will deal with it then. Good news is, he is not dead, God save us there are thousands of homes getting news that their loved one is dead tonight, we are the lucky ones." Mary-Jane took her children by the hand and led them into the house, "Mamie set the table for dinner."

Charlie followed her example. Mary-Jane pulled Charlie to one side in the scullery "Go back out and watch out for Susannah and wee Charlie. They need to be told from us before someone else tells them and word will get around fast."

Charlie went back out the back door but met Charlie in the alleyway, "Son, your brother's name is on the injured list from the Battle of the Somme published today."

"Aw no, Da, Jesus, how is Ma?" Charlie exclaimed.

"Well, first of all, Charlie, if she heard you talk like that, she would say don't take the Lord's name in vain," Charlie quipped.

"Sorry Da, poor James, have we any idea how bad, could be just a flesh wound Da, couldn't it, it might not be too bad, could it Da?" Charlie's questions tumbled out one after the other,

"We don't know anything yet Charlie, get you into the house and help your Ma, I am going to wait on Susannah, here she comes now, hush, let me break it to her gently."

Charlie hushed wee Charlie as Susannah opened the gate into the backyard, but he knew the minute he saw her face that she already knew. Her eyes were red from crying and her whole body was trembling. Charlie put his arms around his daughter and hugged her tight.

"Susannah, don't worry, I know he is injured but as your Ma says it is not the worst news we can get because it means he is alive when so many others are not." Charlie soothed his daughter as she dissolved into deep, heart-wrenching sobs.

When she finally caught her breath she haltingly between sobs told her Da even worse news.

"Da, I know, and I am glad that James is alive, but Martin is dead Da, Martin is dead."

Charlie was stunned into silence. He checked the dead and injured list every day, first for James, then for anyone else he knew. Today when he had seen James name on the injured list any thoughts of anyone else had went out of his head. Now here was Susannah heartbroken at the death of her beau. Father and son placed an arm under Susannah's elbows and led her slowly into the house. Mary-Jane dropped everything and ran to her daughter when she saw her distress. Susannah collapsed to the floor where her mother held her while painful sobs racked her body, Mary-Jane rocked her back and forward rubbing her head and kissing her cheek. Charlie brought the others out of the scullery and into the front room leaving them for a while. Charlie, wee Charlie, Mamie and Ernie sat at the kitchen table listening to their sister's heart breaking in the scullery, each of them numb and unable to say a word yet unable to move away. Eventually, Susannah's tears subsided, and her mother led her upstairs, where she stripped her of her clothing, as she had done when she was a child, helped her don her nightclothes, then tucked her into bed with a kiss.

"I am going to make you a hot drink, stay there and I will bring it up to you."

Mary-Jane whispered softly to her daughter, but Susannah's eyes were already closing, exhausted from the emotional trauma. Mary-Jane stayed rubbing her cheek until Susannah fell asleep before returning downstairs to the rest of the family.

"Puts it all into perspective Charlie, here we were, crying about James and all the time poor Martin was dead. God help his mother, we will have to call there, but we will leave it till tomorrow," Mary-Jane pulled off her apron which was sopping wet with Susannah's tears. She hugged her family one by one then scolded them.

"Why didn't ye have your dinner. It's in the pot. No point in letting it go to waste, Mamie bring me the plates, Ernie is the table set?"

With that Mary-Jane sprang into action, feeding her family, finding relief in doing the normal everyday mundane chores which stopped her mind from wandering into the fields of France and the terror that had befallen her eldest boy and his friend Martin.

Later that evening Alice called in, she had seen Susannah up the alleyway earlier and feared the worse. "God, I am so relieved, I thought it was James and I know that sounds awful but it's the truth. God help Martins Ma, the poor woman, and poor Susannah, her young man dead. When is this awful war going to end? The war to end all wars my foot! How many of our men are going to die before this is over?" Alice ranted, hugging her friend and scurrying out the back door and into her own backyard.

That night Charlie and Mary-Jane sat in their armchairs at either end of the dampened fire. The curtains were closed, and the only light was from the dampened embers.

"Alice is right, where will this all end, Charlie. We don't know how James is, do you realise that if he has a flesh wound they will patch him up and send him back to the front. Do we pray it was only a flesh wound or do we pray that it is worse than that, cause if it is worse they will send him home? What do we pray for Charlie? And Susannah, she is heartbroken, she was really in love with Martin and now he is gone, how will she get over this? Our beautiful daughter distraught, thinking her life is over at 17. Why is life so cruel Charlie?"

Mary-Jane couldn't hold back any longer and tears poured down her cheeks as she cried silently for her son and for her daughter's beau and for all the men and boys who were fighting this war to end all wars. Charlie got up from his chair and knelt in front of his wife pulling her to him and patting her back as she cried on his shoulder.

Several weeks passed before Charlie and Mary-Jane received confirmation that James's injuries were serious. They received a letter from the company sergeant McAllister that his unit had fought bravely at the Battle of the Somme and that during that battle their son had received serious injuries which required medical intervention at the nearest field hospital. A few days later they received a letter from James, well a note really, letting them know that he was injured but okay. It took several weeks before they found out James and Martin's unit had come under major fire during the battle and three-quarters of the unit had died on the field. James had indeed been one of the lucky ones as he had survived but his injuries were severe. Charlie suggested that Mary-Jane take the younger children to her parents in Annalong.

"The break will do you good," Charlie said holding his wife's dainty hand in his large one, "If we get any word on James I will let you know straight away, sure I could be in Annalong in a few hours, plus poor Mamie is not herself, I think all this has had its effect on her, she is quiet and subdued, maybe helping out your mam and the boys will bring her out of herself."

The following morning Mary-Jane wrote to her mother and a week later all was organised. She packed a case for herself, Mamie and Ernie and set off on the train to Newcastle. James and Mary O'Brien stood outside the train station waiting for their eldest daughter and her two youngest children. Mamie held her brothers hand tightly as if she thought that if she let go he would disappear into the steam bellowing from the train. She scanned the platform anxiously for her grandparents. Ernie spotted them first and burst free from Mamie's grasp and ran straight to his Granda James, who swept him up in a bear hug before planting him firmly on the ground in front of him exclaiming,

"Why would you look at him Mary, just look at the height of him, you are getting so big Ernie." Mamie squealed when her brother pulled free from her grip but when she realised who he was running to, she took off and straight into her granny's arms.

"Hello Mamie, let me look at you," said Mary pealing Mamie off her proclaiming "well aren't you just a proper young lady, how grown up you have got, in no time at all."

Mamie beamed at her grandparents and called to her mother. James strode over to Mary-Jane and lifted the heavy suitcase like it was paper, "Come on my lady, let's get you lot home."

After dinner, Mary-Jane stepped outside to the front garden and took a deep breath. Mary had planted a rose bed some years earlier and the heavenly scent was carried into and around the house on a light sea breeze which cooled the heat of the evening sun. Bees were humming in the flowering hedges which surrounded the little garden and separated it from the rest of the smallholding. The hedge stopped the animals from trampling over Mary's precious roses and plants. James had built her a small seat for under the window where she could sit in the evenings, weather permitting, and enjoy the fruits of her labour. Climbing roses each side of the front door had grown into each other and provided a colourful entrance into the cottage and the scent followed everyone who entered and stayed with them in the front room quickly masking any cooking smells. Mary-Jane sat on the garden seat and breathed deeply, feeling the need to ground herself in some way to her roots, before dealing with James's injuries. Poor James, just thinking about him brought a tear to her eye. Later that night, after the younger ones were in bed, they sat in front of the fire while Mary-Jane poured her heart out to her parents. As she talked Mary held Mary-Jane's hand while James patted his daughter on the head and shoulder every so often. Mary-Jane had aged ten years since she last saw her parents only three months ago, her hair greying and lifeless and lines crinkling her eyes.

"James is in good hands. We will say a prayer that he will come back to us soon." Mary lifted her beads and said a decade of the rosary while Mary-Jane joined her in the responses, silent tears running down her cheeks.

Mary-Jane settled into a routine in her parent's home and the days passed quickly. She realised her mother was keeping her occupied so that she had less time to brood about James. The fresh air did them all good. Mamie came out of her shell and Mary-Jane was delighted to hear her laughing heartily at the antics of Will and

Jimmy. The boys adored Mamie and they took great pleasure in making her laugh. As he got older Will was unable to do a lot of the chores he used to do around the small-holding, so Mamie and Ernie helped under his watchful instruction.

That August was warm and dry. Every evening Mary-Jane sat out with her mother on the garden bench enjoying the last of the summer sun. Having worked hard all day both women enjoyed the respite, the last rays of the sun warm on their upturned faces and the ever-present sea breeze carrying the scent of the roses and the honeysuckle in swirls around the garden. Charlie arrived the following Friday. He had two days off work, so he took the train to Newcastle and the whole family travelled to the train station to meet him. Mary had packed a picnic and they found themselves a great spot on the beach where James spread a large blanket and the ladies served the picnic feast. They spent a few hours in Newcastle, the younger ones helped Will and Jimmy make sandcastles, some of them, major engineering feats, while the ladies walked along the water's edge occasionally dabbling a toe into the water. Mary-Jane was glad of the chance to have a catch-up with her sisters. They didn't see enough of each other, not by choice, just simply because of the distance. All too soon it was time to pack up their belongings and head to Annalong with promises to each other to make a bigger effort to see each other more often.

The following night Charlie joined his wife and mother in law as they sat in the late evening sunshine. Charlie lit a cigarette and exhaled with pleasure as he felt the evening sun on his face. It was the first time he had felt pleasure in anything since they had received the news about James. He looked over at Mary-Jane and smiled. His wife looked relaxed, happy even for the first time in a long time. She had her face turned up to the evening sun, eyes closed, and her upturned lips gave a hint of a smile.

"It's the effect of this place," Charlie said, "maybe we should move here, away from Belfast" but as soon as he had it said Mary-Jane dismissed the idea.

"Our problems have nothing to do with where we live, and more to do with the ongoing war to end all wars that shows no signs of ending."

Charlie leaned over and kissed her on the lips.

Mary-Jane gasped, "Charlie behave yourself."

"Never," Charlie replied.

At that, Mamie called out "Tea in the pot" so they all retreated into the kitchen for tea and apple tart, each of them a little more hopeful and little more content than they had been.

Sunday came around too quickly. Charlie and Mary-Jane packed up their belongings and James once again dropped them into the train station together with a parcel from Mary with fresh bread and apples to sustain them on their journey home.

"Thank you, Charlie, I feel so much better, so much more hopeful about the future now," said Mary-Jane when they were nearly home, "The trip was great for Mamie as well, it was a great idea on your part."

Charlie put his arm around his wife and kissed her gently on the cheek.

"As long as we have each other we can deal with whatever life throws at us" Charlie replied. The next morning the McMullen household fell into its normal routine, but Mary-Jane gave herself extra chores so that she was too occupied to think and by evening too tired to even contemplate what James was going through. It was several weeks before they received another letter from James. The letter was light-hearted and tried to diminish what he was going through. The hospital had also written to James and Mary-Jane outlining what had happened to James. The doctors had tried to repair the injuries to his leg at the field hospital, but infection set in and eventually they had to amputate his leg. The intervention worked in that they saved James's life, but recovery was slow.

James arrived home to Belfast just under a year after he had been injured. His parents were waiting on the quayside to meet their son when the hospital boat docked. He walked down the gangplank using his crutch from a distance looking young and relatively healthy. He had been fitted with a wooden leg so that, as he put it, when he walked one trouser leg wasn't swinging in the wind, and his uniform was new, issued to him on the ship on the way home. Mary-Jane watched him coming down the gangplank, noting the grey in his hair which wasn't there just three years earlier when she had seen him last.

She threw her arms around him, "Welcome home James love, you look good."

She stood back from him and looked him in the eyes and was shocked by the depth of pain she could read in his eyes, the lines in his face told their own story and made him look much older than his twenty years.

"Welcome home son."

Charlie shook his son's hand, lifted his case and turned to head out of the port to return home to Sherwood Street.

CHAPTER 27.   *FITTING IN*

James tried his best to fit back in with his family but found it impossible. Susannah and James had been so close growing up but now Martin came between them. James had been with Martin when he had died, and he tried to talk to Susannah about it, but she did not want to hear. He tried to tell her that Martin had died a hero, that his actions had saved the lives of his comrades, but Susannah told James that Martin should not have risked his life, that if he had really loved her he would have thought of her first and not risked his life. James tried but he did not know how to reach her, and he had his own life to think about it.

What James didn't tell his parents was that when he woke up after the amputation he still felt excruciating pain where his leg should be. His leg had been amputated above the knee and it took James a long time to learn to walk again with only one leg and a crutch. He was in constant pain in his leg which didn't even exist anymore. Added to that every time he closed his eyes he heard the shells and the screaming, sometimes he opened and closed his eyes twenty times to try and clear the images of the rats feeding on human flesh, the sound of the shells hitting wooden shelters and human bone, the smell of death and sewerage. But he told no one of the things he heard and saw in his head hoping that in time they would disappear. He had nightmares every night and he knew he woke his younger brothers when he woke screaming during the night, but he could not talk to them about the horrors he had been through.

He had met Maria some time before he had left for war, they had gone out on double dates with Susannah and Martin. While he was away at war he had written to her, witty, chatty letters, telling nothing of the horrific conditions they had found themselves in. He and Martin had made a pact, they knew their mothers could meet and they knew that Susannah and Maria were in constant contact, so they were careful to check with each other that they only wrote home light-hearted words filled with cheer and comradery. When he was injured, Maria had continued to write even when he hadn't replied, and it was those letters, as well as the letters from his mother, that had pulled him through the pain and anguish in the military hospital. He had grown extremely fond of her and was anxious to see her when he got home but he was worried about how she would react when she witnessed his disability in the flesh rather than just heard about from his letters which had glossed over how bad it was. He need not have worried, Maria was so glad to see him, so grateful that at least he had survived. So many of their friends had died in the war she was happy to have him back, maybe not in one piece but at least he was back. She called to visit the Friday evening after he returned home. Susannah welcomed her friend and then retreated upstairs pleading needlework waiting on her attention. Mary-Jane welcomed Maria warmly then made her excuses as she had decided to scrub her already well-scrubbed scullery and enlisted Mamie, wee Charlie and Ernie to help, then sent Charlie down to the local for a pint. Maria and James were left in the front room alone and laughing at the somewhat obvious attempt by his family to give them some privacy. The laughter eased any tensions James was feeling and for the first time since he came home, he felt a gentle awaking of the almost forgotten sensation of happiness. Maria's visits became more frequent over the following weeks and with her encouragement, James eventually decided it was time he rejoined life. His first forage into the Belfast streets was to call on Maria in her home, a short ten-minute walk for normal people that turned into a thirty minute somewhat painful hike for James, but when he knocked on Maria's door he was extremely pleased with himself that he had managed to walk that far on his own. The next day he undertook the same trip and knocked five minutes off the time. After ten minutes spent sitting on the sofa talking to Maria's mother he felt rested and asked Maria to accompany him on a short walk to the local shop. Maria hurriedly put on her coat and hat and the two set off for the short stroll. Every day James ventured out and every day he felt slightly stronger and a little bit more hopeful.

Because of his war injuries, James received a pension from the government so at least he had an income, not a large one but enough for him to consider his future. He donned his army uniform and travelled into the city centre to the Corporation offices to inquire about putting his name on the housing list. Much to his surprise, he was treated like a hero in the Corporation offices. The housing officer shook his hand and thanked him for his service to his country and several strangers approached him shaking his hand and wishing him well for the future. He left the offices assured that he would be assigned a house within weeks. He came home that day feeling better than he had in a long time. He would soon have a home of his own, he had an income and he thought it could be possible that Maria might love him. He certainly was in love with her and thought maybe he should consider proposing to her. His nighttime terrors had started to recede, occurring only two to three times a week instead of two to three times a night. He had adjusted to his wooden leg. The pain was now manageable, and he was able to get out and about without someone to mind him. Maria would make a beautiful bride, he thought, tall and dark like him he reckoned they would make a handsome couple. He couldn't stop the thought "even with one leg" as it jumped unbidden into his head and rebuked himself. James knew that he had to be positive, he had been in the depths of despair for too long and it was Maria that had brought him around. If she loved him, minus a leg, then he should learn to accept his fate and learn to live with it.

It was the autumn before James got up the nerve to propose. It was a fine evening, warm evening sun brought everyone out of their homes and into the parks and walkways. James and Maria sat on a park bench watching children play ball while their parents kept an eye on them, couples walking hand in hand oblivious of the world around them, dog walkers being pulled off the pathways trying to keep their over-excited pets in check, all making the most of the unexpected Indian summer. Maria was laughing at the sight of a small wiry man being pulled along by his very large, energetic dog oblivious to the look of anxiety on James' face.

She started when James suddenly turned to her, "Maria, I can't go down on one knee, because I only have one knee, and if I got down I wouldn't be able to get up again," he joked, "I love you Maria, would you do me the honour of becoming my wife?"

James was dismayed as he watched Maria's eyes fill up with tears, but that dismay quickly turned to joy as Maria whispered, "Oh yes James yes."

He jumped up and threw his cap in the air shouting yippee attracting startled looks from the families around them. "She said yes" he shouted.

The startled expressions changed to smiles and laughter. A young boy retrieved James's cap as his father shook James' hand and congratulated Maria. The chatter rippled around the park spreading from family to family as complete strangers approached James and Maria wishing them joy and happiness. It was as if everyone was in need of some good news and the sight of this very pretty young woman accepting the proposal from a young injured (albeit very handsome) soldier lifted the spirits of everyone in the park. It was nearly an hour before James and Maria managed to start their walk home to Maria's mother's house to tell them their news. Not that it would be a surprise as James had already asked her permission to ask for Maria's hand. He was looking forward to telling his own parents although he reckoned they already had a fair idea.

Mary-Jane and Charlie were delighted when James told them his news later that evening.

"Don't say anything yet to Susannah, Ma, I want to tell her myself. I know she will be happy for us but then there is Martin..." James faltered, unsure how to put into words how bad he felt for his sister, and for himself if he was totally honest, over the loss of his friend Martin. They had been a foursome before the war and now Martin was dead and him and Maria were getting married. He was torn on how to tell her he was getting married but at the same time he knew it would rake up old memories of Martin and how much she had cared for him. The following day James set off to the city. He planned to wait outside Anderson & McAuley's for Susannah to finish work and travel home with her. When the staff door opened James couldn't see Susannah at first in the midst of a large crowd of woman, all chatting and waving goodbye as they set off in their different directions homeward bound. When she spotted him, she was delighted to see him waiting for her and introduced him to her work colleagues. In turn, they shook hands with him, some flirting with him and other just openly admiring his good looks. She linked his arm and they set off walking with Susannah chattering about her day and about the different women she had introduced him to.

James heard little of what she said, concentrating on how he was going to tell her that he had proposed to Maria.

"Sorry what was that?" the word Maria and marry had pierced into his brain but he had no idea in what context.

"You are in another world, do you ever listen to me?" retorted Susannah, "I said when are you going to propose to Maria? You can't keep seeing her indefinitely it's just not right."

James stopped in his tracks and looked directly at his sister.

"I asked her last night."

Susannah hugged her brother, "I am so happy for you, James, a wedding. I can't wait to talk to Maria about her dress, I am going to offer to make it for her. Is she coming over tonight?" James answered his sister's questions in a daze, marvelling at women in general.

"It's okay James," Susannah patted his arm and quietly reassured him, "I am fine, I am happy for you and Maria, you can't bring back Martin and you can't put your lives on hold because Martin isn't here anymore."

It was James's turn to hug his sister, grateful that she was happy for him and thankful that maybe just maybe she was starting to get over Martin's death and get on with her life.

Maria was an only child and her father had been killed in one of the first battles of the war. While they lived only streets away, like James, Maria had been brought up a Catholic and she and her mother were close. They were very happy with Susannah's suggestion that she make the wedding dress and armed with advice from her aunt Bridget, Susannah got started on her dressmaking. James got word that he had been allocated a corporation house. The house was in John Street, off the Falls Road in the west of the city. James brought Maria to see it and they were both happy with it and both looked forward to the day they married and moved in to it together. They had set the date for March 1918 and preparations began. Maria's mother had organised a wedding breakfast in the Grand Hotel, Maria's wedding dress was nearly ready, and Susannah had been delighted when Maria had asked her to be her bridesmaid. Wee Charlie was taking his duties as best man seriously and seemed to have grown up completely to take on the role.

Charlie and Mary-Jane could not have been happier with their eldest sons' choice of bride. Maria was a lovely girl, pretty yet unassuming, and head over heels about James. Mary-Jane knew her son still had recurring nightmares, but he refused to talk to her about them, she hoped and prayed that he would talk to Maria and finally put that period of his young life behind him. Although it was difficult to do with news of the dreadful war on every street corner. Everyone they knew had either lost someone in the war or lived in constant fear of the dreaded telegram telling them their loved one was killed or injured. The so-called "War to end all wars" had been raging over Europe for nearly four years and Germany had the upper hand. They were winning ground over France and people were fearful for their future. The government had brought in conscription on the mainland after the heavy losses at the Somme and there was talk that they were considering introducing conscription in Ireland. Mary-Jane was really worried as Charlie was still of an age where he could be called up and wee Charlie was nearly sixteen so if the war went on for another year then he could possibly end up in France or Belgium and she couldn't face the prospect of losing her husband or her son or see them suffer injuries like poor James, "his injured mind is nearly worse than his physical injuries" Mary-Jane thought to herself although she would never voice that to Charlie.

The day of the wedding dawned with a hard frost. Mary-Jane woke James with a cup of tea.

"Up you get James, it's your big day today."

James rubbed his eyes and sat up to drink his tea.

Wee Charlie stretched and yawned, "Eh Ma, where's my tea," and gasped in astonishment when his mother handed him a cup of tea.

"It's a big day for you as well, Charlie."

The brothers drank their tea in companionable silence. Their suits were hanging on the back of the bedroom door, perfectly pressed and ready for them to just step in to. Mary-Jane returned to her room to get herself ready. The ceremony was in Maria's parish church, St. Matthews, which was the same church the McMullen family attended. Charlie's parents were not attending the ceremony but would meet them afterwards for the wedding breakfast in the Grand Hotel.

"You would think after all these years my Ma would have relented a bit especially where James is concerned," huffed Charlie.

"Ah Charlie, she is entitled to her beliefs, just be thankful that she's not boycotting the whole thing," retorted Mary-Jane.

Susannah had stayed with Maria the night before so that she was on hand to help Maria get ready. Mary-Jane couldn't wait to see them in their finery. She had glimpsed the dress briefly when Maria had called for her final fitting and was justifiably proud of her daughter's creation. With the war still raging, dress fabric was in short supply. Susannah had used every contact she had to get her hands on some white silk and teamed it with delicate Carrickmacross lace supplied by her aunt Bridget. Maria's mother had given her daughter her lace veil and a beautiful silver tiara that her mother had worn on her wedding day. The veil was edged with Carrickmacross lace and perfectly complimented the silk dress.

Mary-Jane checked her reflection in the mirror before donning her hat, a gift from her sister Bridget and pulling on her gloves, a gift from her parents the previous Christmas. Charlie whistled as she ascended into the living room. Mary-Jane laughed in delight, pleased that her husband still appreciated her.

"Give over Charlie, you're looking extremely handsome yourself," she retorted, kissing her husband on his proffered cheek. Before long it was time to leave for the church. Charlie locked the front door after him and Mary-Jane tucked her arm in his as they set off down the street behind their brood. The neighbours all came out to wish them well and their progress down the street was slow and joyful. James was well respected in the neighbourhood. His war service and his obvious sacrifice were acknowledged and respected by all. Most of his neighbours agreed that they could do with more young men like him, so on this cold frosty morning they turned out on their street and paid their respects, shaking his hand and wishing him well. Mary-Jane was touched by the warmth and good wishes extended to James and to the whole family. She vividly remembered the Sundays she had walked to mass when the only acknowledgement from their neighbours were whispered comments after they had passed, "Fenian" and "papists" and other much more hateful comments that she prayed her children had not heard but knew by the set line of James's jaw that he had heard but chose to ignore. James had not been inside St. Matthews since the week before he had been shipped overseas. His experiences in the fields of France had made him question if there truly was a God and on his return to Belfast, he refused to accompany his mother to church on Sundays. Mary-Jane had pleaded with him at first but then realised that he was an adult and was entitled to make his own decisions. Maria, however, was a regular attendee at Sunday mass and Mary-Jane felt sure that James would return to the church if his new wife requested him to do so.

They arrived at the church in good time and hurried inside to await the arrival of the bride. Alice was already seated as were Mary-Jane's sisters Susan, Maggie and Bridget together with their husbands. Charlie's brothers Randal and John were there with their wives and when Charlie went over to greet them he stopped in shock when he saw his mother and father sitting in the middle of them. Mary-Jane could not believe her eyes thanking God for their attendance on this special day in her son's life. She knew that Margaret still regretted her behaviour when James and then George were born, and she deeply regretted that she never got to meet her little grandson George who had died as a baby, so she hugged Margaret tightly and thanked her profusely for being there.

"You being here will mean so much to James, he adores you both," Mary-Jane told a tearful Margaret. Charles hugged his mother, shook hands with his father just as the organ started to announce the arrival of the bride.

Maria was a beautiful bride. Her joy was evident in her smile as her mother walked her down the aisle and handed her over to James who was beaming from ear to ear. The ceremony went off without a hitch and the whole party set off for the Grand Hotel. After the meal had been eaten and before the speeches, Mary-Jane sat back in her chair and surveyed the room around her. James was chatting quietly to Maria while Susannah chatted to Maria's mother. Charlie was in deep conversation with the priest who was had kindly joined them after the ceremony. Alice was talking to Randal and she could see Margaret laughing at something that James O'Brien had said. The whole bridal party had left all talk of war outside the door and the result was a happy gathering, hopeful and happy to share in the joy and love of the newly married couple.

Before long the time came for them to leave and go their separate ways. Maria changed into her going away clothes, a stylish suit in dark purple with a full skirt and a long jacket, this time designed and made with love by her new aunt Bridget. They were going by train to Newcastle and were booked into the Slieve Donard Hotel at the end of the promenade. Maria stood at the top of the stairs with her back to the wedding party and threw her bouquet in the air. The bouquet landed in Susannah's hands without her even trying to catch it and everyone cheered. The wedding party broke up as the happy couple left for their short honeymoon and every person there went home with a smile on their face and joy in their heart.

CHAPTER 28
THE END OF THE WAR TO END ALL WARS

The following month the papers reported that the United States had joined the war on the side of the allies. There was jubilation at the prospect, especially in the McMullen household.

"Thank God, Charlie, maybe this is what is needed to put an end to this debacle," Mary-Jane said as she kneaded the bread for the tea.

"I hope so love, I dearly hope so."

Charlie shook his head while reading the latest war reports from the newspaper. In work that week all the men were talking about the Americans joining the war. The papers had carried reports some weeks earlier about the torpedoing of the Lusitania off the coast of Queenstown in Cork. Grainy photographs showed the bodies recovered by fisherman of women and children who had drowned when the Lusitania went down. All were agreed that it was a horrific deed, and many debated how any man, even a sailor or soldier at war, could be so lacking in human decency as to believe it was okay to fire a weapon at a ship carrying civilians, women and babies. The sinking of the Lusitania outraged most people and Mary-Jane and Charlie were no different from their neighbours in their horror and outrage at this tragedy. Of course, many now believed that it was the sinking of the Lusitania that pushed the Americans into joining the war effort. Mary-Jane pondered that point as she and Charlie read the headlines of the Sunday newspaper outlining the American declaration of war.

"It's awful to think that maybe it took such an awful tragedy to bring the Americans into the war effort or was the sinking of that ship just the last straw for them? Would they have joined the war effort anyway?"

Charlie shook his head in quiet contemplation.

"Who knows, love, let's just pray that this will give us the extra manpower we need to defeat the Hun and bring this inhumane war to an end."

The bang of the back door startled them both.

"Ma, is dinner ready, I'm starving," shouted Ernie as he banged the back door shut. Mary-Jane laughed and wiping her hands on her apron went back to the kitchen to check on the dinner for the family. Thirteen-year-old Ernie was getting taller by the day and was constantly hungry. Mary-Jane deftly cut a thick slice of bread, slathered it with butter and handed to Ernie, "here that will keep you going until I get dinner organised." Hearing the commotion Mamie and Susannah came downstairs from where they had been reorganising their wardrobe. Susannah had bought some new items and gave Mamie a dress and two shirts that she no longer wanted to wear. Mamie was delighted with the "grown-up" clothing and arrived down to the kitchen to her mother to show off her new dress.

"That is lovely on you, just lovely," said Mary-Jane as Charlie let out a wolf whistle. Mamie blushed and then grinned with delight.

"I'll set the table Ma," as she lifted the cutlery and began to set the table for dinner.

The months passed slowly, and every day Mary-Jane heard of another death from Spanish Flu. Her nerves jangled if she heard just one sneeze or cough from her children. Alice had been left devastated when her only daughter succumbed to the illness. Bright and full of life on Sunday, struck down too ill to lift her head from her pillow on Monday and dead by Tuesday. Mary-Jane had practically lived in Alice's house for weeks. Forcing Alice to get out of bed each morning, making her get herself dressed and practically dragging her to the shops to get food to feed her husband. Alice and Willy had seen three sons go off to fight with the 36th, one was now missing in action and one was a prisoner of war, the third son was fighting in Flanders and Alice dreaded a knock on the door, but she spent so much energy worrying about her boys that she never considered that her precious Emily was in any danger. None of them had ever experienced anything like this flu. It wiped out the young and the healthy with sudden viciousness. Every household told stories of young people in their prime struck down by the illness while older people suffered what appeared to be the same symptoms and made full recoveries. Mary-Jane was really looking forward to getting out of the city and spending time in Annalong in July and actively encouraged James and Maria to join them. Susannah had already agreed to take her holidays in Annalong with them this year. She had stayed in the city the previous year and had missed spending time with her aunt Bridget. James and Maria had eventually relented and were travelling down on the train with the whole family the Sunday before the 12th July orange marches.

James O'Brien was waiting on them at the train station in Annalong along with Sean, Susan's eldest son. Sean was looking forward to spending time with his cousin, rekindle their childhood fishing exhibitions if Maria was agreeable. It was Maria's first trip to Annalong, although she had met the whole family at the wedding she was still a bit apprehensive at the prospect of spending a week with them. As they pulled up outside the cottage, the door opened, and Mary O'Brien threw open her arms trying to encompass them all with a welcome and a warm hug for everyone.

"Welcome, welcome, so glad to see you," she beamed at them. "Maria, you look a picture, welcome so much to our home." Mary hugged her family one by one beckoning them into her home. The rose garden had matured over the years with bushes forming an archway over the front door framing the red front door. Will and Jimmy were excitedly waiting and after greeting them all they lifted their bags and carried them inside. Mary had a pot of soup on the range and bread just out of the oven, the aroma wafting out from the kitchen made mouths water and they quickly washed up after their journey and sat down to the table for their meal. James O'Brien sat at the head of the table, saying nothing but paying close attention to the chatter around him. He paid particular attention to his eldest grandchild, James and his new wife Maria. He was already fond of Maria and noted that James was very attentive to her, as any newlywed man should be, but he was concerned that James did not fully engage in the conversation around the table and frequently seemed to be staring into space, oblivious of the chatter around him. He noticed Maria touching his hand gently on several occasions like a little reminder to focus on what was going on around him rather than some distant memory. He had seen local men home from the war who showed signs of the same type of behaviour and knew of at least one man who had been committed to the asylum after he not only failed to fit back into family life but walked the roads occasionally screaming and hitting out at his demons. He made himself a mental note to have a chat with James if only just to put his own mind at ease.

The days passed quickly, Mary-Jane quickly fell into a routine with her mother, wee Charlie and Ernie helped Will and Jimmy with the animals and in the vegetable plot. Charlie went for long walks with his father-in-law while James took great pleasure in introducing Maria to all his childhood haunts. They even went fishing with Sean and his younger brothers, sitting on the peer on the long summer evenings, rods in the water and chatting away until the sunset. Each evening Mary-Jane and her mother sat on the bench outside the front door, drinking in the scent of the roses, sipping tea and talking about everything and nothing. At different times they were joined by other members of the family unless of course, it was raining. On those nights they congregated in front of the fire in the parlour. Mary-Jane felt the tension seep out of her. She always felt that way when she went home to Annalong. The sea air blew away all her worries or at least reduced them to a manageable level. This trip was no different and she felt refreshed and renewed as the time drew near for them to return to Belfast. On their last night in Annalong Mary-Jane and Charlie walked down to the harbour. Mary-Jane stood on the pier looking out to sea, Charlie wrapped his arms around her, dusting her neck with a kiss and drinking in her scent.

"Ah Charlie, can we not move here, it's so beautiful and peaceful. Have you noticed the change in James since we got here, he seems more at ease, more in touch with everyone?"

Charlie sighed, "I know love, but my work is in Belfast, Susannah and Charlie both work in Belfast, Annalong is great for a holiday but there are no jobs here for us, how would we live?"

Mary-Jane sighed, she knew he was right, she was just being selfish, but she couldn't help herself. She missed Annalong even though she had lived in Belfast as long as she had lived in Annalong. She realised she was harking for a life that wasn't possible, turning into Charlie's arms she kissed him gently and they turned for the walk home arm in arm.

The return journey to Belfast was subdued, they all were going back to Belfast refreshed and renewed. Mary-Jane sat back in the train carriage looking around her family. Charlie, dosing in his seat, was sporting a dark tan which contrasted nicely with his silver flecked curls. Susannah protected her pale skin with a wide brimmed bonnet on sunny days, so her skin remained untanned but with a healthy glow. James had inherited his dad's ability to turn a golden brown without much exposure to the sun and he looked more healthy and happier than he had since he had gone away to war. Maria had her arm linked into the crook of James' arm and patted his arm gently as she daydreamed out the window at the passing landscape. Mary-Jane said a prayer each night that they would be blessed with a child but to no avail so far. Mamie copied her older sister in every way and Mary-Jane smiled as she watched the two discuss some fabric and dress designs that Bridget had given them. Wee Charlie, as he was affectionately called, was a larger man than his older brother or his Dad. He outstripped his Dad by a good two inches and that's if he had stopped growing, but Ernie was going to be the biggest of them all. Mary-Jane smiled as she surveyed her two younger boys. Ernie was as tall as wee Charlie but at only fifteen he had more growing to do. They were both mad into soccer, Charlie had two caps playing for Ireland at schoolboy level and still played for Belfast Celtic. Ernie hadn't the same talent as wee Charlie but loved the game and the two of them were strong members of their club. Both had benefited from their weeks in Annalong, they both looked healthy and happy and ready to get back into work and soccer. Charlie had just finished his apprenticeship as a welder in Eastwoods that summer and Ernie was due to start when they returned to Belfast. Ernie was looking forward to it. He looked up to his big brother Charlie and Mary-Jane was grateful that at least Charlie would be there to keep an eye on Ernie and show him the ropes because Ernie could be a bit of a hothead and she hoped that Charlie would keep him out of trouble. Her smile turned into a frown at the thought of the trouble Ernie could get himself into just as Charlie woke from his doze and glanced over at her.

"Worrying again woman," he teased her, waking her out of her reverie

"Ah no, Charlie, just counting our blessings," she retorted, blowing him a kiss. They both burst out laughing just as the train pulled into the station bringing their journey to an end.

Bags were unpacked, and the house was aired out and fires lit and within a day or two Mary-Jane felt like she had never been away. Each day she scrubbed her house from top to bottom before venturing out to the front of the road to check what meat and vegetables were available today. The war had brought shortages, but Mary-Jane knew how to make the most out of the cheapest cuts of meat and whatever vegetables she could get her hands on. She never failed to have a dinner on the table every evening for her family. There was a nip in the air coupled with the shortened evenings that reminded her that autumn was on its way. Every evening over dinner they sat around the table and each evening the latest news on the war was debated and analysed. The allies were starting to turn things around and it looked like the tide may be turning in their favour. Mary-Jane often blessed herself when she considered how lucky her own little family had been during the last few years compared to others she knew, especially Alice next door. Alice was a shadow of her former self. The death of her only daughter earlier that year had taken its toll on her. Her once thick golden hair was pure grey with no shine or life, her eyes were watery and heavy and her skin the colour of oatmeal. Mary-Jane and Alice discussed the latest news on their way to the shops the following day. Alice was hoping that the war was in its final days. She wanted her sons home, her middle son, Arthur had been missing in action for three years and she held little hope of him ever returning or his body being found. Alice was convinced that he was one of those unknown souls given a Christian burial in France. It was only by believing that to be true that she could carry on, not knowing where he had died or when. Fred was a prisoner of war so at least he was safe until the hostilities had ended and she prayed every day that John would survive the latest battle. The end of the war could not come quick enough for her.

Every day brought the end of the war closer and at 11 am on the 11th November 1918 when the war ended there were cheers and celebrations in every household. As the news filtered through people came out into the streets, hugging their neighbours and raising their voices in joyful thanks. Charlie heard the news in work and every passenger who ascended his tram that day were greeted with the great news. On his walk home from work people were out in the streets singing and dancing and celebrating the end of this hateful war. It took him an hour longer than usual to make it home to be greeted by Mary-Jane and Alice dancing around the living room. Susannah and Mamie sat in the middle of them laughing and were overjoyed when Charlie joined in. James and Maria arrived into the middle of the mayhem. Maria had heard the news when she went to the shops and in her haste to get home to tell James she forgot what she had gone out to buy. They both called into her mother's home and brought her with them to join in the celebrations. The whole street was alive with music and dancing until late into the night. The following morning it seemed to Mary-Jane that the whole city was on a go slow. Tired from the celebrations yet anxious to get life back to a new normality, a normality without war, without the fear and pain that they had endured for the last four years and four months. Any uneasy future lay ahead of them.

CHAPTER 29.   GENERAL ELECTION

The Great War was over, and Ireland had changed completely from the country it had been only four years previously. Before the great war commenced in July 1914 Ireland had been on the brink of civil war. The outbreak of the great war had meant the suspension of the enactment of Home Rule until after the war but in the interim Unionists Edward Carson and James Craig had campaigned and received promises of the exclusion of the north west of the country from the rule of Dublin. Immediately after the end of the war the government called for a general election and the date was set for Saturday 14th December 1918. Charlie laughed at the reaction of Mary-Jane and Alice who were astounded when they learnt that women would be allowed to vote for the first time, albeit women over thirty who owned property, so it didn't apply to them or anyone they knew. They had read with interest about the suffragettes on the mainland and they had both read the Sinn Fein manifesto along with the literature from the Irish Parliamentary Party and the Unionist parties.

In the weeks leading up to the election, the debate around the McMullen dinner table became very heated at times. On the Sunday before the election James and Maria joined them for dinner. James was firmly behind the Irish Parliamentary Party.

"Da, I have always been a supporter of Home Rule and of John Redmond. Redmond had encouraged us Irishmen to join the war effort, to fight for the rights of small nations. I deliberately chose the Irish Royal Rifles to make the point Unionist and Nationalist could work together. I know Redmond's dead, but the party isn't. What we fought for is still on the table."

Susannah voiced her support for her brother, but wee Charlie and Ernie thought differently.

"Ach James, you did what was right for you, but times have changed. The Dublin uprising changed that. We Irish will never get fairness from the British unless we take it. We have earned our right to self-determination. The Unionists are already looking for parts of the country to be partitioned with the northwest staying British and the rest of the country being ruled by a devolved government in Dublin," said wee Charlie.

Ernie took up his point, "Sure that would cause chaos. What we need to do is break free once and for all from British rule. Have you read the Sinn Fein manifesto, sure it's the only way forward."

Mamie sat silently listening to each of her brothers debate the future, a worried frown on her little face. Charlie sat at the head of the table saying nothing but taking in every word and gesture. One part of him was proud to hear his sons voice opinions and back those opinions up with reasoned argument but he also worried that this argument was ongoing in every household, particularly in this corner of Ireland and he wondered where it would all end. He knew Mary-Jane's thoughts were in the same vein as his but was surprised when she piped up.

"you know I really do wonder sometimes. Can any of ye tell how, in this little corner of the world, we had jumped from the threat of civil war to the enactment of a world war on a scale never before imagined, to the prospect of a renewed threat of civil war."

"Well said Ma," Susannah said, "I know you don't really approve of women having the right to vote Ma, but do you ever wonder if women ruled the world would the world be a safer place for everyone."

Election day dawned and those that could vote set off and cast their votes. It was over a month later before the votes were counted and the results announced. The result in Ireland was a resounding victory for Sinn Fein, winning 73 out of 105 seats. Wee Charlie and Ernie were ecstatic even though neither of them were old enough to vote. James had the right to vote for the first time and he cast his vote in favour of the Irish Parliamentary Party. His candidate Joe Devlin retained his seat, beating Eamon DeValera, but he was one of the few members of his party to do so. Mary-Jane and Charlie decided to pay a visit to James and Maria when they heard the election results. They were living in a little house in John Street, just off the Falls Road in the west of the city. The area they lived in was mostly Catholic and many were of the same political persuasion as James, following Joe Devlin. James and Maria had settled into their surroundings and had made some good friends in the area. Charlie wondered if James still had his nightmares and mentioned it to Mary-Jane, but she was reluctant to ask Maria about it.

"Sure, if Maria was concerned surely she would say something to us," she told Charlie. Charlie was also concerned that there was no sign of any children as was Mary-Jane but again she was reluctant to say anything to Maria about that. James had chatted about the election results to his Da and teased Maria about her view that allowing women to vote for the first time was a good thing. Charlie and Mary-Jane were surprised to learn that Maria was a fan of Countess Markievicz who had been elected as a Sinn Fein candidate. Maria regaled them with her stories of how the countess was a lady from a wealthy family, born in London but brought up in Sligo, of how she was an artist who had lived in London and Paris and had married a polish prince, of how she worked tirelessly for the poor in Dublin, how she fought in the Easter Rising side by side with the men, of how she was sentenced to death for her part in the rising and then pardoned and now was the first woman elected to the British houses of parliament. Maria was obviously enthralled with the woman, Mary-Jane pondered.

"They seem happy enough, don't they Charlie?" she voiced her concerns to Charlie on their way home.

"Of course, they are. It was a lovely visit, stop worrying," Charlie teased his wife. Maria was a good cook and housekeeper and their little house was kept spotlessly clean and tidy. She had made them tea and fresh scones from the oven and Mary-Jane noted how James had helped Maria, setting the table and carrying dishes to and from the little back kitchen and said so to Charlie.

"You, my man are a wonderful husband and father but never in your life have you helped her out in the kitchen or with any household chore."

Charlie laughed, "I know better, that is your domain."

They exchanged smiles as they turned into Sherwood Street, both thinking that times are changing. Men helping about the house and women not only having the vote but putting themselves forward for election and winning a seat in the house at Westminster.

Charlie smiled at his wife, "What is the world coming too?"

CHAPTER 30   *STRIKES*

1919 started off cold and wet. The rain was incessant, and Mary-Jane felt like the damp was getting into her very bones. She had a constant chill in her back and neck no matter what she wore. Charlie came in from work every night drowned to the skin. His uniform and overcoat had to be dried in front of the fire so that he could wear it again the following day. The steam from the clothes drying in front of the fire filled the whole house and caused the dampness to seep into every nook and cranny. During the day when Mary-Jane was in the house by herself, she opened all the windows to try and air out the house, but the cold damp air outside did nothing to ease the damp within the house. As darkness fell the soot from all the fires gathered in the air above Belfast and caused a thick smog that caught in your throat and in your eyes and dimmed the light struggling to generate out from the street lights. Mary-Jane longed for the spring and for the fresh air in Annalong. The winter weather seemed to match the general atmosphere in Belfast. Mary-Jane and Alice could talk of nothing else but the impending strike and the ongoing violence on the streets. The general strike was called for 25th January 1919.

"In fairness now, all we want is a maximum working week, 44 hours. You know Alice, I never see my family, working from early morning until night six days a week, if the working week was limited to 44 hours then more jobs could be created and all those men coming back from war would have a chance of a decent job with pay that you could live on."

Willy was sincere and grateful for the support of Alice his wife and their neighbours. Most of the men on the street were on strike and they gathered each morning to compare notes on the effect of the strike on their places of employment. The first day of the strike was a Saturday and the shipyards closed at lunchtime anyway, so the effect of the strike wasn't noticed until later that afternoon when the electricity and gas supply was affected. The power supply to the trams was lost and the trams had to return to their depot. The gas lights were not lit so as darkness fell anyone still outside had to find their way home in complete darkness. Charlie got back to his street shortly after dark and was heartened by the sight of a warm glow emanating from the window through the curtains. Smoke bellowed out the chimney and Charlie sprinted the last few steps to back door, gratefully anticipating the heat and a welcoming smile from Mary-Jane.

It was tough being on strike and he was not looking forward to the next few weeks. He did not like confrontation, but he was not afraid to stand up for himself or for others. He had listened carefully to the union officials as they outlined the position all workers had found themselves in after the war. They had all worked longer hours for less money than before the war. Now all those thousands of men were returning from war, looking for work and there were no decent jobs available for them. The general consensus amongst the workers was that fixed working hours and decent wages would lead to more jobs. The Unions said that it was time for workers to demand a shorter working week and decent employment for all. Mary-Jane smiled as Charlie outlined everything he had heard at the meeting that week.

"Fair play Charlie, good on ya," she patted his head as he settled himself into his armchair.

"I just hope it doesn't go on too long Mary-Jane, I'm worried about money, we can't afford for it to drag on for a long time."

"I know," agreed Mary-Jane, "but you can't afford not to strike, because with the hours you are working we never see you and when we do, you are too exhausted to talk to me at all."

The strike brought the city to a standstill. The shipyards had to close, the engineering works, the electricity station and the gasworks all closed. The trams stopped running and Charlie found himself at home under Mary-Jane's feet. Even the newspapers were affected. Mary-Jane and her neighbours got their information from word of mouth and they were anxious to know more about what was happening in Dublin. Sinn Fein had refused to take their seats at Westminster, instead, setting up a new government "Dáil Eireann" in Dublin, a completely independent Irish government. Wee Charlie and Ernie were delighted.

"Its great news Da, we are at war but this time we are fighting for our own freedom, not some country in Europe we had never heard of before and will never see again."

Charlie was worried about the two younger boys and implored them not to get caught up in politics. He knew he was wasting his breath and said a silent prayer that if they did get caught up in it all that they would remain safe.

"Charlie, I feel like I have been praying for peace for as many years as I can remember. Seven years ago, we were praying that the country would not dissolve into civil war, then five years ago praying that the great war would be over quickly and praying for the safe return of all those thousands of men, including our son and all those other sons and husbands, and now, here we are, praying once again that the country would not disintegrate into a bloody war against the British."

Charlie hugged his wife to him in the darkness of their bedroom, hushing her to sleep.

After the second week of the strike with no end in sight, the British army were called in to man the electricity stations and the gasworks so that at least transport was running, and street lights went back on. There had been strikes all over the United Kingdom, but Belfast was by far the biggest, however within the next two weeks the strike was defeated, and workers went back to work without their demands being met.

"Terrible state of affairs I tell ya, the crowd in Glasgow went back to work before us. What else can we do, at the end of the day we have to put food on the table," Willy told Charlie and Mary-Jane as news of the end of the strike broke. Willy was disheartened at the defeat but always practical, so with a heavy heart, he returned to work.

CHAPTER 31 HOMECOMINGS

The next day Alice heard her back door open in the middle of the afternoon and jumped from her place at the kitchen sink where she was washing spuds for the dinner. She shook her head and blinked twice, convinced that she was dreaming, but no, when she opened her eyes again there they were in front of her, in uniform, with kitbags over their shoulders and the biggest grin imaginable on their faces. She opened her mouth to scream her delight, but no sound came out. Her boys were home. Home from the war, standing in her scullery grinning at her. She yelped and threw her arms around both of them at the same time, jumping up and down laughing hysterically. "Ma, calm down, calm down," they both said in unison, returning her hug with fierce joy. Alice stood back and looked them up and down, then hugged them again just to be sure she wasn't imagining their presence in her little scullery.

Suddenly she let them go and pushed past them out the back door and into the yard, calling, "Mary-Jane, come here quick." Mary-Jane had been standing in her kitchen preparing her dinner when she heard Alice calling. On hearing the tremor in Alice's voice, she dropped the knife from her hand into the sink and ran out the backyard and into the alley, wiping her hands on her apron as she ran.

"Whatever is the matter Alice?" she exclaimed as she ran in the back door towards Alice who stood with a large grin on her face. She stepped back to reveal her two sons standing further along the scullery. Mary-Jane hugged both boys in turn welcoming them home then turned to her friend and hugged her and joined her in her tears.

"Oh boys you have no idea how much your ma has missed you," Mary-Jane told the boys, her voice breaking with emotion as she hugged her friend, both laughing and crying in unison.

There was a party that night in the Russell household as well as twenty other households in the area, with all the neighbours calling in to each home to welcome home their sons and fathers. Willy and Charlie toasted their safe return as did James and Maria. Neighbours spoke in hushed voices of Fred, the Russell's' eldest boy who had been a prisoner of war since early on in the war but there was no word on his return yet. Alice was praying for his safe return soon but at least the two younger boys were home. The singing and dancing went on until the small hours of the morning with Mary-Jane and Alice leading the singing and all the neighbours joining in the celebration of the safe return from war of these two young men.

The next morning Mary-Jane was late getting out of bed, which was so unusual for her that Charlie joined the children in teasing her about it. At least it was a Sunday and the pace was more relaxed than the normal workday. Mary-Jane went to a later mass with wee Charlie, Mamie and Ernie, leaving Charlie at home to light the fire and Susannah to start preparations for the Sunday dinner. Mary-Jane tried to hurry home, but she met more people who stopped and chatted about the celebrations the previous night that it took her twice as long as usual to get home. She put away her outdoor clothes and went down to the kitchen to see how far Susannah had got with dinner. Charlie took her hand and led her to her fireside chair.

"Now Mary-Jane, have a seat, there is a cup of tea on its way, everything is under control in the kitchen, you just relax there."

Mary-Jane gratefully accepted the cup of tea that Susannah handed to her and got herself comfortable on her chair. She sipped her tea and read the Sunday newspaper with a little soft smile on her face. It was the first time since Charlie had carried her over the threshold as a young bride that she hadn't cooked Sunday dinner. She relished the sheer luxury of sitting doing nothing but engrossing herself in the newspapers. She managed to keep her mouth firmly closed and not offer any advice as Susannah went back and forth preparing the vegetables and checking the roast whilst Mamie set the table. When dinner was ready Charlie led her again by the hand to the table where dinner was served to her by her daughters. I have taught them well, she thought as she tucked into a delicious Sunday roast with all the trimmings cooked to perfection by her daughters.

CHAPTER 32   THE WAR OF INDEPENDENCE

The following week Mary-Jane attended her usual mass in St. Matthew's with her children hurrying home in the rain to prepare Sunday dinner. It was a cold, dark Sunday morning with grey clouds blustering along the rooftops and rain pelting off the footpaths intermingled with stinging sleet. They were all soaked to the skin on their return, but Charlie had the fire lit and surrounded by a large wooden clothes drier he had engineered himself the previous autumn in his little shed out in the backyard. He took Mary-Jane's coat and hat and draped it carefully in front of the fire to dry, then held his hand out to his daughters for their coats, leaving the boys to fend for themselves. Within minutes steam was rising from the wet garments and the air turned sticky and damp. Mary-Jane withdrew into the kitchen to start dinner preparations while Charlie settled into his armchair with the Sunday newspaper. The girls retired upstairs to their room ostensibly, so they could prepare their clothes for the week ahead. Charlie and Ernie sat at the table playing cards and the only sound was the occasional "Snap" breaking the comfortable silence. After saying grace before their meal, they all tucked into Sunday lunch and the conversation slowly turned to the latest news contained in the Sunday newspaper of the ongoing violence in the country.

Mary-Jane tried to steer the conversation away from the violence and intervened with the good news that her nephew Sean's wife had a new baby boy. They were having the baby baptised the following weekend, so Mary-Jane and Charlie were travelling down to Annalong to attend. After the strike, they had very little money, but Charlie reckoned a trip to Annalong would do them both the world of good, so they planned to travel down on the train on Saturday afternoon when Charlie finished work and then get the last train back to Belfast on the Sunday. Susannah said she would go too and so did Mamie and Ernie, but wee Charlie had other plans but told Mary-Jane and Charlie that he had to work late on Saturday, so he was going to stay in Belfast. Susannah has some suspicions about her brother's plans and challenged him.

"Please don't join the Irish Volunteers. James isn't a member since he came back from the war. It's a different army now to what it was before the war."

Wee Charlie disagreed with her.

"Sinn Fein have set up an Irish parliament "Dáil Eireann" in Dublin and have declared the Irish Republic, an independent Irish Republic. The old notion of Home Rule is dead. Those Unionists will never allow it, they call it Rome Rule. You have read what it said in the papers, they have even suggested that if Home Rule goes ahead then the northwest of the country should be left out of the arrangement. How would that work? No, the only way forward is complete independence from Britain."

Ernie nodded his head voicing his agreement with his brother.

"What do you know Ernie, you are only thirteen, you have no idea what's going on." Susannah rounded on Ernie.

"I am entitled to my opinion Susannah, it might not be the same as yours but that doesn't make it wrong," Ernie retorted.

Susannah jumped to her feet, "This country has seen enough bloodshed, just think about this street alone and the number of men who didn't make it back from the war. You don't even remember what life was like before the war, the constant threat of violence, the discrimination, year after year, going back as far as even Da can remember. And for what? The right to self-determination? Will our lives become suddenly better? Or let's just imagine you get your independent Irish state, would the Unionists suddenly decide that they will live quietly and peacefully in an independent Irish state considering the mayhem they have been causing the best part of the last forty years because it was suggested that Ireland should be self-governing but still under the British crown."

Susannah banged her fist on the table, spots of anger of her flushed cheeks.

Wee Charlie was quick to answer her.

"So Ireland remains under British rule just to keep the Unionists happy, they are not even Irish, they were planted here by the British and if they are so fond of British rule maybe they should go and live there."

Susannah was completely taken aback by the strength and passion behind wee Charlie's words. Normally wee Charlie had a much quieter disposition than his siblings and seldom raised his voice.

Mamie's quiet little voice interjected, "Maybe we should talk about something else," but her comment was overtaken by Susannah, whose quick temper got the better of her.

"How can you say something like that Charlie, Granny and Grandad McMullen are Unionist, should they be shipped to England. They were born in Belfast, same as their parents before them, they don't want to live in England, they have never been outside Belfast. What about all our aunts and uncles Randal, Ernie, John, Tommy, Susan, Lily, all our cousins, will I list them out for you. They are Protestant, and most of them probably Unionist as well, you know they are. Do you really believe the answer to the problems this country has is to ship anyone who wants to remain part of the Union out of the country?"

Wee Charlie rose to his feet, "That is a simplification of the problem Susannah, and you know it is, but letting the Unionists dictate to the rest of us is not the answer either," with that he lifted his coat and walked out of the house.

Ernie grabbed his coat running after him, "wait for me, Charlie," slamming the back door shut behind him. Susannah sank back into her chair deflated and with tears building up behind her eyelids she turned to her mother with a trembling whisper, "What about Martin, he went to war to fight for Home Rule, he gave his life fighting in a foreign land in the belief that by doing just that he was achieving something for Ireland. Was that all for nothing?"

Tears slid slowly down her cheeks as her mother pulled her close, rocking her like she did when she was a baby. Charlie rose from the table squeezing Mary-Jane's shoulder on the way past to the kitchen.

"Mamie come on we put the kettle on for tea. Tea makes everything better." Charlie and Mamie left Mary-Jane rocking her daughter gently.

There was a strained atmosphere over the next few days whenever Susannah and wee Charlie were in the same room together which was every night for dinner. By the end of the week, Mary-Jane had enough,

"Come on, this is a sad state of affairs when brother and sister stop speaking to each other. I will not tolerate this atmosphere in my home, you will sit at this table and you will talk to each other. You have to learn to agree that you disagree and respect one another's opinions."

Susannah started to object but was silenced by her mother who raised her hand upright and spoke firmly.

"I mean it Susannah, I know how hurt you are, but wee Charlie is hurt too, Mamie and Ernie are caught between the two of you and Mamie is so upset. Me and your Dad brought all of you up to treat each other with respect. We will not tolerate you and your brother not speaking, so sit, talk to each other, sort this out."

Susannah closed her mouth firmly pulling out a chair and sat opposite wee Charlie, who was already seated at the table.

"Sorry Ma, I meant no disrespect to you and Da, and neither did Susannah," wee Charlie murmured, glancing at Susannah as he spoke.

"No, Ma, we didn't" Susannah agreed with her brother.

"Good, now that's a good start, at least you are agreed on something. Ernie is out, Mamie is gone to the shop for me and I'm going in next door to Alice for a cuppa, you two sit there and talk." On that note, Mary-Jane left the room closing the door behind her. Susannah and wee Charlie looked at the closed door in silence for a minute.

Wee Charlie was first to break the ice. "Look Susannah I didn't mean any disrespect to you or the family, it's just that times have changed. We live in a different world than the way we lived before the great war. Back then we all believed in Home Rule, now we know it's not going to happen. Your Martin was a member of the Irish Volunteers, sure that's the main reason he joined up and went off to war. I am a member of the Irish Volunteers now, but the British have reneged on their promise and Home Rule is not going to happen. That is unacceptable, and we cannot just sit back and do nothing."

Susannah let her brother speak, listening intently and then sat in silence for a minute. The only sound was the ticking of the mantel clock and the occasional hiss from the fire. When Susannah finally spoke, it was in a quiet subdued tone.

"I hear what you are saying Charlie, and I do understand but after everything this country has been through, do we have to go through more violence. My Martin went off to war along with our James and thousands of other Irish Volunteers. Was that for nothing? Did my Martin die for nothing?"

Wee Charlie looked at his sister in horror, "No, Susannah no, they fought for the right of the Irish nation to self-determination and that fight goes on, just in a different way. Martin died a hero and don't let anyone tell you any different," wee Charlie took his sister's hands in his, "I am so sorry if I made you feel like that, that was not my intention. I liked Martin, he was a good sort, and I look up to James, he has shown us what real courage is, they both have. But at the end of the day they fought for the rights of small nations, like us, our right to rule ourselves, and me, and others like me, are now going to take up where they finished off. That doesn't mean we disrespect what they did, nothing could be further from the truth."

Susannah squeezed her brothers hand, desperately trying to avoid crying. She had thought she had moved on and had stopped grieving for Martin but the last few days had made her realise how much she still missed him.

"I think I understand you better now, I don't agree with you on some things, but I do understand," Susannah murmured.

"Are we friends again?" wee Charlie held her hands tighter with an imploring expression on his face.

"course we are," Susannah replied with a grin. Wee Charlie lifted her right hand and kissed it gently.

"I am sorry Susannah,"

"me too."

The moment was broken with the sound of the back door opening and Mamie's voice echoing into the room in singsong fashion, "Hello, anyone home." Susannah and wee Charlie smiled at each other then went into the kitchen to give Mamie a hand with the shopping.

CHAPTER 33   CONFLICT AT HOME

A certain amount of normality returned to the McMullen household with Susannah and wee Charlie doing their best not to upset each other. The whole family had always sat down to eat dinner together every evening and Mary-Jane had always encouraged discussion over their meal with everyone contributing in some way. At first Susannah and wee Charlie made a conscious effort not to say anything which could offend the other but eventually, they fell back into their old ways and conflict was inevitable.

As the evenings grew longer wee Charlie excused himself from the table earlier than usual several evenings a week, citing a pressing engagement with a colleague or football training at the club. Wee Charlie enjoyed training and loved playing, but he attended training two nights per week, the other two nights were spent on a different type of training. As a part-time member of the Irish Volunteers wee Charlie trained with his unit two nights per week. His unit was small, well trained and well-armed, charged with fighting the British forces in the Belfast area and protecting the nationalist community from attack by Unionist gangs. He tried to keep his involvement secret from his family as he knew it would upset his parents and his sister but eventually as he spent more and more time with his unit and little or no time at home his parents tackled him one night as he crept back into the house in the early hours. It was a good autumn, dry weather and sunshine which turned the leaves a glorious red shade before falling to the ground in bundles of red and gold which rustled as you walked through them and made a walk in the park a delight for adults and children alike. The nights were cold though and the fires were lit as soon as the sun went down. Not that Charlie had the time to enjoy the park. That night his unit had a particularly violent encounter with the Black and Tans and wee Charlie had taken a beating before being rescued by members of his unit. He wasn't surprised to see his Da sitting in the dark in his armchair waiting for him, but he was surprised to see his mother sitting in the opposite armchair.

Mary-Jane gasped out loud when she saw the state of wee Charlie.

"Oh my God, what has happened to you?" she exclaimed as she took in the sight of his bloodied coat and bruised face.

"Its fine, Ma, it's nothing a bit of ointment won't fix," he tried to reassure his mother.

Mary-Jane led him to the table pulling out a chair and sending Charlie to fetch her first aid kit. Charlie returned minutes later with a bowl of warm water, disinfectant and a cloth. Charlie helped his son out of his coat and Mary-Jane wrung out the cloth and started to tenderly dap his bloodied face so that she could get a better idea of the damage. Charlie checked his limbs to make sure there was nothing broken and between them they assessed the damage.

"Yes, you're okay, Charlie, no lasting damage as far as I can tell but God almighty you're going to be in some state tomorrow."

Wee Charlie looked gingerly in the mirror over the mantle. His eyes were already turning a purplish-black and a deep gash on his forehead was covered by a bandage which his mother had expertly wrapped around his head. His lip was still bleeding slightly, and his knuckles were raw and throbbing.

Mary-Jane and Charlie had asked no questions as they had administered to him but now they stood beside him waiting expectedly on an explanation. Wee Charlie considered lying to them but just as quickly dismissed the thought. His mother would see through any lie he could dream up. He was battered and bruised from the blows he had taken before his comrades had come to his aid. He held his head up and proudly announced the fact that he was in the Irish Volunteers. Mary-Jane and Charlie didn't say a word. They exchanged glances which wee Charlie realised meant they had already been aware of his membership, but they didn't say a word.

"Well, I'm sure you don't approve, Ma, Da, but I am doing what I am meant to do. This is important to me."

Charlie just shook his head, "Away to bed, son, it's late, we will talk tomorrow."

Mary-Jane patted her son gently on his one good shoulder before climbing the stairs to her bedroom. Charlie followed her telling his son to dampen the fire and blow out the oil lamp before he retired.

Wee Charlie sat in the dark, going back over the events of the evening. It had been an eventful night. His unit had broken into a small British army outpost based in an old RIC house earlier that evening. They had been surveying the outpost for several weeks and had hit the outpost on a night when they knew that the majority of the soldiers based there were out at a function in the city centre. Overcoming the handful of soldiers on duty was relatively easy and they had left them tied up in the basement unharmed. The weapons room was easily accessed, and they had made off with a sizable collection of pistols and rifles. The whole unit were jubilant, the mission had been a success, and no one got hurt. They had secreted the weapons in their hiding place and parted company close to the park. Charlie had only just walked through the gates of the park when he came across the band of Black and Tans. They were an unruly bunch and had obviously been drinking. Charlie knew straight away that he was in trouble. He tried to ignore them, but they wouldn't let him pass. He knew he was in trouble, so he threw the first punch then ran for this life back the way he had come shouting for his comrades. The Black and Tans caught up with him easily tripping him but luckily a large bundle of fallen leaves broke his fall. They were upon him in minutes kicking him on the ground and he thought his life was over. The barrage of boots rained down on him and he curled into a ball to protect himself as best he could. He heard the shouts of the lads arriving seconds before the kicks stopped and he jumped to his feet punching as hard as he could, the cuts on his knuckles, proof that his fists had made contact with his targets. It was over as quickly as it had started, the alcohol had slowed the reflexes of the Black and Tans and their courage was induced by alcohol so when they realised that Charlie and his comrades were not afraid to use their fists they made off, shouting threats and abuse as they ran. It was a much more subdued group of men who bade their goodbyes to each other after that. Charlie eased up off his chair and went to bed, his arms and legs painful from the kicking he had received, his head throbbing and his cut lip was stinging from the antiseptic. He stripped and climbed into bed trying not to moan with the pain. The last thing he wanted was to wake Ernie and have to answer his questions. He was stunned at his parent's reaction tonight but realised that the lack of questioning tonight meant he was in for an in-depth interrogation tomorrow. He sighed, wincing as he turned over on to his side closing his eyes and succumbing to the sleep his battered limbs so badly needed.

The next morning wee Charlie woke early and headed off to work early before the rest of the household got up. Every one of his muscles ached and he was thankful it was a Saturday and would finish work at 12.30. He had never been so glad to hear the horn sounding the end of the work week. He had told his work mates what had happened but had left out everything that had happened before he had walked into the park. They all had stories to tell about the brutality of the Black and Tans and all sympathised with him, each of them volunteering to take on some of his work which really helped him get through the morning.

He made his way home, his mind racing, wondering what his parents were going to say to him. He held his head a little higher, he was proud of his involvement with the Irish Volunteers and his involvement in this war, this fight against the British Empire for an independent Ireland. He was aware of how Susannah felt about the war and he did not want to cause her any pain, but he was also confident in his belief that the time was right for Ireland to demand their independence with Britain. He turned the corner into their back lane at the same time as Ernie who halted abruptly when he saw Charlie's face.

"Jesus, what happened to you?"

Charlie ignored his brother's question, putting his arm around Ernie's shoulder.

"All in good time Ernie. You are going to hear all about it when we get home."

The smell of hot soda bread assaulted their senses wafting out the back door and down the passageway.

"ah Ma, can I have the first one off the griddle?" Ernie begged as he opened the back door. Mary-Jane laughed and put out two plates for her boys, split open two sodas and slathered them with butter. The boys stuffed their faces before heading to the yard to wash up in the hot water Mary-Jane had left out for them. Most of their neighbours had their Saturday baths in front of the fire during the winter but as the family started to get older Charlie had converted his little shed in the yard. He had installed an old pot-bellied stove that he had picked up in a scrap yard, his brother had helped him install the chimney which ran from the back of the stove up through the roof and over the back wall. The shed was so small it only took a small fire to heat the whole shed to a comfortable temperature. The top of the stove was flat and was the perfect size for the kettle that Mary-Jane kept on top of it filled with water. On Saturday's she lit the stove early and repeatedly boiled the kettle and emptied the hot water into the tin bath that sat in front of the stove, so that by the time the boys got home from work the tin bath was full of hot water and the soap and towels were laid out ready for use. When the boys finished their absolutions, they took the bath out of the shed, emptied it down the shore, cleaned it and set about filling it up again with hot water for the girls.

Wee Charlie was quiet that afternoon waiting on his parents bringing up what had happened the night before. Mary-Jane and Charlie waited until the boys had bathed and eaten before they spoke. Charlie spoke first asking wee Charlie simple direct questions about his role in the Volunteers.

Charlie spoke quietly but firmly.

"Da, when James signed up with the Royal Irish Rifles, he did so in the firm belief that serving with the British army was the way forward for Ireland, that when the war ended we would have Home Rule. The British changed the goal posts Da, not us. Men like our James did what was asked of them, but the British did not follow up with their side of the bargain. You know that Sinn Fein won the election last year Da, but they didn't take their seats in Westminster, but set up an Irish government in Dublin. They declared an Irish Republic. I know you voted for Joe Devlin of the Irish Parliamentary Party Da, and he did take his seat in Westminster but let's face it, he is one of the very few over there now representing us. The rest of them are in Dublin and yes, Britain did declare that Dáil Eireann is illegal, but they are still there, functioning as best they can. That's where we should be looking for leadership. There's a fella there by the name of Michael Collins, he is the Minister for Finance and he has just been made the Director of Intelligence. And he is a great man Da.

He fought in the rising. He won the poll in Cork and he will help us win this war, for war it is."

Ernie has listened intently to everything his brother said, saying nothing but nodding his head in agreement at different times. Charlie and Mary-Jane exchanged glances across the table. Theirs had always been a marriage of compromise, their differing religions was the original stumbling block for them and their individual families, but they had gotten over that, confident in the knowledge that they loved each other and that was enough to conquer any trials and tribulations that came their way. They had hoped they had passed on that capacity for compromise to their children but now there didn't seem to be any room for compromise. The Unionists were firmly of the opinion that Ireland should be ruled by Britain and the Nationalists wanted independence from Britain. Charlie and Mary-Jane sat firmly in the middle and they knew they were not alone. Mary-Jane shivered inside as she remembered the pain and worry they had went through when James went off to war. Now as she listened to wee Charlie she knew in her heart that he was going to take the same path only his path led to a different army and a different war and that by choosing that path, heartbreak lay ahead for her family.

"I am doing much the same thing as James did Da, and you supported him, and I am asking you now to support me. He signed up and fought for what he believed in, now I must do the same."

Charlie offered his hand to his son.

"Charlie, always remember that me and your Ma will always be here for you. I don't know what to make of it all, but I know that you are a man of your word and if you believe in this cause then you fight for it. I'm proud of you son."

Charlie shook his namesake's hand and rose from the table. Mary-Jane followed suit hugging her son before pulling on her apron and heading to the kitchen to prepare the evening meal. Ernie and Charlie remained at the table as Ernie badgered Charlie with questions.

"No Ernie, you're too young yet, sure your only 14 next month. Wait another while, I promise you I will speak for you when the time is right."

Charlie slapped his brother on the back and headed out to check the fire in the shed.

Charlie and Mary-Jane said nothing to Susannah. Wee Charlie told her the same story he had told his workmates, which was the truth of what had happened, he just left out the reason he was in the park in the first place. Susannah was sympathetic, she had heard similar stories in work and fussed over Charlie, making him tea and bathing his hands. It was several weeks before Charlie's injuries healed. He still left the house every evening returning in the early hours. Mary-Jane lay awake until she heard him creep quietly into the house trying to avoid waking his younger brother or disturb his parents.

CHAPTER 34   CHRISTMAS

Christmas came with a visit from James and Mary with the boys, Will and Jimmy. Mary-Jane was delighted to have them stay and grateful for the opportunity to discuss the ongoing sectarianism in the city and her worries about wee Charlie. James was delighted to hear wee Charlie was a volunteer.

"They call them the Irish Republican Army these days, Mary-Jane you should be proud," James admonished her,

"Ach I am Da, I'm just worried about it, worried about how this all will end. We have had enough of war, I can't bear to even think of the possibility of anything happening to wee Charlie."

Mary agreed with her daughter,

"Ye men think differently, we women are the ones sitting at home, keeping everything together."

James shook his head,

"That's changing too, love, that Countess, the one that fought in the rising, sure isn't she in the new Dáil. A government minister no less."

Mary argued with her husband,

"Ach sure James, she is landed gentry, them women think differently too. Women like her can vote as well, imagine that, and there's men like you only got the right to vote for the first time in the last election."

Charlie laughed at his mother in law's incredulous expression. Mary-Jane put a fresh pot of tea on the table along with a plate of scones fresh from the oven.

"No more talk of war, the girls will be home soon, and I don't want them worrying, especially Mamie, she is so sensitive."

They all happily took their places at the table and tucked into the scones and the blackcurrant jam Mary had brought with her from her store cupboard. Susannah arrived home shortly afterwards and was hailed heartily by her grandparents.

"Hope you are packed and ready to go. Susie?" Mary asked her granddaughter for Susannah was accompanying her grandparents back to Annalong. She was staying with Bridget for a few days and had picked up some beautiful dress trimmings for her in the sale in Anderson and McAuley's Department Store.

"I am nearly ready Granny. I can't wait to show Bridget these and I want her advice on some dress designs I've been working on." She had a full portfolio of drawings that she had been working on over the last few months, but she hadn't shared them with anyone yet.

"You and your auntie Bridget, thick as thieves ye are. You'll be a great help to her for a few days, sure she is extremely busy, between alterations, curtain-making and you should see the latest dress she is making."

"I'm looking forward to it Granny," Susannah hurried upstairs to finish packing. They were setting off early the next morning, so Susannah wanted to be ready at first light. Her grandparents were sleeping in her room, so Susannah was sleeping on the sofa and Mamie was staying with James and Maria for a few days.

The next morning Mary-Jane rose early and made breakfast for everyone, making sure that her parents and her brothers were well fed before departing to catch the next train to Newcastle. She had packed them some sandwiches to have on the train and handed them to her mother, then hugged Susannah to her, suddenly anxious for her but at the same time knowing she was safe in her parent's company, for they adored their grand-children. Charlie gave Mary-Jane a quick kiss on the cheek, then set off with them, accompanying them part of the way as he went to work. Mary-Jane stood at the door and waved goodbye until they rounded the corner. Wee Charlie and Ernie had left for work earlier so Mary-Jane had the house to herself. She busied herself cleaning away the breakfast dishes and raking out the fire. She hummed as she worked. Her household chores soothed her, she had been feeling anxious, worried about Susannah who still grieved for Martin over three years after he died, about James who hadn't found work and was still having nightmares, about wee Charlie who spent every minute he could spare with his IRA comrades, about Ernie who idolised his older brother and couldn't wait until he was old enough to follow him into the IRA, and about Mamie, sweet, gentle little Mamie who said so very little but took in everything. It was a busy day and by the end of it Mary-Jane felt exhausted physically and emotionally. Charlie noticed her lethargy when he got in from work and after dinner he led her to her armchair, asking Mamie to make her Ma a cup of tea.

"Sit for a while love, me and the lads will do the washup." Mary-Jane started to laugh at the idea of any of the men in her life helping out with the household chores.

So did Mamie "Don't worry Ma, I will clean up, you sit there and have your tea.

CHAPTER 35   MARY-JANE

The evenings started to stretch but the weather remained cold and wet. Mary-Jane and the girls got soaked yet again walking back from mass on Sunday morning. Their wet coats and hats draped over the clothes horse in front of the fire as they set about preparing Sunday dinner. James and Maria were coming for dinner today and Mary-Jane was looking forward to seeing them. Wee Charlie had left early that morning, but he had promised to be home for dinner. Mary-Jane felt the anxiety in her throat at the thought of her son and the danger he was putting himself in. Belfast was a powder keg once again with violence erupting at the slightest provocation. In mass that morning she had prayed for wee Charlie, prayed to God to keep him safe. She felt selfish in asking for her son's safety, so many men had died in the great war, so many young and healthy people had died from the influenza epidemic the previous year and she had been fortunate, yes James had a serious injury, he had lost his leg and his poor mind was demented but they were all still here. Poor Alice next door had lost her daughter to influenza and her son to the war. Her other two sons arrived home from the war uninjured, in any physical sense, but her eldest boy never returned. So, yes, she felt guilty and selfish but that didn't stop her from asking God to watch over her son and keep him safe.

Wee Charlie didn't arrive home for dinner. Mary-Jane put out a plate for him and put it to one side to heat up for him when he got home. Anxiety started to build up in her again wondering why he was late, but she hid her anxiety from the rest of the family. The conversation came around to the latest reports in the Sunday papers. Charles read the newspaper aloud, "The Government of Ireland Act 1920, has passed its second reading in the House of Commons, quite the mouthful, isn't it? Why didn't they just stick with the 4th Home Rule Act, that's what everyone is calling it anyway." No one was happy with the new act. The Act would finally give Ireland the Home Rule that had been campaigned for, for so many years, but not in the form they had wanted. There was to be two jurisdictions, six counties in Ulster would have their parliament in Belfast and the rest of the island would have their parliament in Dublin, both jurisdictions would remain part of the United Kingdom.

It was a compromise that neither side wanted. The Unionists had never wanted self-determination, they wanted to remain in the United Kingdom ruled by Westminster. The Nationalists didn't want to see the country partitioned they wanted independence from the United Kingdom for the whole island.

"It's a mess Da," James intervened, "It's not the Home Rule we signed up for, it's not what we were promised when we signed up with the British army. Even the Unionists don't want it."

Susannah agreed with her older brother but also voiced her anxiety that it would also cause more violence. There was an ongoing guerrilla war between the British forces and the IRA which showed no signs of abating, quite the opposite in fact with news daily of battles, shootings, ambushes and general mayhem. The Black and Tans were making matters worse.

"I thought they were supposed to aid the Royal Irish Constabulary" queried Mary-Jane.

Ernie spoke up before anyone else could reply, "They were recruited on the mainland, Ma, mainly ex great war veterans who had been unable to adjust back into normal society and they jumped at the chance of a steady income, ten shillings a week plus room and board, sure they couldn't earn that money at home. So nearly 10,000 of them are now in Ireland supposedly aiding the RIC fight the IRA. And they are violent men, brutalised by war, without family or loved ones to pull them back to reality."

Mary-Jane shuddered with the realisation that her son had a lucky escape last week, while Charlie's mouth fell open in awe at the knowledge Ernie had of the ongoing situation. They were all startled by the sound of the back door opening and wee Charlie stuck his head around the door.

"Sorry I'm late Ma, Mick had a puncture and it took us ages to fix it."

Mary-Jane let out a sigh of relief and hurried out to the kitchen to check on his dinner. Wee Charlie watched from the sink where he was washing his hands.

"Smells good, Ma I'm starving."

Mary-Jane went to admonish him for being late then thought better of it, patted his shoulder and turned away thinking, do I really want to know the truth of where he was and what he was doing, if I query him, and he answers honestly, will that just anger Susannah and upset Mamie. He will confide in us when he wants to but for now, I will let it go. She paused, formed her mouth into a smile and joined the family who were still sitting around the table discussing the contents of today's newspaper.

Every day appeared to bring more bad news of shootings and reprisals. Mary-Jane hugged each member of her family as they left for work in the morning, praying for their safe return that evening. Mary-Jane and Alice met every day to go to the shops for the makings of that evening's dinner but were reluctant to travel any further. They used to go to the park every day but this year they decided they would stay close to home, it was just too dangerous to leave your street, let alone wander to the parks. Alice seemed to have aged ten years in the last two. Her once glorious hair was completely grey, her face lined like an old leather bag and her eyes dimmed by grief and sorrow. Mary-Jane refused to let her sit and brood on her misfortune, calling every day and dragging her out to the shops on days when she didn't want to do anything, baking her bread and scones, propping her up on days when the weight of the world seemed to be on her shoulders.

"Thanks Mary-Jane, I don't know what I would do without you," Alice said to Mary-Jane on their way back from the shops one fine July day. The sun had made an appearance and it was a pleasantly warm day. Mary-Jane and Charlie were going to Annalong the next day for their annual holiday in her home place, but Mary-Jane was worried about leaving Alice. She said as much to Charlie that evening over dinner.

Susannah piped up, "But Ma, I will be here, I will pop into Alice every evening after work and check on her, sure I can whip up a few scones, didn't you teach me, and I can get her to help me with some crochet I am working on. She was really good at crochet a few years back, I'm sure that with a bit of practice she could be just as good again if not better. What do you think?" Mary-Jane paused then beamed a radiant smile at her daughter.

"Do you know something Susie that is a great idea, I have the makings of a little blanket I was going to make for the McAllister girl's new baby, I will tell Alice tomorrow that I don't have the time to do and ask her to do it for me. I will tell her that you will call into her and show her what has to be done."

"And will you call into James and Maria if you get a chance love?" Mary-Jane asked Susannah. Mary-Jane would never discuss her worries about James with Susannah, but she knew they were close although James had never discussed his nightmares with his sister. Mary-Jane had a quiet word with Maria every few months, they met in town on days when Maria managed to get out without James by her side. He was still having nightmares although they were not as frequent, maybe once a month, which Mary-Jane reckoned was progress. His biggest problem was he had too much time on his hands. He had a war pension so financially they were managing and outwardly they seemed happy. Maria never spoke a bad word about her husband reassuring Mary-Jane that all was fine but Mary-Jane worried. Maria had mentioned his moods, days when he would not speak to her or to anyone. He would sit in his front room and stare at the wall for hours on end, rocking back and forth, occasionally flitching, putting his hands over his ears as if he could still hear the shelling. It was only gentle persuasion from Maria that brought him around. If she spoke loudly or touched him he would flitch and curl up into a ball, whining like a scared dog. She had learned to never touch him or alarm him when he went into those trances as she called them. She let him be for a few hours then called to him in a voice no louder than a whisper, gently humming his name like she was singing a lullaby to a baby. She could see the life gradually coming back into his eyes first as he recognised his name, then the rocking would stop and finally her James was back, sweet, gentle, loving James. There was still no sign of children and Mary-Jane didn't like to intrude on Maria's privacy by asking why. She had attempted at one time to ask how things were in the bedroom, but Maria started to cry and was so upset that Mary-Jane never asked again. She knew Charlie had a more practical approach. He called into James and Maria and got James involved in building a shed in the backyard similar to the one he had built at home. The project kept James busy for weeks and got Charlie thinking of other projects he could get James involved in.

CHAPTER 36   MAMIE'S DATE

Susannah was a good friend to James and Maria. She adored her older brother and Maria was her best friend, so she spent as much time with them as she could. The fact that they had known Martin helped as well. Susannah still grieved for Martin and could not contemplate the prospect of dating anyone new. Maria implored her to put Martin behind her and move on, telling her that it was what Martin would have wanted but Susannah found it all so difficult. She had plenty of offers and at times had been tempted but every time she looked at another man Martin sprang into her thoughts and she felt guilty, as if she was cheating on him in some mad way. She knew she was wrong in thinking that way but that was how she felt and for the time being, she could not shake it off.

Maria had just finished lecturing Susannah for the hundred time when Mamie arrived at the door, "I have a date" she squealed. Susannah and Maria clambered for more information.

"His name is Eddie, and he comes in the shop every day. He is really nice, chatty and mannerly and he has asked me to go to the pictures with him on Saturday night," Mamie was ecstatic.

"What are you going to wear?" was Susannah's first question and the other two women laughed.

"Typical of you Susie, and now I panic, I don't know what I will wear, I've never been on a date to the pictures before, what will I wear?" Mamie started to look anxious. Susannah and Maria laughed and the three sat down with a cup of tea and discussed plans of how to walk, talk, how to dress, what to say and what not to say until Mamie's head was spinning. Susannah and Mamie set off home several hours later with loads of advice and several items of clothing on loan from Maria.

Susannah met up with Mamie after work on Saturday afternoon and they walked home together. Mary-Jane had the hot water ready for Mamie's bath and Susannah helped her wash her hair and brush it to perfection. Susannah lent Mamie a beautiful silver clasp for her hair and Mary-Jane had washed and pressed Mamie's pink dress. The dress was complemented by a rich dark cream shawl which was on loan from Maria.

"Och bless, you look as pretty as a picture Mamie," Charlie exclaimed as his youngest daughter walked into the room. Wee Charlie let out a wolf whistle while Ernie took his sister's hand and made her do a pirouette showing off the full skirt of her dress and her sisters shoes. The laughter and joviality was interrupted by a knock on the front door.

"Lad's I'm warning ye, do not tease this boy, you will only embarrass your sister and if you do you will answer to me, I mean it."

Charlie scowled at the boys who grinned back at him, "as if Da." Charlie opened the door and shook Eddie's hand. He knew Eddie's father, he was a conductor on the trams, so Charlie had no worries about Eddie taking Mamie out on a date.

"If he's anything like his father he's a good sort," Charlie told Mamie. The boys knew Eddie as well for he had been at school with them, so introductions were not really needed and within a few minutes, they were ready to leave.

Mary-Jane handed Mamie her bag, "Have fun, love, see you later." Mamie and Eddie set off down the street walking side by side, chatting away like old friends.

Susannah turned to her mother and smiled,

"Isn't that great Ma, to see Mamie so chatty and comfortable."

Mary-Jane agreed, "Mamie on a date and you keeping an eye on Alice, I can go to Annalong and enjoy the break knowing life is on the up." Susannah laughed as her mother hopped up the stairs with a spring in her step.

CHAPTER 37   SUMMER IN ANNALONG

The weather in Annalong that week in July was glorious. Mary-Jane and Charlie went walking every morning, some days they took the route along the coast and others they headed up to the lower slopes of the mountain trails. They always made it back to the house in the early afternoon so that Charlie could help the lads on the smallholding and Mary-Jane could help her mother prepare the evening meal.

"Charlie, did you notice a big change in Ma and Da since the last time we were here?" Mary-Jane asked on their first morning walk.

"Yes, but sure they are getting on. Your Da may be retired from the quarry, but he never sits still."

Charlie listed the numerous projects around the land, James's efforts were clearly visible in the beautiful rose garden and the meticulous vegetable garden.

"Mary-Jane, you have always pictured your father as this big, strong, invincible man who towered over everyone and provided for everyone but now he is getting on in years."

"I know Charlie, but it's like he has shrunk in stature and he's just so much slower, more measured. When did that happen?" she wondered.

"I noticed it too, love, it's just that we haven't seen them in nearly seven months and then it was in our house and it was winter, so we weren't out and about. But don't forget they are a fair age, sure you Da must be pushing 70." Mary-Jane agreed and added another worry to her list.

Charlie laughed, "You're not happy unless you're worrying," but he too was worried that if anything happened to James, how would Mary be able to manage on her own with just Will and Jimmy.

They decided that they would have to talk to her sisters and soon, find out if they had any worries about their parents because they lived close by, they saw more of them and they might have a better idea of how life was going for them. Although there was absolutely no sign that they were not managing, quite the opposite in fact. The house was spotless, the pantry was full of the usual jams and preserves, the rose garden was amazing, and the various gardens were well kept and the animals healthy and well looked after, so maybe they were worrying unnecessarily. The week was over too soon, and Mary-Jane and Charlie packed up to head back to Belfast. They hadn't seen a paper all week and were glad of the break from the violence that had erupted and the naked sectarianism that surrounded them at home. Mary and James had offered them sanctuary if they wanted to leave Belfast, but Mary-Jane and Charlie were both agreed, their children were adults with jobs and roots in Belfast and they couldn't leave them. Mary-Jane thanked her mother and father for their generosity explaining why they couldn't leave Belfast and her parents understood for they knew that if they were in her shoes they would do the same. Family comes first. James left them into the train station and Mary-Jane hugged him before he left, "Take care Da, mind yourself."

The journey to Belfast was short and uneventful and Mary-Jane and Charlie stepped off the train relaxed and happy only to be met by mayhem. The cobbles on the streets had been ripped up and were being flung by a crowd of young men at British soldiers and RIC men who were preparing to baton charge the stone throwers. Mary-Jane and Charlie had to run ducking for cover as the baton charge progressed towards them. They ducked into a shop and took cover behind the counter along with several other people who had also been caught up in the riots. It took them several hours to get to the safety of their own home. Susannah and Mamie were already there, they had been sent home from work as the rioting had closed the shops and businesses across the city. Luckily Susannah had bought provisions the day before so, between those and the cold cooked ham and preserves Mary-Jane had brought home from Annalong, there was enough food in the house to keep them going for a few days.

There was no sign of Ernie or Charlie and Mary-Jane said a silent prayer for their safety. It was an hour later that Ernie arrived at the back door. He had a cut over his eye where he had been hit by a stray stone but otherwise, he was fine. He told them about the large riot that he had witnessed just outside the shipyards.

"What triggered it this time?" Mary-Jane asked.

"I heard, and I don't know if it's true of not but, there was an RIC man killed in Cork by the IRA, it seems he was stationed in Cork, but he was from here and that's what kicked it off," Ernie replied.

Susannah interrupted, "But the women in work were saying that it started over work, the shipyards not employing Protestant men or employing too many Catholic men or something like that."

Mary-Jane sighed as Charlie spoke, "It's always been the same, as far back as I can remember, Catholic against Protestant. Instead of uniting as working-class people and being a real force for change, the ruling classes stir up this ridiculous divide pulling the working classes apart. There is no sense to it," Charlie spoke despondently, shaking his head as he sank into his armchair by the fire.

As night fell they could hear the bangs and crashes of rioting going on in the streets outside. Like most of their neighbours, they closed their curtains and locked their doors, sitting in front of the fire, talking quietly, in the hope that somehow the violence would die down and life could return to some sort of normality. Although Charlie wondered what normality was. Life had not been normal for so many years he wondered if he would recognise normality if he found it.

The violence continued over the weekend and the McMullens didn't venture out at all. Wee Charlie arrived home on Saturday night late when everyone had gone to bed except Charlie. He was sitting in his armchair doing something he hadn't done in years. He was saying a prayer that his son would return home safe. Charlie had never been one for praying. He thought of his mother who prayed enough for the whole family and was so wrapped up in her Church that she had very nearly not attended his wedding. She knew she regretted never having seen her second grandchild George who had died in infancy, she had never seen him because he was a Catholic, her own grandchild, and it was then that he had lost faith in the Church. He figured that if your religion made you hate a little baby, your own grandchild, then it was a religion he wanted no part of. He respected Mary-Jane, respected that she wanted her children brought up in the Catholic faith and he had never objected when she brought them to mass every Sunday or that they attended Catholic school. He had even attended mass with them on occasions particularly when they were in Annalong. So tonight, he prayed, they hadn't seen wee Charlie in over a week and with all that was going on across the city, he was worried. He knew Mary-Jane was worried too so he said nothing to her other than to reassure her that wee Charlie would be fine. It was a relief when he heard the back door open and the sound of his son tip toeing in through the scullery.

"Good night Charlie," he said in a quiet clear voice,

"Da, what are you doing up?" wee Charlie was limping and there was blood from a cut over his eye slowly dripping down his face, over his chin and onto this shirt. Charlie sprang into action, stripping his son of his coat and shirt, mopping his forehead and checking his limbs for damage. He cleaned him up as best he could and led him to his bedroom where he tucked him into bed like he had when he was a small child. Wee Charlie fell asleep as soon as his head hit the pillow, exhausted from forty-eight hours of running battles with the RIC and the British army. Charlie stood over him, worry etched on his face, looking down at his son and wondering where it would all end. He tiptoed upstairs and crept into bed beside Mary-Jane. Mary-Jane woke and went to jump out of bed, but Charlie stopped her.

"Its fine, love, Charlie is home and he is fine, go back to sleep." Mary-Jane cuddled into her husband's arms and fell back into a deep sleep, something which eluded Charlie for a very long time.

The next morning wee Charlie left straight after breakfast. Charlie and Mary-Jane never commented when he said he was going. Mary-Jane hugged him to her tightly begging him to stay safe, Charlie shook his hand and told him to be careful. Susannah stood in the scullery watching and unable to speak. She was furious at her brother for getting involved in the IRA, feeling he was letting down James and her beloved Martin but he was also her brother and she was fearful for him. She felt Mamie touch her arm and gave her sister a brief little smile, grateful for the support. She turned back to the sink full of dishes and started the washing up while Mamie lifted the tea towel and dried them putting them away as she worked. Both were slightly later than usual heading out to work but they had wanted to help their mother out this morning. She looked tired, the stress of the last few days had taken their toll. Mary-Jane waved the girls off to work and turned back to her clean kitchen. She was appreciative of the girls help this morning, but she decided there and then that she would have to hide her feelings better, she didn't want the girls worrying about her.

"No, this is not happening, it's my job to worry about them not the other way around," she said to Charlie as he pulled on his uniform jacket, "Be careful today Charlie."

Charlie reached out to her and pulled her close

"Don't worry love, if this rioting continues today they will pull the trams back to the depot, if that happens I will be home straight away."

Mary-Jane and Alice went to the shops earlier than usual that day, anxious to get some supplies in, just in case rioting broke out again. It was the first time they had a chance to have a good talk since before Mary-Jane's week in Annalong and Mary-Jane was anxious to hear how she was feeling.

"Susannah asked me to help her with that baby blanket for you and I said no at first, but she was telling me that she was really behind and that she had promised you she would get it done for you and she really needed my help, so I said I would give it a go. Do you know, it all came back to me in a flash, the minute I picked up that crochet hook it was like I had never stopped. I'm nearly finished it now, so I might pick up some more supplies and dig out my old patterns. Your Susie called in every evening after work to see how I was getting on and by Friday I was giving her crochet tips," Alice confided in Mary-Jane as they walked to the shops.

"Ach sure that's great Alice, you were always so good with your hands, do you remember that lovely shawl you made me for Mamie, I still have it, beautiful it is, everyone admired it."

Mary-Jane was delighted for her friend, pleased to hear some purpose in her voice. It's a start, she thought. The main road was quieter than usual for a Monday morning, but Mary-Jane and Alice didn't notice at first, they were so busy chatting with Alice bringing Mary-Jane up to date with all that had happened in the city while she was in Annalong.

Mary-Jane groaned inwardly as they entered the greengrocers and saw Sadie Bennett standing talking to Mrs Ward behind the counter. The two women stopped talking when they saw Mary-Jane and Alice coming in the door.

"Morning ladies," Mary-Jane called out an upbeat greeting even though Sadie Bennett was not someone she had any time for. She knew instinctively that Sadie had been talking about her, she could read it in her slightly flushed face and the hesitant reply. Mrs Ward had the grace to look embarrassed and turned away to put more potatoes in a basket that was already well stocked. Sadie pulled herself up to her full height, straightening her shoulders and jutting her chin forward, she stared into Mary-Jane's eyes.

"Well, haven't you the nerve, prancing around here, Mary-Jane McMullen, you should have stayed down country where you belong. We don't want your lot round here."

Mary-Jane was taken aback by the venom in the other woman's voice.

"I beg your pardon, Sadie, what on earth are you talking about it?"

"You know what I'm talking about, we don't want Fenians around here." Sadie spat the words out and stalked out of the shop, the bell over the door jangling until she was out of sight.

"Well I never," Alice shook her head in amazement, "Who does that one think she is."

Mary-Jane stood silently in the middle of the shop watching the door as if expecting Sadie to walk back in and spit more venom her way.

Alice took her hand, "Don't mind her, that one is just vicious, ignore her."

Mary-Jane shook herself and approached the counter where Mrs Ward was busy wiping the already clean countertop, pretending she hadn't heard anything, only looking up when Mary-Jane asked her for 5lb of potatoes. She silently filled the bag and handed it over to Mary-Jane without comment, embarrassment obvious on her face. She threw in 2lb of carrots as well, before giving Mary-Jane her change. Alice paid for her purchases quickly and they left the shop without speaking another word. Mary-Jane had been a customer for over twenty years and Alice for even longer, yet Mrs Ward had obviously been gossiping about them with Sadie Bennett, a hateful, bigoted woman who liked nothing better than to spread spiteful gossip. Nobody had ever heard Sadie speak well of anyone and that included her own family.

Mary-Jane and Alice stepped into the butchers, their local butcher Robert, a cheerful man with a penchant for friendly banter. But today Robert had nothing to say, no friendly smile, his face devoid of any emotion, he ignored Mary-Jane's greeting and turned to Alice.

"What can I get you Mrs?" Mary-Jane was completely flummoxed.

Alice was incensed, "What on earth is going on?" she demanded of Robert, who had the grace to look embarrassed.

"Nothing Mrs, but this is my livelihood, I have a wife and children to feed, if I am seen to be serving Fenians they will burn me out. I am sorry Mrs McMullen, you have been a good customer for many years, but I have to think of my family."

Mary-Jane's mouth fell open in surprise, tears suddenly springing into her eyes. She turned and left the shop before anyone could see how distressed she was.

Alice was hot on her heels after first telling Robert in no uncertain terms that he had now lost the business of both families for neither woman would set foot in his shop again. Alice tried to reassure Mary-Jane on the walk home, but Mary-Jane couldn't bring herself to speak. Mary-Jane said her goodbyes to Alice at the back gate and as she closed her door she dropped her shopping on the floor and slid down beside it sobbing. In all her years in Belfast, she had never been on the receiving end of this type of abuse. The venom in Sadie Bennett's voice was hard to take but her butcher completely ignoring her had really upset her. His confirmation that he had been threatened made her wonder how many other shops would stop serving her. What was she to do, were her children subject to the same treatment? Her tears gradually receded, and she picked herself up from the floor together with her shopping, physically shook herself, and started to prepare the evening meal for her family. It will have to be meat free today, she thought to herself as she peeled the potatoes.

CHAPTER 38   THE BELFAST POGROMS

Charlie arrived home in the early afternoon.

"The city has erupted, love, all trams have been sent back to depot and we have been sent home..." he stopped when he noticed the red eyes and forlorn expression on his wife. "Whatever is the matter."

Mary-Jane poured out her story while Charlie held her hand trying to reassure her. "What about the girls Charlie, if there is rioting nearby are they going to have to walk through it to get home." Mary-Jane wrung her hands with worry. Charlie told Mary-Jane to stay in the house, close the curtains and lock the doors after him as he put on his coat to head out again to find Susannah and Mamie. But he didn't have to leave the backyard. The back gate opened and there was Ernie with Susannah and Mamie in tow.

"I was in work Da and we saw what was happening, so I left and went straight to the city centre to see if the girls were still in work. All the shops are closing their doors with staff inside afraid to leave in case they walk straight into a violent mob. I arrived at Anderson and McAuley's just as they were closing their doors and got Susannah and two of her workmates and we collected Mamie on the way."

"Good lad, Ernie," Charlie clapped his youngest son on the back. He was a big lad, tall and broad and it would be a brave man that would tackle him, but he was still only a young lad and Charlie was relieved that no harm had come to any of them. The four of them hurried home and locked the door behind them.

Alice and Willy from next door called into them later that night. They had even worse news, after a lunchtime meeting in the shipyards Orangemen had forced the expulsion of all Catholics working there, any Protestants who were seen to have been friendly with Catholics got the same treatment, Willy included. Those men were beaten and stoned as they made their way out of the yard and into the streets. Some men had been beaten back into the water with some having to swim for their lives while the Orangemen pelted them with rocks as they swam. The same had happened to women in the Linen Mills. The city was a mess with Unionist pitted against Nationalist and running battles on the streets. Fires were burning, cobblestones uprooted and used as weapons.

"I tell you Charlie, that Carson has a lot to answer for. That yard was a great place to work, Protestant and Catholic went on strike together only last year but it's the rich and powerful that stir up the sectarian divide, it suits them to keep the workers divided and those bloody Orangemen fall into the trap every time." The horror of what had happened in that yard haunted Willy but had been powerless to do anything about it. He had a black eye and a split lip from trying to protect workmates who were being pelted with sticks by other shipyard workers. Mary-Jane put tea on the table and some scones and they sat together dejected at the state of their city.

"I couldn't believe it Charlie, I saw Sean Murray being pushed into the water by James McFarland, they have been working on the same team for years for God's sake, he pushed him in and then the rest of the team pelted rocks into the water at him."

Willy put his head in his hands, incredulous at the events of the last few weeks. He looked up, anguish plain to see etched in the lines in his face.

"It has been brewing a while, that Carson fella has been stirring it up. Him and Craig, they're behind it." Alice took his hand in hers stroking the back of his large hand as she held it in her lap.

"I don't know if I can go back to work tomorrow, I don't know if they will let me into my own work."

Charlie sympathised, shaking his head.

"Willy, I don't know what to say to ye, the only thing I can suggest is that you just go back, keep your head down and hope that common sense will return and soon."

CHAPTER 39   VIOLENCE CONTINUES

The next morning Mary-Jane woke early and dressed quickly and quietly so as not to disturb Charlie who was still sleeping. She opened the back door and stood on the back step listening to the sounds of the city waking. She shivered in the early morning chill, the morning mist was just clearing, and it was going to be a fine day: the sky was slowly turning a bright shade of blue with no visible signs of clouds and the pigeons in Martin Hughes backyard at the top of the street were awake and calling for breakfast, their gentle cooing breaking the silence. She closed her eyes and was instantly transported to Annalong imagining she could hear the chattering sound of the birds waking and calling to each other: the sound of waves crashing against the rocks. She could practically taste the salt from the sea air on the breeze. She opened her eyes and exhaled. Maybe it was time to run to Annalong, run to safety, out of the madness that Belfast had become. She decided she would talk to Charlie when he woke.

She jumped as she heard the back gate open, breathing out in relief when she saw it was wee Charlie. Shooing him into the house, she fussed over him for a few minutes, then turned to light the fire and prepare breakfast for her family.

"I think I might take Susannah and Mamie and head back to Annalong for a few days."

Wee Charlie nodded, "there were people killed yesterday and today is going to be more of the same. I'm going to grab some sleep then I am gone again."

Ernie popped his head into the room, "Thought I heard you Charlie, what about ya."

Wee Charlie grinned at Ernie, "I'm good, Ernie, heard you were quite the gentleman yesterday, escorting Susie and her workmates from work. Well done."

Ernie shrugged as if Charlie's opinion didn't matter to him but he turned away, his face flushed with embarrassment, happy to have been acknowledged by his older brother. They sat and chatted while Mary-Jane cooked breakfast and called the rest of the family to eat. Susannah acknowledged wee Charlie with a curt nod as she came into the room but never spoke to him after that, choosing a seat at the end of the table where she was out of his direct line of vision. Mamie chose to sit beside her sister in a move of unspoken support. If wee Charlie had noticed anything amiss he chose not to comment on it. Mary-Jane fussed over her brood, glad to have them all under her roof, if only for a little while. Charlie agreed with her that Susannah and Mamie should not venture into work today. It was just too dangerous. Mary-Jane had suggested that they all go to Annalong, so Charlie said he would check if the trains were running but his main worry was that even if the trains were running they would have to negotiate the city to get to the train station which would be just too dangerous.

"They even attacked the Church, Ma, St. Matthews."

Mary-Jane was horrified as wee Charlie relayed what he had seen the previous night, hundreds of men, shipyard workers, firing stones at St. Matthews Church, a group of them had climbed the railings and got access into the grounds of the church before the army arrived. They opened fire, dispersing the rioters, who then set off on a spree of looting and burning local shops.

Charlie decided that their best course of action was to stay indoors, keep curtains closed and pray for an end to the rioting. Mary-Jane had enough food in the house to keep her family well fed for a few days and got out her griddle pan to bake fresh soda farls for lunch. Susannah said she might as well use her unexpected time off productively, so she retired upstairs with Mamie to sort their wardrobes and work on some new designs Susannah had in mind.

Wee Charlie slept until evening then bade his parent's goodbye as he set off again. Mary-Jane handed him a bag packed with fresh sodas, cold cheese and preserves to keep him going until he got a chance to return home. No one else entered or left the McMullen house for the next two days. After nightfall, the sound of men shouting and women screaming could clearly be heard carried on the night air. The crash of stone into glass and erratic gunfire punctuated the air which was filled with the acrid smell of smoke and sulphur. Mary-Jane was worried, she had never seen such violence. She prayed that the area where James and Maria lived had been spared as she feared for James and the effect of the sounds and smells would have on his fragile mind. It was several days before any of them ventured out of the house and it was Charlie and Ernie who ventured out first to check on James and to shop for some food. Mary-Jane was relieved to see them return several hours later both ashen faced.

"We managed to get over to the west of the city, but it looks to be even more badly damaged than here. James and Maria were safe for now, but the neighbouring streets had been burnt out, the families tossed out on the street and their homes burnt in front of them" Charlie said. James and Maria decided to stay at home, Maria's mother had abandoned her home and was with them.

"I tell ya, ma, I'm glad to be back home," Ernie said, "the city is in ruins. Rioting and looting going on everywhere." They had found an open shop in Castle Street and had bought some milk, eggs, vegetables and the newspaper to bring home to Mary-Jane and had met some men they knew along the way, men like themselves, out for food for their families, worried, scared for their futures and anxious to get what they needed and return home as soon as humanly possible. They all exchanged stories of their own experiences of what was happening around the city, each narrative building a picture of a city in turmoil.

"They attacked St. Matthews again, love, tried to break into the convent, burnt out two rooms before the army arrived and put a stop to it. There have been Catholic families burnt out of the homes just two streets over. Maria's mam had to run for her life, she is with Maria and James now, thank God. Over where James lives on the Falls, streets of houses have been burnt and the families scattered. People have died, thousands of men have lost their jobs, thrown out of work for no other reason than they are Catholic." Mary-Jane stood with her hand over her mouth, shock and despair on her face as she listened to what Charlie was telling her.

The rioting abated after four or five days and people gradually came out of their homes to survey the damage. Shops and factories re-opened and people returned to work.

"Or at least those who still have jobs can go back to work," said Mary-Jane as she waved off Susannah and Mamie the following Monday morning with stern warnings to be careful and with Ernie to escort them. Ernie had been thrown out of his job, he wasn't long working there and now he had no prospect of getting his job back. Reports on how many had been thrown out of their jobs the previous week varied, depending on who was telling the story, but the estimates she had heard varied from 7,000 to 10,000. Catholic businesses had been targeted specifically and many were burnt and sacked. Charlie and Mary-Jane were incredulous, how could relations between Catholic and Protestant have gotten to this stage where they were tearing the city apart in this fashion. Ordinary working man pitted against his workmates, churches attacked, homes burnt, he could not see how the city could ever recover. And as for all these displaced families, what would happen to them, where would they go. The men who had lost their jobs, how would they feed their families with no income and no prospect of earning an income in the foreseeable future. The violence continued in a continuing spiral of riots, looting, tit for tat murders. The Sunday newspapers gave differing views on what had happened, and Charlie angrily tossed one paper directly into the bin declaring he had never read such rubbish.

"Pure rubbish, Mary-Jane, I tell ya, trying to whitewash what happened in this city, disgraceful." Mary-Jane just nodded and returned to the kitchen, fear eating her up inside.

While the girls had returned to work they still hurried to and from the city with their heads down accompanied by Ernie who had taken to walking into town with them and going back in the evenings to make sure that neither of his sisters had to negotiate the treacherous streets alone. Mary-Jane was anxious for their safety until they arrived in the back door. Both girls breathed a sigh of relief when they got home without incident. There were days when they had to make abrupt changes to their route home due to riots or shootings. Charlie was back at work but at some stage, every day he had to return his tram to the depot because of riots, then set off again when the rioters had dispersed. Every evening after dinner and before the sun went down, the McMullens locked their doors and closed their curtains locking out the mayhem which continued unabated outside in the city streets. Mary-Jane made sure that her family, with the exception of wee Charlie, adhered to the curfew imposed by the authorities.

Wee Charlie only got home intermittently, usually in the early morning for some much-needed sleep. Mary-Jane and Charlie knew he was in B company of the IRA Belfast Brigade and they were now trying to protect Catholics from the ongoing attacks by the Unionists. There was an ongoing war against the British being fought in every corner of Ireland but in Belfast it was different.

"There have been shootings all around the country, but the shootouts are between IRA and armed forces, here its civilians who are being shot and burned out of their homes, Catholics who are being targeted deliberately whether they are involved or not," wee Charlie explained to his parents, "We cannot stand by and let this continue, we have to defend ourselves, if we don't there won't be a single Catholic left in this corner of the country."

Mary-Jane stayed inside her home as much as possible and when she had to venture out she kept her head down and made her trips quick and short. She never returned to Robert's butchers and walked an extra twenty minutes to get her weekly roasting joint. Mrs Wall in the greengrocers continued to serve her but kept conversation to a minimum. Mary-Jane kept a watchful eye out for Sadie Bennett and avoided her at all costs. She had no wish to listen to Sadie's vitriolic abuse ever again.

On top of worrying about her family, Mary-Jane feared for her dear friend and neighbour. Alice was struggling to cope with everything that had happened. Willy had been driven out of the shipyard tagged as a leftie and a Fenian lover. He had worked at the shipyard on and off for over forty years. His years as a trade unionist had led to him being unemployed and unemployable on several occasions particularly after the general strike in 1907 and he was a vocal socialist activist during the massive strike the previous summer. Willy was unusual in Belfast as he was a Protestant but not a Unionist and certainly not an Orangeman. His socialist viewpoints led him to look forward rather than backwards and his heroes were Jim

Larkin and James Connolly. He had been driven out of the shipyard pelted by rivets by a gang of Unionists blinded by sectarian hatred, but some weeks later his manager sent for him, recognising his leadership qualities were badly missed. It was a difficult time for Willy, half of his workmates declined to even recognise that he existed while others kept contact to a minimum for fear of being ejected from the yard themselves.

As summer gave way to a cold autumn rioting continued. The British government replied by following the advice of James Craig, a Unionist politician with a seat in Westminster, by setting up a volunteer, armed police force, the Ulster Special Constabulary, operational only in the six counties. Recruitment commenced in November and the former Ulster Volunteers flocked to join the Ulster Special Constabulary.

"Why do they need another police force?" Mary-Jane asked as Charlie poured over the newspaper.

"The Unionist community don't trust the RIC, they say that its members are mainly Catholic," and Charlie and he read from the newspaper. 'The RIC is under fire from Nationalists right across the island and particularly in Belfast and Derry for standing by and not intervening when the Unionist mobs burnt Catholic homes and business and drove Catholics from the shipyards and linen mills. The Ulster Special Constabulary will aid the RIC.'

"Just in time for the enactment of the Government of Ireland Act," Charlie sighed as he put down the Sunday newspaper. "Unbelievable, they have set up two states, the six counties here where the unionists are in the majority have a parliament in Belfast and the rest of the country have their parliament in Dublin, both still under the United Kingdom flag but self-governing. How the hell is that going to work."

"Hush now Charlie, don't upset yourself for there is nothing we can do about it," Mary-Jane tried to soothe
her irate husband to no avail.

"It can't work, Belfast is industrialised and there is work here but the rest of the country relies on agriculture and we need that too. Sure, didn't Ireland feed the whole of the United Kingdom during the war? What is wrong with these people, have they no sense."

Ernie spoke up, "He is right Ma, we have to fight against this. They already have their enforcers in place, those new Ulster Special Constabulary are all Ulster Volunteers and Orangemen. Carson and Craig made sure they were in place before the Home Rule became law, they knew what they were doing. It's time to join wee Charlie. This is a complete cop-out, just to appease the Unionists."

Susannah walked into the room from the kitchen where she had been washing up the dinner dishes and hearing the last few words spoken by Ernie, she flung the tea towel she was holding at Ernie.

"How can you talk about fighting for freedom Ernie, what do you know about it, ask James what it was like to fight for king and country," she shouted her voice quivering with rage, "We need measured, reasoned arguments for the Home Rule we were promised, not more talk of war."

Mary-Jane sprang immediately to her side, trying to hold her close and calm her but Susannah was so angry she lifted a half cup of tea from the table and flung it at Ernie's head. Ernie ducked, and the cup narrowly missed her father, crashed into the wall, shattering into pieces and the tea dripped down the wall in dark rivulets.

Charlie jumped to his feet, "Susannah, stop this instant, I don't care how strongly you feel about this, there will be no fighting in this house," his voice raised at his daughter. Mary-Jane led her crying daughter out of the room and back to the kitchen as Charlie sank back down in his chair, shaking his head, annoyed at himself for raising his voice at his daughter. Ernie got up and picked up the broken pieces of china whilst Mamie, ever the peacemaker arrived beside him with a cloth to clean off the wall and the floor in front of it. Mamie gave Ernie an encouraging smile as she helped him clean up.

"Thanks Mamie, you're a pal," Ernie said as he put the pieces in the bin and went in search of Susannah.

"Ma, Susannah, I'm sorry, I didn't mean to start anything," Ernie said in a low voice, head bowed.

"No Ernie, it's my fault, I shouldn't have lost my temper," Susannah managed to voice through her tears, "Where is Da, I want to say sorry," Susannah ran back into the front room and knelt on the floor beside her Da's chair choking through her tears.

"Ah Da, I am so sorry, I nearly hit you, I didn't mean it Da, I'm sorry."

Charlie put his arms around his daughter wiping her tears as he spoke, "Ach love, it's me that's sorry, actually I think we all are sorry. Just goes to prove how easily good people can react violently when they are pushed where they do not want to go. Maybe there's a lesson for us all in that."

Peace was resumed when Mamie returned to the front room with a full teapot and some fresh cups, "To quote you Da, tea makes everything better," which brought a smile to everyone's face.

Christmas was a quiet affair in the McMullen household like most other households in Belfast. An uneasy truce was informally in place and wee Charlie returned home on Christmas Eve to spend Christmas day with his family. His parents were overjoyed to see him and fussed over him, getting his bath ready and preparing his favourite food.

"I honestly don't know what all the fuss is about," sniffed Susannah, "Talk about the prodigal son," but Mary-Jane was much too happy to chastise her. She was just happy to have all her brood at home for Christmas Day, for James and Maria were coming to them for Christmas dinner as well, along with Maria's mother. Mary-Jane's family normally travelled up from Annalong for Christmas day, but this year had decided against it, choosing to stay close to home with Mary-Jane's sister Susan. Mary had written to her daughter earlier that month explaining that she was fearful for their safety travelling to Belfast, as even travelling into their nearest town of Newcastle was fraught with danger these days. Mary-Jane understood completely and wrote back to her mother enclosing Christmas cards for her sisters. Christmas day fell on a Sunday this year and the shops and businesses closed early on Christmas eve. Ernie still escorted the girls home every evening from work and Mary-Jane had hot water ready for them when they arrived in the early afternoon. The girls were bathed and in their nightclothes by the time Charlie got home shortly after dark. When wee Charlie arrived home the girls left their parents to fuss over him while they made sure all was ready for the following day. The day dawned bright and mild for the time of year. Charlie woke early, dressed quickly and went downstairs to clear out the ashes and set the fire for the day. He loved Christmas day. Years ago when the children were small it was his favourite time of year. The look of joy on their faces when they opened their stockings to find their presents from Father Christmas. A shiny penny, an exotic orange, a doll or a toy soldier. They had some really good Christmases over the years and he hoped today would be another one.

He had the tea brewed when Mary-Jane ventured down the stairs and he greeted with a cup and a kiss, "Merry Christmas, my love, here's to us."

Mary-Jane accepted the cup gratefully, "Merry Christmas to you love." They sat companionly in their armchairs in front of the fire listening to the tick-tock of the mantel clock and the hiss of the fire, enjoying some time together in quiet reflection before the occupants of the house awoke and the Christmas bustle began.

Mass in St Matthews was packed that morning with families of all ages squeezed into the pews. Mary-Jane smiled at the baby in front of her who gurgled and gooed over his mother's shoulder for most of the mass, remembering the days when she had bounced babies on her knee and over her shoulder to keep them quiet in the church. Susannah beside her started making funny faces which made the baby laugh more, Mamie could scarcely contain her laughter and had to hide her face from the scowling look she received from the baby's Grandmother, who was sitting further along the pew and had heard the baby's little gurgle and had quickly spotted the instigator. It was a good mass, joyful and hopeful for the future, despite the turmoil in the streets outside. Mary-Jane was escorted home from church linked on each side by her sons wee Charlie and Ernie, with her daughters, Susannah and

Mamie linking arms behind them. Behind them came James, Maria and her mother Kathleen. They chatted about the presents they had received from each other and the day they were about to enjoy and they all arrived home in cheerful form. Susannah put away her mother's coat and hat for her while Mary-Jane got started on the dinner preparations. The goose was ready for the oven and Mamie helped her mother peel the potatoes and prepare the vegetables. Susannah and Maria set the table with the best linen tablecloth and water glasses lent by Maria. The boys joined their Da in a glass of stout as they sat talking while watching the women work. Dinner was served, and Charlie said grace before meals and added a special thank you to Mary-Jane for her efforts in creating a beautiful meal for the family to enjoy. They all tucked in to roast goose, mash and roast potatoes, carrots and brussels sprouts all covered in delicious gravy. Desert was trifle dripping in sherry, Kathleen's contribution to the feast and everyone practically licked their bowls clean. They all helped with the cleaning up before settling down to rest, the large meal leaving them all contentedly drowsy.

Later that evening Alice and Willy came in and they played cards around the table, talking and laughing as they played. Alice and Willy's sons had dined with them but after dinner went to visit their prospective in-laws. Arthur was getting married in February and John's wife Lily was pregnant with their first child. Alice and Willy were delighted at the prospect of becoming grandparents. Alice had a full baby layette ready and the baby wasn't due for another three months. John and Lily lived close by, just a few streets away and Alice was looking forward to helping her daughter in law out in any way she could. Lily was the eldest of her family and her mother still had young children so would not have the same time on her hands as Alice had. The news of the pregnancy had lifted Alice out of the deep depression she had been under for so long.

"New life brings hope and hope is what we all need to get us through the day," she told Mary-Jane when she had told her the news as they had shopped for more wool and patterns for the knitting and crochet Alice had planned.

They sat in the front room until the early hours. Mary-Jane even indulged in a small glass of sherry, she quite liked the taste and decided to have another, Alice and Susannah joined her, but Mamie declined. She took a sip of her mother's drink and decided it was not for her and chose elderflower cordial instead, a gift from Mary O'Brien which was delicious and reminded her of her Grandmother's pantry. Willy arrived with a bottle of Black Bush, his favourite whiskey from Bushmills in Antrim, a present from his son. The men clinked glasses and drank to peace and prosperity for all men. The Russell's weaved their way next door late that night singing out Merry Christmas to their friends and neighbours. The McMullens retired to bed, Mary-Jane happy in the knowledge that her family were healthy and happy, knelt beside her bed and asked God to keep her family safe. Charlie watched his wife from the bedroom door, a faint smile across his face, grateful to see his wife relaxed and happy for the first time in months. Both fell into a deep sleep the minute they lay down helped along no doubt by the whiskey and the sherry.

CHAPTER 40   SANCTUARY IN ANNALONG

Within months of the Ulster Special Constabulary hitting the streets, the B specials were feared by every Catholic household in the six counties. They proved themselves to be vehemently anti-Catholic perceiving anyone who was Catholic to be Nationalist and an IRA supporter. Mary-Jane and Charlie kept their heads down and only ventured outside their home when they had to. Charlie was still working on the trams, but his route was often suspended due to rioting and he came home on numerous occasions with cuts and bruises from missiles hurled at him by the rioters. Ernie continued to accompany the girls to and from work as he was still out of work and finding it difficult to find employment in a city were three-quarters of the population were Protestant and distrustful of Catholics.

"Don't worry Ernie, something will turn up, why don't you go down to Annalong to your grandparents, I'm sure they would be glad of the help," Charlie said to Ernie on a day he was particularly dejected about his employment status.

"Ach Da, I am training with the football club couple times a week, sure what would I be doing in Annalong, they don't even have a football club."

Charlie's mind flashed back to a similar conversation with wee Charlie only a few years earlier when wee Charlie claimed he was at football training but was training with the Irish Volunteers instead.

"Have you joined up with your brother?" he demanded of Ernie.

"Why Da, would that be so bad?" Ernie pleaded for understanding.

"Ach Ernie, it's bad enough worrying about Charlie without you being in the mix as well. This'll kill your mother."

"What'll kill your mother," Mary-Jane asked as she entered the room, looking at her husband and son with a no-nonsense frown.

"Ernie has joined up with his brother," Charlie told her wearily.

Mary-Jane stood directly in front of Ernie where he stood in front of the fire, her arms folded and her face stern.

"Are you in the same unit as your brother?" she asked him.

"Yes, Ma, I am or rather I will be, I am getting some training first," he raised his head and pulled himself up to his full height.

Mary-Jane deflated, her arms fell by her sides and she sighed.

"Ok so Ernie, I am not going to argue with you about it, if you feel this is something you have to do, then that is okay by me, but make sure you look after each other, do not put yourself in harm's way, be safe."

At that Mary-Jane hugged her son to her, taller and broader than his father and his two older brothers he was still her baby and probably always would be.

The fine spring led to a beautiful summer. The rioting in Belfast had eased somewhat with the fine weather and the ordinary people, Catholic and Protestant alike, were starting to come out of their homes and use their city again. The news was that the British government and authorities from the Irish Republic were in negotiations. Charlie had been delighted to hear the news hoping it would mean the boys would return home soon. Charlie overheard the men in work talking about the proposed truce, saying that the British government shouldn't be speaking to anyone representing the Irish Republic because they had declared them illegal two years ago and they were terrorists. The conversation ceased when Charlie's presence was noticed. Most of his workmates didn't speak to him anyway and it no longer bothered him. If the fact that his wife and children were Catholic offended them then he wanted nothing to do with them.

That evening he was working late, he did the late shift every third Friday, when the news came in of a shooting on the Falls Road of three RIC men, one fatally, by the IRA. Violence once again erupted, and chaos reigned for the next few days with reprisals by the Ulster Special Constabulary, uncontrollable riots and destruction to property. Once again Mary-Jane and Charlie kept themselves and their family indoors and out of harm's way as much as they could. Because of the late shift on Friday, Charlie was off work until Monday so at least they could all stay home those two days. Charlie wouldn't let Susannah and Mamie go to work on the Saturday, telling them there was no point, with the sporadic riots. There were no shoppers, only rioters, in the city so there was no point in opening the shops. Ernie and wee Charlie did not arrive home all weekend and Mary-Jane fretted over them as did Charlie, although he didn't share his thoughts about his sons with Mary-Jane figuring she was worried enough for both of them without him adding to it. The following week some form of normality returned but there were random shootings and rioting sparked at the slightest provocation. It was nearly time for the Orange Order's 12th July marches, always a tense time in Belfast, but this year the city felt like it was on a powder keg. It was a sigh of relief when the news came that a truce had been called between the British Government and the Irish Republic, due to start on 11th July.

Charlie was delighted, they were due to travel to Annalong for their annual holiday on Saturday 9th. The girls were coming with them and Charlie was hopeful that with a truce in place maybe Charlie and Ernie could join them in Annalong.

James and Maria were already there as they had travelled down several days earlier. Charlie was thankful to get out of the city that Saturday. Their walk to the train station had been fraught. The streets in the city told the tale of the ongoing civil disruption in the city, with cobbles torn up, burnt buildings and broken windows. The residential areas were worse with the shells of whole streets of burnt out homes littered with broken glass and soot. The McMullen family picked their way silently through the destruction saddened by the sheer scale of the damage to their city and to the lives of those who were now homeless, destitute, with no homes, no jobs and no hope. The acrid smell of smoke lingered in the air and gathered in their throats leaving a bitter aftertaste. As the train pulled away they all said a silent prayer for the truce to hold and for an end to this senseless violence.

Alighting from the train a short time later was like stepping into a different world. James O'Brien was waiting for them to bring them on the final leg of their journey to Annalong and he looked well. A golden tan covered his face and hands and he looked fitter and healthier than he had in years. They all crowded around him, hugging him, happy to leave the toxic atmosphere of Belfast behind them. As they made their way out of the station and out the road to Annalong the sun was shining, and the air was warm and clear. The sea sparkled in the sunshine and the beach and promenade was full of people, young people, families, older couples, children and babies, all talking and laughing and enjoying the sunshine. Charlie chatted happily to his father in law while Mary-Jane chatted to her daughters suggesting days out in Newcastle with Susan and her family and visits with Maggie and her family and with Bridget in her shop. Susannah had brought fabric and trimmings to show Bridget as she wanted advice on dresses she was planning to make for herself and for Mamie. Mamie couldn't wait to tell her aunt Bridget all about her boyfriend Eddie and to show her the beautiful watch he had bought for her at Christmas. The time went by in a flash and before they knew it they were pulling up outside the house in Annalong. Charlie watched Mary-Jane's face as they travelled the last mile of the journey, smiling to himself. Mary-Jane had confided him years before that she always felt a warm glow in her chest welcoming her home. That feeling had never faded for her and he could see that warm glow and frizzle of excitement build up in her on that final part of the journey. Mary-Jane hugged her mother warmly and then Jimmy and Will who immediately wanted their presents. She always brought presents for her brothers. They were a lot older now but the same type of present still excited them, marbles or chocolate, and she always brought both. Jimmy was his usual exuberant self, but Will seemed quieter than usual and Mary-Jane commented on his flushed complexion. Her mother agreed and fussed over Will, setting him down with a drink and a blanket.

They all enjoyed their annual holiday in Annalong and this year the weather was excellent, the best weather they had ever experienced. They made the most of it, walking out every day, eating outside, fishing and swimming. On the following Thursday, they made their way to Newcastle to spend the day on the beach with Susan and her family. It was another glorious day and they were looking forward to their picnic, their walk along the seashore and of course the promenade, for no day in Newcastle would be complete without a walk along the promenade. Susan had arrived on the beach before them and had set up a little camp, with blankets to sit on, sunchairs for the older ones and umbrellas to protect the ladies from the strong rays. It was close to the water so that they could dip their toes in the sea to cool them down if they got too hot. After greetings were exchanged they made themselves comfortable with Mary-Jane and Susan organising the picnic. Their mother offered to help but the women wouldn't hear of it, coaxing their mother into sitting down and enjoying the rest. They ate and drank and talked. The younger children played in the sand and the older girls went for a walk down the promenade enjoying the attention they gathered. The cousins were fairly close in age and sisters all laughed at the memory of a day, a beautiful sunny day like this one, when they had walked the length of the promenade and back again before having a picnic with their parents and the boys Will and Jimmy. It seemed so long ago and here they were, on another beautiful sunny day watching their daughters walking the same promenade. Mary-Jane remarked to Susan,

"Wonder will they get the same attention we did, do you remember?"

Susan burst out laughing, "God, that was a lifetime ago."

When the best of the sunny day was over, and it was time to head back to Annalong, Charlie and Sean went to the nearest shop to pick up some cold lemonade for the journey. As he walked into the shop the headlines on the newspaper shouted out at him. Charlie was totally dismayed. He bought a copy but hid it from sight of the women not wanting to spoil the mood of the entire party. He decided he would wait till he got home and read it then and digest it before he mentioned what was going on to anyone.

It was later that night when the women were clearing up after the dinner that Charlie went outside and read the newspaper. The headlines read, "Bloody Sunday Aftermath," and his hands were trembling as he opened the pages to read further. The truce had started the previous Monday, but Belfast was in flames. The evening they had left Belfast there had been an IRA ambush of a police truck, one RIC man had died and two more were injured. That incident sparked rioting and B Special reprisals, the result of which was, 16 people died, and 161 homes were destroyed, their residents left homeless and it wasn't over. There were gun battles raging and fierce fighting, particularly in West Belfast.

James joined Charlie on his bench handing him a small whiskey, "What's up Charlie, you look like you've seen a ghost."

Charlie filled him in on the contents of the paper and the two men talked until the women joined them.

"Why the glum faces?" Mary said as she sat with her cup of tea, patting the seat next to her for Mary-Jane to sit down and gestured to another bench for James and Maria. Charlie showed them the paper and told them what was in it. They sat up until the early hours talking about the War, about the boys, trying to figure out what they should do. Mary O'Brien was adamant that they should stay in Annalong and never go back to Belfast.

"Your Da and Charlie could go up and clear out the house and bring all your belongings back here. You could live here with us."

Within minutes she had it figured out, that Susannah would live with Bridget, Bridget had married and was living in a little cottage in the town centre close to the shop.

"Sure, Susannah would love that, Bridget is looking for someone skilled to help out in the shop with the alterations and that sure Susie would be perfect"

Mary thought this was a great idea, "And Mamie could help me around the place until we find her a place in the village and there is plenty of room here for her."

James piped in, "You could transfer to the train service Charlie and drive the trains from Newcastle," he elbowed Charlie chummily, "Sure it would all work out fine."

Mary-Jane and Charlie listened to their arguments, but it was James and Susannah that decided them on the right course of action.

"Granny, I know you mean well, but Belfast is our home, me and Maria we have our own home and Kathleen lives with us, we can't go anywhere. Da loves his job, why would he leave, and what about Charlie and Ernie, they arrive home to be fed and to sleep, what would they do? and anyway this all has to stop sometime, it cannot go on indefinitely, sure there would be nobody left in the city."

Susannah put up her own argument.

"Granny I know it would be great to live here and to work with Bridget all the time, you know how much I love Bridget, but it's not for me. I've been promoted in the shop Granny, I'm not just a shop girl anymore, I am a buyer, I choose what the shop buys to sell to women, I am the first woman to hold that position, I have influence, and respect and I love it. I don't want to leave it, even though working with Bridget would be great, I feel like I would be running away. I accepted this position and challenging though it is I really enjoy it."

Mary O'Brien sat back looking directly at each of her family and smiled, "Thank God we raised strong women James, who also raised strong women who know their own minds and who raised men who are equally strong and sure of their place in the world." James smiled in return,

"Just remember each and every one of ye, if it ever gets too much for you or even if just need a few days break, we are here, you are more than welcome anytime."

Charles shook the outstretched hand of his father-in-law and they all raised a glass, "to the future, whatever it may hold."

The next morning Mary called the boys for breakfast as well as the rest of the family. Jimmy arrived into the kitchen in an agitated state.

"Ma, Will won't get out of bed."

Mary-Jane laughed "Don't worry Jimmy, I will go wake him, you have your breakfast."

Mary-Jane opened the bedroom door.

"Up you get Will, it's too nice a day to stay in bed," pulling open the curtains as she spoke. She turned and screamed. James and Charlie both came running. Charlie gasped at the realisation that Will was dead, his features frozen in time yet peaceful. Charlie put his arms around his wife while James checked his son for a pulse even though he was cold. Mary came into the room calling Will's name and stopped in shock as she witnessed James closing her son's eyes for the last time. Jimmy was inconsolable. His brother was his best friend and his childish mind could not comprehend why Will had to be laid out in a box and buried in the cemetery. He wanted Will to wake up and play with him and it took some gentle explanation and persuasion from his sisters to make him understand what had happened to Will. The family united in grief to celebrate the life of their sweet, gentle brother and to support their parents in their grief. All were agreed that at least they all had the last day in Newcastle together as a family before Will died and they would treasure those memories. After the funeral, Mary-Jane and her family had to return to Belfast with her parents offer of sanctuary ringing in their ears.

CHAPTER 41   CHARLIE'S TRAUMA

After a week back in Belfast with the violence continuing unabated, Mary-Jane questioned her judgement in not taking her parents up on their offer. Getting to the shops was a major chore not just because she was running the risk of running into a riot, but the riots were causing transport problems and the shops weren't getting their normal deliveries. Eventually, after numerous wasted trips Alice and Mary-Jane discovered that early morning was best when the men were just going to work, the shops were managing to receive their deliveries in at that time and the rioting seemed to start in the late afternoon or early evening and lasted till the early hours of the morning. Like many other women, Mary-Jane and Alice changed their routines, going out to the shops in the morning when their husbands were leaving for work and doing their chores when they returned. She never went to the butchers anymore. James went for her, buying the Sunday roast and the vegetable roll. Everyone treated James with respect. His wooden leg a badge of honour which was respected by all sides. On days when the riots continued all day, James would arrive with vegetables, potatoes or eggs knowing his mother would be able to feed the family on whatever he brought.

Wednesday was vegetable roll day. She had never heard of it before she came to Belfast. It was Alice who had introduced her to the delicacy which Belfast people were reared on. It was a cheap dinner and Mary-Jane doubted if there was much meat in it, but every butcher made their own version, some better than others. It was a large spicy sausage cut into large round slices the size of a large biscuit and those slices could be fried or cooked in the oven. It was spicy and delicious and Mary-Jane's family loved it. She preferred to oven bake it with vegetables and herbs which gave a lovely flavour to the gravy she made from the juices. Served up with mash it was a favourite dinner in her house.

The fine weather continued as autumn approached and so did the violence. The truce had held firm in all other parts of Ireland, it was only in the six counties that hostilities continued. Mary-Jane feared every day for her family. The trams were regularly attacked, and Charlie often arrived home early after the trams were taken off the streets. Susannah and Mamie were working in the city centre, which regularly closed when violence erupted, but then they had to face the gauntlet of the rioting crowds to get home. The family regularly discussed the option they had of packing up their belongings and going to Annalong but each time they made the decision to leave there was a lull in the violence which led them to believe that maybe just maybe there was an end in sight. Inevitably something would spark off more rioting and the violence would start again.

Then just after Halloween Charlie arrived home one day ashen faced and shaking.

"They bombed the tram Mary-Jane, there were bodies everywhere, blood everywhere."

Charlie fell into his chair and sobbed. Mary-Jane dropped to her knees in front of him, stroking his hair and trying to soothe him. She had never seen Charlie cry before and she was shaken to the core. They remained in that position for what seemed like an age before Charlie's sobs subsided.

"Sorry, sorry oh God," he wiped his eyes with the back of his hand and blew his nose on the hankie he always kept in his trouser pocket along with his pocket watch.

"Ach whist Charlie, you cry as much as you need to. I am here for you, such an awful sight to witness, you dear, dear, man," Mary-Jane hugged her husband to her.

"I tried to move one lad, he was lying under the seat, but his legs were missing, and he was bleeding and I watched him die, I saw the life leave his eyes."

Shock engulfed Charlie and he shivered and struggled to breathe.

"I thought of our James, Mary-Jane, I realised how scared he must have been, how much pain he must have been in," he paused struggling to take in another breath, "For all we know our boys could have planted that bomb. Our sons could be responsible for killing some other father's son. I can't sort that out in my head, Mary-Jane."

Charlie dissolved into more sobs, heartfelt sobs that started in the depths of his stomach and erupted through his throat. Mary-Jane tried to soothe him, silent tears pouring down her cheeks, she held him close until his giant sobs subsided once again. He sat back in his chair exhausted from the trauma he had been through. Mary-Jane got her shawl and draped it over him, tucking it in then removing his shoes, she sat and stroked his face until he fell into a fitful sleep.

She heard the back door open and moved quickly to the kitchen to shush the girls, anxious that Charlie should sleep for just a little while. In an urgent whisper, she gestured the girls to stay quiet then told them in hushed tones what had happened. Susannah and Mamie were shocked and scared. They tiptoed to the door of the front room just to look at their father who was muttering and jumping in his sleep as if he was reliving the events of the day in his dreams. The girls retreated upstairs for a while, returning to the kitchen an hour later. They found Charlie awake but still in his chair staring into the flames of the fire that Mary-Jane had kept going. They both gave their father a silent hug then went into the kitchen to help their mother serve dinner. The dinner table was uncharacteristically silent that night as they all ate their food in silence, conscious of Charlie, sitting at the head of the table staring at his plate and unable to eat more than a mouthful.

Mary-Jane was expecting James to visit the next morning, so she watched out for him out the bedroom window and when she saw his familiar gait in the laneway she rushed downstairs grabbing her coat and caught him before he came in the back gate. She told him what had happened the day before.

"Will you talk to him James, I don't know what to say to him to try and make it better and he hasn't spoken a word since yesterday," Mary-Jane pleaded with James.

"Course Ma, go you into Alice and get a cuppa and I will sit with Da for a while."

Alice had the kettle on and listened to her friend as she poured her heart out about Charlie.

"Go, Mary-Jane, take Charlie and go to Annalong for a few days, maybe the change of air will do him good. Let's face it he needs to get out of Belfast for a few days. This place is toxic, and you are lucky that you have the opportunity. Go."

Mary-Jane thanked her friend for listening and for her good advice.

James thought it was a great idea. Susannah and Mamie had insisted that they go, just for a few days to give Charlie time to heal. Mary-Jane had wanted her daughters to go with them, but Susannah refused, and Mamie insisted she would stay to look after Susannah. So, after assurances from the girls that they would look after each other, Mary-Jane packed a bag and told Charlie that they were going to Annalong for a few days. Charlie didn't argue, he had talked to James the day before and he was trying to act normally but his eyes were haunted in his grey face and he moved like an old man, forgetful and hesitant. Mary-Jane was worried about him. Alice and Willy said they would look out for the girls so there was nothing standing in their way. They arrived in Newcastle late afternoon and made their way to Susan's home on the edge of the town.

Sean opened the door and exclaimed in shock when he saw Mary-Jane and Charlie on his door step. He opened the door widely, calling out to Susan, and took the suitcase from Charlie, pulling them into his home. Susan was thrilled to see them and insisted that they stay the night, offering the services of Sean to bring them to Annalong in the morning. Before long she had shown them to a bedroom and made them food. Susan and Sean remarked on Charlie's pallor as they sat over a cup of tea after dinner.   Hesitantly Charlie told them what had happened on the tram two days previously.

"Oh my goodness, Charlie, that is just dreadful." Tears formed in Susan's eyes as she listened to Charlie. Sean got up from the table and disappeared into the larder, returning a few minutes later with a bottle of whiskey and four glasses. He poured a small measure into two glasses and handed one to his wife and one to Mary-Jane. He poured a large measure for himself and Charlie, who took a sip then downed the rest in one large gulp.

"Steady on Charlie..."

Sean cut Mary-Jane short,

"he's grand Mary-Jane, let him be, what's seldom is wonderful as my mother used to say to me."

Sean refilled Charlie's glass getting a smile from Charlie and a grateful smile from Mary-Jane. They sat for several hours around the table debating the War and the truce, the violence, trying to make sense of what was happening to their country. They eventually retired to bed, Charlie once again exhausted fell into a deep but restless sleep. Mary-Jane lay awake for a long time just stroking his cheek, watching him as demons chased him in his dreams.

The next day Sean brought them on the short trip to Annalong. Mary O'Brien was baking bread in the kitchen and heard the sound of their approach down the laneway. Wiping her hands on her apron she went to the door to see who was calling for she was not expecting any visitors particularly on a day like today when the rain was coming down in sheets. She was overjoyed to see Charlie and Mary-Jane, calling to James who was out in the shed. Sean stopped and had tea and a chat with his father in law before taking his leave shaking Charlie's hand and wishing him all the best. They were soon ensconced beside the fire enjoying hot soup and fresh baked bread and Mary-Jane watched Charlie as the stress slowly drained out of his body. He had always loved Annalong and he particularly loved his in-laws. They were good people who brought out the best in everyone, including him. Charlie told them briefly what had happened and how dreadful a sight it had been and how he couldn't get the vision of that young man with his legs blown off out of his head. He told them of his worries about wee Charlie and Ernie and his horror at the thought that they may have been responsible for shooting or bombing and his confusion at how that made him feel about his sons.

James understood completely.

"Och Charlie, I think I understand for I think any right-thinking person would feel the same. You brought up your boys to be fine, young men, with strong Christian values, you taught them the Commandments, the 5th Commandment, thou shalt not kill, sure they know that, we all know that. But, we live in strange times, we have spent the last seven years at war, first on a grand scale, think of all the young Christian men who went off to fight, young men like your James. Now we have this war in Ireland, wee Charlie and Ernie are no different than James. They are fighting for what they believe in. James's war was fought in foreign lands, so we didn't see the bodies as they fell from gunshots or bombs. This war is being fought in our own country, in our streets and we can see first-hand the damage to human life. You have seen first-hand the horror of death and destruction."

James stood as he spoke pacing up and down the room.

"What you have to remember is that they are fighting for something they believe in. I remember many years ago hearing a quote from an Irish politician, Burke was his name, something along the lines of "the only thing necessary for evil to triumph is for good men to do nothing" and that is as true today as it was a hundred years ago. And your sons Charlie, are good men."

Mary-Jane looked up at her father with gratitude. She knew Charlie set great store by James and respected his point of view. She hoped that listening to James would help Charlie put everything into perspective for him.

"Thank you, you are making sense of it all for me now James and I thank you for that." Charlie stood and shook his father-in-law's hand.

Mary wanted them to stay for a few days, but Mary-Jane and Charlie were conscious that the girls were alone, even though Alice and Willy were keeping an eye out for them, and they wanted to get back to them. They couldn't rest in Annalong knowing that the girls were in Belfast going about their normal daily activities in the midst of the mayhem. The following day Mary-Jane and Charlie made their way back to Belfast arriving home in the middle of the afternoon with plenty of time to shop for provisions and have dinner ready for the girls arriving home from work. Charlie walked in to meet them and escort them back home. It was a dark, wintery night with intermittent rain and blustery winds. The streets were quiet with all of the people they passed muffled up in hats and scarves and hurrying through the rain, anxious to get indoors and out of the cold. Charlie opened the back door ushering the girls inside. The warmth of the kitchen hit them the minute the door opened and the delicious smell of the stew bubbling away on the range assailed their senses.

"Och Ma, it is so good to have you home," Mamie ran straight into Mary-Jane's arms, "No one can make a stew like you."

Susannah laughed "Hey you, I make a good stew," she joined her sister in a group hug. Mary-Jane felt Charlie's eyes on them.

"I am so lucky."

Charlie smiled as he joined their group hug. There was a loud knock at the back-door startling them all. The door opened, and wee Charlie put his head around the door, followed closely by Ernie.

"Och lads, what about ya?" Charlie's delight at seeing his sons evident in his expression. The family spent the evening together, Charlie lit the pot belly in the shed for hot water, so the lads could bathe before dinner. Mary-Jane put extra dumplings in the stew and the girls set the table everyone working in harmony.

CHAPTER 42   CHARLIE AND HIS MOTHER

Once again, the O'Briens declined Mary-Jane's invitation to spend Christmas Day in Belfast, this time going to Bridget's home for dinner. Mary-Jane didn't mind.

"Mam and Dad have to share out which daughter they spent Christmas with," she told Charlie. James and his wife and mother-in-law were coming for dinner again and Kathleen had promised to make her delicious sherry trifle for dessert. Just like the previous year, the violence abated in the run-up to Christmas and everyone was glad of the respite. The violence of the previous three years had worn everyone down, thousands had left the city, burnt out of their homes and businesses, many had ventured as far as Dublin and were being housed in buildings around the city.

"Charlie, do you know they housed refugees from Belfast in a place called Fowler Hall, a building owned by the Orange Order, imagine, Orangemen burnt these people out of their homes and now they are living in an Orange Hall." Mary-Jane laughed at the thought.

Charlie nodded in agreement, he had read about that in the papers although some of the papers were printing complete rubbish trying to say that there were no refugees, no burnt-out homes but the evidence was there for everyone to see. Streets upon streets of burnt out homes, streets littered with stones and bricks. British troops patrolled the streets to try and restore some sort of order. Now the treaty had been signed and the Irish Free State had been set up, a dominion of the British Commonwealth of Nations. More importantly for Charlie and his family, the six counties had exercised their right to opt out of the new state so instead of living in a country with a Nationalist (mainly Catholic) majority, they now lived in a state with a Unionist (mainly Protestant) majority, a Unionist majority who hated Catholics.

Worry lines creased Charlie's brow, he wondered how he could talk his adult children into leaving Belfast. He knew Mary-Jane would not leave Belfast without them. Annalong was an option for them but he wondered now if they should head to the Irish Free State. County Down was within the six counties. The violence of the last three years had touched every county, but it had been worse in Belfast and Derry. His own brothers and sisters had stopped speaking to him, branding him a traitor for marrying a Catholic. His mother had stopped calling when she discovered that wee Charlie was in the IRA. Charlie still remembered her rage that day. She had slapped Mary-Jane across the face, accusing her of raising a terrorist, of ruining her grandchildren's lives by bringing them up Catholic. Charlie sprang to his wife's defence, ordering his mother to apologise to Mary-Jane and when she wouldn't apologise he ordered her out of his home. They hadn't seen her since and Charlie had no wish to see her ever again.

Charlie despaired of Ireland, the sectarian violence had been going on since before he was born and was now worse than it had ever been with no end in sight. He was tired, tired of worrying about his family, particularly his sons. James had sacrificed his future for his country, albeit in a British uniform, but that was the uniform of his country at the time. Charlie wondered how he would be judged in the future, would future generations understand he wore a British uniform to help Ireland? Wee Charlie and Ernie, they fought a different war but for the same reason, for Ireland. Charlie voiced his concerns to Mary-Jane who agreed with his view but confirmed what Charlie had feared, that she would not leave Belfast without her children, even if they were adults. Mary-Jane favoured Annalong rather than the Free State, arguing by going to Dublin they could be going from the frying pan into the fire. They both agreed to talk to the family after Christmas Day was over and find out what their opinions were.

Christmas was a joyous day. Mamie's young man Eddie had proposed the month previous. He had asked Charlie for permission which Charlie had gladly given. They were planning to marry in the spring and Susannah was already busy designing her sister's wedding dress. Charlie had been a little concerned at first thinking his youngest daughter was too young to marry, she had just turned eighteen, but Mary-Jane had talked him around.

"Mamie is mature beyond her years and madly in love with her Eddie."

Susannah had spoken up for her sister, reminding her father that her chance of love and marriage had died with Martin on a field in France. Mary-Jane hugged her daughter to her, it had been nearly four years since Martin had died and Susannah still grieved for him.

"I pray at mass every week that Susannah would find peace and an end to her grief, I pray that Susannah could meet someone worthy of her who would make her happy again," Mary-Jane told Charlie as they discussed their daughters late one night. It was Susannah who made Charlie and Mary-Jane realise that Mamie was right not to wait, in the turbulent world they lived in, they needed to nurture happiness.

The boys arrived home late on Christmas Eve to a joyful family. Wee Charlie and Ernie both knew Eddie and they were happy for their sister. The joyful atmosphere in his home was contagious and Charlie felt the faint stirring of hope for the future. He thought about his mother and reckoned if he could make peace with his mother then it bore well for the rest of the country and maybe, just maybe there was some hope for them all. The next morning, they all set off to Christmas Day mass on a fine morning which felt more like spring than the depths of winter. Charlie parted company with them at St. Matthews and went on to his mother's house. His sister Maggie met him in the street as she and her husband made their way to the house for their Christmas day visit. Maggie hugged Charlie wishing him a merry Christmas. She offered to walk in with him but warned him that their mother had become increasingly bitter. Maggie knocked the door as she opened it to find her mother standing in the kitchen.

"Morning Maggie love, your early, come in, come in," she hesitated as she saw Charlie walking in behind Maggie.

"Charlie," she said curtly, "What brings you here?"

Charlie smiled at his mother, "Merry Christmas Ma, how are you?"

"Fine, Charlie, Merry Christmas." Charlie's younger brother Tom heard Charlie's voice and entered the kitchen.

"Well Charlie, where is the taig, did you not bring her with you?"

Charlie bristled with anger, "Do not speak about my wife like that Tom, do not disrespect me."

Maggie stood between her brothers, "For God's sake, do I have to remind you that it is Christmas Day. Even the Germans and the British called a truce on Christmas Day during the war, surely you two can do the same, you are brothers" she implored them. Both brothers had the grace to appear embarrassed, Tom apologised to Charlie and offered him his hand. Charlie hesitated for just a fraction of a second then accepted his brother's apology and shook his open hand.

Charlie decided the time was right to tell them some good news.

"I'm here to let you know that our Mamie is getting married next May. Eddie popped the question last month, he is a good person, lovely young man and the two of them are so happy."

His mother's reaction surprised him as tears sprang to her eyes.

"I can't believe it, little Mamie, just seems like yesterday she was toddling around with her little doll and her big blue eyes. Thanks Charlie, thank you for telling me. I will get her something for her bottom drawer in the sales."

Charlie thanked his mother and after wishing them all a merry Christmas he left for home, pleased with how the visit had gone regardless of the cross words with Tom. He couldn't wait to get home and tell Mamie, she would be pleased, always the peacemaker Mamie hated the fact that her paternal Grandmother wasn't in her life. She had been part of their lives for so long, looking after them for a morning once a week when they were smaller so that her mother could get run errands and she missed her. She had been there in the front room the day of the argument and had been horrified when her Grandmother slapped her mother. She had welcomed her Da springing to her Ma's defence while she had put her arm around her mother showing her support and her abhorrence for what had happened. Charlie remembered her face that day, a mixture of shock and hurt at anyone hurting her Ma, let alone her Grandmother being the culprit. He knew that Mary-Jane would never forget that day, but he also knew that she was a compassionate woman who always saw both sides of every argument and would be quite willing to forgive even if she couldn't forget.

The family had all returned from mass when Charlie got back. He hadn't said where he was going so they were quite surprised when he told them.

Mary-Jane smiled broadly,

"Charlie, that is great news, hopefully you and your Ma can sort things out between you now," planting a kiss on Charlie's cheek.

Mamie hugged her Da, "Thanks Da, I might try and call to her and show her my ring, if that's okay with you Ma," sudden confusion on her face, delighted as she was to hear her Grandmother's positive reaction to her engagement, she wouldn't dream of doing anything that would hurt her mother, so if her mother had told her to stay away from Margaret McMullen she would have. But she shouldn't have even considered it, Mary-Jane quickly reassured her daughter.

"Of course you should show your Grandmother your ring, she will be delighted to see you." Mamie beamed her pleasure and put her hand in front of her, moving it to and fro so that the diamond caught the light and glittered on her smooth, white fingers, delight dancing on her upturned face.

Susannah laughed with joy at her sister's pleasure,

"We will go over after work next week, I would quite like to see granny as well."

Mary-Jane smiled at her two daughters.

"Now I'm glad that's settled but if I don't get started on this dinner shortly we won't be eating until after dark."

They all got started on their various jobs, Mamie singing as she laid the table with wee Charlie and Ernie joining in on the chorus. James and Maria arrived and soon joined in with the joviality. Charlie sat in his chair by the fireside beaming with pride as he watched his family singing and talking while they worked. Life is good, thought Charlie, it may be mayhem outside on the city streets but in here, in our home, life is good, and we have a lot to be thankful for.

The inevitable return to violence came early in the new year. Refugees continued to flood into Dublin, most of them with no belongings other than the clothes on their backs. Charlie tried to arrange his shifts so that either himself or Eddie were available to walk Susannah and Mamie to work and back. Everyone kept their head down and prayed for a resolution. Wee Charlie and Ernie arrived infrequently to bathe and sleep. Wee Charlie told his father that Michael Collins was sending guns from the Irish Free State so that they could protect the Catholic population.

"But I would say he is hoping to destabilise the government here as well Da."

The short days of winter were fraught with danger, but the long nights were even worse. Every evening as soon as darkness fell Mary-Jane pulled the curtains and the minute Charlie and the girls got in from work they locked the doors as if by doing that they were locking out the horrific violence going on outside in the streets.

CHAPTER 43   THE SHOOTING

The milder than usual winter brought plenty of rain but no frost or snow.

"There hasn't been any hard frost to kill off the germs," said Mary-Jane and Alice agreed as they walked to the shops, the light rain soaking into their coats and scarfs.

"I hate these drizzly days, the rain just soaks through, making everything damp and miserable, a bit of frost would be welcome if you ask me."

They paid a visit to the greengrocer who didn't have a lot to offer and were just turning off the main road when they heard the shots. Both women ran for cover into a newsagent's shop and hid behind a shelf unit as far back into the shop as they could. Mary-Jane lifted her head and peered out around the corner of a shelf, she spotted a B Special crouched behind the corner of the building directly opposite. He flinched as shots pinged off the corner of the building, then stood out away from the building and fired several shots in their direction, jumping back behind the building within seconds. Mary-Jane heard the whiz of the bullet as it passed her inches from her ear. She dropped down lower, and on her hands and knees, crawled further back into the shop dragging Alice with her. They heard the returning fire come from somewhere outside the building they were in. The exchange went on for a few more minutes and then suddenly all was quiet. Both women sat with their backs against the wall and their hands over their ears, wide-eyed with fear they slowly moved to a standing position, slowly lowering their hands. The newsagent was beside them and he peered around the corner before moving cautiously into the centre of the shop.

"All clear ladies, it appears to be over, for now, but I would advise you get yourself off the streets just as quick as you can."

Mary-Jane and Alice thanked him profusely, gathered their bags and practically ran the whole way home.

They sat in Mary-Jane's kitchen trying to drink a cup of tea with hands shaking both conscious of their lucky escape. Once again Mary-Jane thought of leaving Belfast behind her and going to Annalong and decided that she would talk to Charlie that evening after work and devise a plan to get all her family out of Belfast and if not to Annalong then to the Free State. Susannah had applied for a position in a department store in London called Selfridges and was quite excited about the prospect of living and working in London. Mamie was getting married in May and would be well looked after by Eddie, she had no fears there, but she could talk to Eddie about getting a transfer to the train service and moving out of Belfast and out to Newcastle or Newry. James and Maria were settled and had Maria's mother living with them, but Kathleen was sick and was unlikely to see the winter out so maybe when Kathleen passed James and Maria would consider moving, work was not a problem for them as they lived on James's war pension. As for the boys, they were never at home and if they moved to Annalong surely the boys would follow them, for neither were working, spending all their time fighting with the Belfast Brigade of the IRA. She had every argument reasoned through but was totally surprised when Charlie said he was totally against the idea. He saw it as fleeing Belfast and abandoning their family.

"But Charlie, we will bring them with us."

But Charlie was adamant,

"No Mary-Jane, Eddie just got the house in Cawnpore Street and he is fixing that up for him and Mamie, they won't leave Belfast. James and Maria are well settled, they won't go and as for the boys, there is no way they would leave Belfast, particularly with the way things are at the minute. You know this Mary-Jane, you have always told me that we can't leave without them, why now."

Mary-Jane knew he was right, but she felt deflated somehow and helpless. She had come to hate her adopted city and longed for the fresh air of Annalong.

Charlie saw the dejection in her face,

"It's this damp, dark weather, it's getting everyone down, love, you wait and see, only six months until we go to Annalong for our summer holiday. Once the weather picks up you will feel better."

Mary-Jane said nothing, hoping that Charlie was right in what he was saying but unable to shake the feeling of impending doom that was twisting her insides and giving her an uneasiness that she couldn't shake.

Wee Charlie and Ernie arrived home on Saturday night after darkness fell, wet and cold and hungry. Charlie got the fire going for hot water while the lads stripped off their damp and dirty clothing. They wrapped up in blankets until they could bathe and put on clean clothes. Mary-Jane had hot soup ready in twenty minutes to heat them up while she prepared something more substantial. Wee Charlie woke the next morning with a high temperature and a dreadful cough. Ernie left to return to his unit leaving wee Charlie in bed delirious with Mary-Jane administering to him. It was the best part of a week before wee Charlie could put his foot on the floor and into the second week before he was fit to re-join his unit. The day he left Charlie felt unwell but went on to work saying nothing to Mary-Jane.

That night on his return he could barely stand up he felt so bad, every muscle ached, his head felt too heavy for his shoulders and was pounding on the inside as if there was a miniature orange march on his forehead. Mary-Jane put the back of her hand on his brow.

"Och Charlie, you are burning up," she helped him into his nightclothes, fed him some soup and left him to sleep. Charlie's fever stayed with him for nearly the whole week and Mary-Jane was seriously worried about him. She climbed the stairs several times a day, bringing water and soup and fresh linens. He sweated profusely which Alice said was a good sign and eventually he started to feel slightly better. Mary-Jane helped him down the stairs and into his armchair by the fire. She got him comfortable then left him reading the newspaper by the light of the fire and snoozing in between each article.

Mary-Jane was slightly behind in her usual busy Saturday schedule so was slightly later than usual getting out the griddle pan to make the sodas for the evening tea. Ernie had arrived home without wee Charlie, which alarmed Mary-Jane at first, but Ernie explained that wee Charlie would be home later that night. Mary-Jane sent Ernie straight out to the shed to check the water for their baths.

"Done Ma, What the hell?" Ernie jumped at the loud knock on the front door. Mary-Jane tried to push Ernie back out the door into the yard, shouting, "Run, Ernie, run." Mary-Jane felt her heart sink as she heard the crash of the front door being kicked off its hinges. Her world felt like it was in slow motion as she heard the raised men's voices from the front room, shouting and screaming, although she couldn't process what they were shouting. She heard the shots, loud and roaring around the room and she became aware of Ernie running past her into the danger. She heard the crash of broken glass underfoot as the two men ran back out over the remnants of the front door. She looked past Ernie calling Charlie's name. She heard Charlie's cup crash against the floor as Charlie slipped sideways in his chair, blood pouring from his side. Ernie stopped in full flight as he heard his mother's scream out. He caught Mamie at the bottom of the stairs and propelled her out the front of the house, "Mamie, go get help." Ernie ran to his father's side, calling him, feeling for a pulse, trying to stem the flow of blood from his side. Mary-Jane stood in shock in the middle of the room watching her beloved Charlie gasping for breath.

Alice came running in and caught her before she fell, wrapping her arms around her friend, feeling her pain. There were screams and shouting from outside as Mamie screamed for help and someone went to call an ambulance. Ernie nursed his da in his arms, waiting and praying for help, tears falling unchecked and mixing in with the blood on his Da's clothes. The ambulance arrived and took Charlie from Ernie's arms. Ernie went to his mother, holding her for a minute and then in a quiet gentle voice told her to get her hat and coat and they would go in the ambulance to the hospital. Alice quickly got Mary-Jane into her coat and putting her handbag over her arm she helped Ernie lead her from the house. Alice's husband Willy had taken Mamie into his house out of the street so that she didn't see her father being carried out. As Ernie led his mother through the little crowd that had gathered outside the house Mary-Jane could hear her neighbours.

"They were shouting Fenian lover," and Mrs McConvey saying, "I heard the shots and the men shouting fenians get out, God bless us, what's to become of us all."

Several women reached out and patted Mary-Jane sympathetically on the arm as she passed, but Mary-Jane could not look anywhere but in front of her at her beloved Charlie.

CHAPTER 44   NEIGHBOURS

As the ambulance pulled away, its siren blaring, the crowd moved to let the ambulance through then gathered together in front of the house gossiping about what they had just witnessed.

Mrs Regan recounted the shouting she had heard, "and the gunmen ran straight past me then ducked around the corner into an alleyway."

Mrs Harkness nodded, "That Charlie was a good sort, a lovely man with a smile and greeting for everyone."

"Aye, he was that," agreed Mrs Magill adding, "it was just a pity he had married a Catholic, he would have been better to leave Belfast when he married, sure Sherwood Street is no place for a Catholic family."

Mrs McHenry interjected, "I recognised one of the gunmen, he's a B Special."

Mrs Duncan agreed with her, "Yes, he is, and I think I know who he is, but I tell ye, I don't think it was Charlie they were after. No, I reckon it was the young lad, Ernie, sure I heard he was in the IRA."

Mrs Turner was amazed that Mrs Duncan was so well informed and believed every word that was uttered.

Mrs Anderson called them all, "silly stupid gossips with not an ounce of compassion, The McMullens moved into this street around the same time as most of us, nigh on thirty years, they have always been good neighbours, good people. How can ye stand here spreading gossip when that poor man had been shot, could be dead for you all you know. Poor Mary-Jane," and after subjecting the gathered women to a look of pure disdain she turned on her heel and walked away.

Her outburst resulted in complete silence from the offending group for thirty seconds before they all burst into chat again.

"Well, I never."

"Who does that one think she is."

"huh, don't mind that one," and the chatter rose to a crescendo.

Alice shook her head in despair and opening her door glared at the women with contempt before going inside to comfort the distraught Mamie. Arthur had called in to visit her, so she dispatched him to go and see James and tell him the news while she sent Willy to fetch Susannah from work.

"The last thing that lass needs is to walk into her home and see her father's blood all over the front room floor."

She held Mamie gently while she sobbed and when her tears subsided made her tea, all the while watching for Willy and Arthur to return. Willy arrived with Susannah, her eyes red with tears, she fell upon Mamie, the two sisters rocked each other, each trying to comfort the other. Susannah hushed her sister,

"It will be okay Mamie, we will go down to the hospital and you'll see it will be fine."

Alice insisted that Susannah and Mamie have a bite to eat before they made their way to the hospital and put out bowls of stew for them both. Neither girl could manage more than a few mouthfuls and apologised to Alice and thanked her for kindness. Will escorted them both down to the Falls Road to the Royal Victoria Hospital and they were grateful for his company. James and Maria were already at the hospital when the girls arrived, and they huddled together, united in their shock as they waited on word from the medical staff on when they could see their father.

CHAPTER 45 THE ROYAL VICTORIA HOSPITAL

Mary-Jane was devastated. She stayed by Charlie's side for as long as the matron would let her. Eddie had arrived and told them they were going to his house as it was close to the hospital.

"My house is close by, Mrs McMullen. My mother is there waiting for us. She has the beds aired and a nice pot of stew on the range."

Mary-Jane looked up at Eddie as he spoke, her face blank, then turned her gaze back to Charlie, where he lay, still unconscious.

She rubbed his hand, "What do you think Charlie, will I go to Eddie's?" And she searched his face for some sort of reaction. The only sound she could hear was Charlie's laboured breathing, while in the background the noise of the hospital receded. Mary-Jane could not hear the crying of the injured, the praying of their loved ones, the clatter of hospital trolleys or the click of footfall on the polished floors as the hospital strained to cope with the victims of the violence in the surrounding city. Silent tears wound their way down Mary-Jane's face as she held her breath waiting on her Charlie to reply to her.

Mamie put her arms around her mother, "Let's go Mam, we will come back tomorrow."

Mary-Jane allowed Mamie and Eddie to lead her away. The family made their way to Cawnpore Street. Mary-Jane ate little and barely slept, anxious to get back to the hospital to her beloved Charlie.

The following afternoon Mary-Jane sat beside Charlie's hospital bed, stroking his hand and whispering silent prayers when Margaret and Thomas walked in. Thomas put his hand on Mary-Jane's shoulder and squeezed as Margaret walked over to the foot of the bed and stared at her son. She ignored Mary-Jane who was sitting at his bedside stroking his hand. Margaret drilled the attending nurse about his treatment then turned and left without saying a word to her daughter in law or her grandchildren. Thomas followed her, his face grey.

The days blended into each other in a blur of doctor's white coats and week canteen tea. Mary-Jane spent every minute she could at Charlie's bedside, stroking his hand and smoothing his hair. The Ward Sister told them Charlie's immune system was already weakened by influenza, and sepsis had set in. He was unlikely to survive. Mary-Jane took in what she said, nodding, but never uttered a word. Susannah and Mamie clung together, tears flowing unable to comprehend how their world had been destroyed so suddenly.

The Ward Sister gave the family some time alone with Charlie to say their goodbyes. Ernie had got word to wee Charlie and he arrived at the Royal Victoria Hospital just in time. They were all with him when he died and for that Mary-Jane was grateful. Charlie loved his family and it was only fitting that they were all with him when he took his last breath. She watched as the doctor recorded time of death and nodded as the Doctor sympathised with her, unable to process his words. They left the hospital in a daze, retiring to Eddie's house to plan the funeral.

Mary-Jane gathered her daughters to her, "Susannah, your granny Margaret and Granda Thomas need to be told. I know it is a lot to ask of you, but can you call to them. They don't want to see me or the boys."

"We'll both go, Mam," Mamie said.

"I will go with them Mrs McMullen, don't worry."

Later that evening Eddie accompanied Mamie and Susannah to their Grandmothers' home to tell her the dreadful news. Mary-Jane could see the anguish in Mamie's face on their return.

"She threw us out on the street, screaming at us. She called us Fenians and traitors. She said that our brothers caused her son's death. The gunmen were looking for them, not her Charlie," Mamie sobbed.

Susannah was red with temper, "How can she treat us like that, her own grandchildren, on the day our father died," shaking her head in temper as the tears welled up in her eyes

"She was distraught, people in that frame of mind sometimes react in unexpected ways," Eddie tried to make excuses for Margaret's behaviour, but Susannah was having none of it.

"I am so sorry girls. I should not have sent you, I should have told them myself. I am so sorry," Mary-Jane tried to comfort her daughters. She was furious with her in-laws and heartbroken for her daughters.

Eddie was a rock for the whole family in the following days. He helped plan the funeral and his parents could not do enough for the McMullen family. Mary-Jane knew that they could never return to Sherwood Street, but she was at a loss to know what to do. Eddie put her mind at ease.

"Mrs McMullen, this is your home now. You and your family are my family and I promise I will look after you," Eddie told Mary-Jane.

Mamie hugged him, "Thank you Eddie."

Mary-Jane couldn't find the words at first, but she took his hand in both of hers and thanked him from the bottom of her heart for his generosity.

The day of the funeral dawned wet and cold.   Charlie's mother Margaret attended the funeral along with his brothers and sisters but none of them spoke to Mary-Jane either before or after the service.   Thomas approached them at the graveyard.   He silently squeezed Mary-Jane's shoulder and shook James's hand. Mary-Jane turned away, more concerned with looking after her daughters than with how Margaret and Thomas were faring.   It was some weeks later that James told her that Thomas had taken Margaret to task for her treatment of her grand-daughters but to no avail.   Mary-Jane no longer cared.

"Margaret's treatment of Mamie and Susannah on the day their father died was despicable.   I don't care how grief-stricken she was, how upset, how could she treat her grand-daughters that way.   How could she be so cruel, so selfish?"

James had no answer for her.

CHAPTER 46   MARY-JANE'S GRIEF

In the weeks after the funeral, the girls became increasingly concerned for Mary-Jane. She didn't appear to be functioning and they asked Alice to intervene.

"All I can think of is Charlie, my handsome husband, the love of my life. I adored him from the night I met him. He swept me off my feet, we were so happy. He had made me feel loved and special and we built a home together, a family," Mary-Jane sobbed, "I am bereft, alone, with no future, nothing to live for now that my Charlie is no more."

Alice held her, trying to comfort her.

"But Mary-Jane, I know, it is awful, but you have to keep going through the motions, your girls need you."

The girls kept an eye on her as she sank into a deep depression.

"I'm worried Susannah, she is rising and dressing, eating and drinking when it's handed to her, the rest of the time just sitting in another world oblivious to those around her."

"Maybe we should contact Granny, she will know what to do," Susannah said, and Mamie nodded her agreement.

Mary-Jane had taken to sitting in a chair in Eddie's front room silent and unmoving, simply sitting in a trance like state, not reacting to anyone around her.

"Ma, why don't you go to Annalong for a little while, stay with Granny and Grandad," Susannah gently coaxed her mother. Mary-Jane just looked at her, her face a totally blank page.

Mamie joined in, holding Mary-Jane's hand she gently asked,

"Ma, Granny is coming to Belfast tomorrow, why don't you go back with her, keep her company on the way back."

Mary-Jane starred at each of her daughters in turn, comprehension slowly dawning in her eyes. She nodded her agreement then sank back into the chair closing her eyes.

On Sunday morning the girls waited patiently at the train station for their Grandmother to arrive. The girls were so relieved to see her step off the train that they both ran into her arms crying, nearly knocking her off her feet. Mary was startled but quickly calmed her grand-daughters taking each of them by the arm. Talking at once and across each other Mary struggled to understand them.

Putting them both at arm's length she implored,

"Whist girls, one at a time, Susie you start, what's wrong."

Susannah took a deep breath and told her Grandmother about Mary-Jane's behaviour, Mamie interjected with the detail and how worried they all were about their mother. Mary said nothing until the girls stopped talking, then hugging them both to her in one single motion she comforted them.

"Now girls, take me to your mother," she straightened up with her shoulders back and her head held high, the girls automatically copied her pose, and the three women left the station for Cawnpore Street.

Susannah showed Mary into the front room and Mary-Jane lifted her head as the door into the room opened. Slowly her dead expression changed to pure grief as if the realisation hit her once again that Charlie wasn't coming through the door and was never coming back to her again. Her mother crossed the room in seconds folding her first born in her arms and rocking her back and forward murmuring words of endearment. Susannah and Mamie left them alone, closing the door on the heart-breaking scene. Some hours later Mary emerged calling for Mamie to make tea and Susannah to go upstairs and pack a bag for Mary-Jane.

"Your mother is coming back to Annalong with me for a few weeks. Her poor mind is in a very dark place and she can't find her way out. I think Annalong will do her good. She can work in the vegetable garden, feed the animals, help Jimmy with his chores. Even mingling with her sisters will help her find her way. I want you two to come down next month, get word to the boys as well and we will all sit down together and figure out what is to be done."

Mary insisted that Mary-Jane sat up to the table and had some food with her daughters before she left. Mamie had baked some sodas and she had set the table with Mary-Jane's own china tea set and a Belfast linen tablecloth.

"Why Mamie, the table looks lovely, well done sweetheart." Mary praised her grand-daughter, conscious that Mamie's gentle soul was as upset over her mother's current demeanour as she had been over her father's death. Susannah agreed with her Grandmother.

A shy smile crossed Mamie's face, "Thanks Susie, thank you Granny, Ma?"

Mary-Jane slowly focused her eyes on Mamie and recognition dawned in her dead eyes. She nodded.

"Lovely dear, just lovely."

The women sat at the table and Mary said grace before they had their lunch of soda and blackcurrant jam washed down with strong hot tea. Mary asked the girls about their work and quizzed Mamie on Eddie, advising her to go ahead with her wedding plans, all the while keeping an eye on Mary-Jane, who sat motionless pretending to pick at some bread and sipping the tea, absolutely disconnected from everyone around her. When Mary-Jane retired upstairs to fetch her coat, Mary turned to the girls and thanked them both for contacting her, assuring them that they had been perfectly correct in having concerns for their mother's well-being but also assuring them that everything would be fine. The girls were relieved to hear their Grandmothers comforting words hugging her and confirming that they would travel to Annalong the following week.

CHAPTER 47   HOME TO ANNALONG

The journey to Annalong was a quiet one. Mary-Jane said nothing, and Mary sat beside her holding her hand not expecting any conversation from her. Every so often Mary would glance at her daughter's face and see silent tears running down her cheeks which she wiped away with the handkerchief she kept bunched up in her left hand. On their arrival at the house Jimmy came tearing down the pathway, calling out to Mary-Jane in his usual boisterous manner. As he came closer and noticed the dead expression in Mary-Jane's eyes he stopped abruptly and held his large arms to his sister,

"Mary-Jane is sad, Jimmy will make you better,"

and he hugged his sister gently and then taking her arm he walked her up the garden path and into the house. James stepped aside to let them enter and his eyes met Mary's with a question to which Mary shook her head, shrugging her shoulders "She's in a bad way James." James put his arms around his wife, kissing her lightly on her temple and they went into the house closing the door behind them.

Over the next few days, Mary kept a close eye on Mary-Jane. The first morning Mary-Jane did not get out of bed only rising that evening for the evening meal which she barely touched before retiring once again. The next day, she would have stayed in bed all day again if Mary had not practically pushed her out of bed, pleading that Jimmy needed help planting the spring vegetables and that she and James were just too old and not able for that type of back breaking work anymore. Mary-Jane got up and got dressed reluctantly, ate little, then went with Jimmy to the large vegetable garden. There was a lot of hard, physical work, planting seed potatoes and sowing carrots and onions and Mary-Jane fell into bed that evening exhausted. The following day Mary-Jane rose when her mother called her, again ate little then followed Jimmy out to the garden. Jimmy chatted away to his sister, delighted with the company but also aware that his sister was sad because Charlie was dead. His mother had told him about that a while ago and he had been sad too because he had really liked Charlie. Charlie had always bought him marlies and played football with him in the back field, so he understood why Mary-Jane was sad and wanted to help her feel better. At the end of the second day he asked Mary-Jane if she was feeling a little better.

"When Will died I was sad. I worked in the garden, I planted carrots and cabbage and watching them grow made me feel better. Will was watching me from heaven and helping me when it got really hard. He cried with me when I was sad, and he laughed with me when I laughed," Jimmy told her, his hand stroking her arm. "Charlie is watching over you from heaven and he doesn't want you to be sad all the time."

Mary-Jane stopped what she was doing, listening to Jimmy's simple words and smiled for the first time since Charlie had been shot.

She gave her brother a hug,

"Thank you Jimmy, I will try and remember that," and she turned back to the chore in hand. Mary listened and smiled. Jimmy's simple logic made perfect sense and was just what Mary-Jane needed to pull her out of this deep depression that overwhelmed her. Mary and James talked each night trying to figure out how best to help their daughter and they came to the conclusion that she shouldn't go back to Belfast, but they would need to talk to the grandchildren and get their opinion on what was best for their mother. Mary spoke to Mary-Jane every evening after dinner. She spoke about Charlie and about the children and kept pushing Mary-Jane to open up, to pierce through the fog that appeared to cloud her head.

James and his sisters travelled to Annalong the following week. Maria stayed at home to nurse her mother who was gravely ill and unable to be left alone. Susannah and Mamie were relieved to see their mother with colour in her cheeks and some semblance of life in her eyes.

They all sat down to dinner that evening around the grandparent's table and the conversation reverted to the ongoing violence in Belfast. The previous Sunday they had all attended the funeral of the McMahon family.

"Massive funeral Granda, over 10,000 people turned out to show their respects," Susannah told her grandparents.

"And the British army had to line the funeral route in case the B Specials attacked the funeral," said Mamie, "Six members of the one family, shot because they were Catholic,"

"Aye Catholic and supporters of Joe Devlin," interjected James as he read aloud from the paper a statement from Joe Devlin in Westminster where he said that "if Catholics have no revolvers to protect themselves they are murdered. If they have revolvers they are flogged and sentenced to death."

"And that's the truth of it Granda, it is a dangerous country we live in, the papers said that thirty people were killed in Belfast last month and its close to sixty for this month."

There was a brief silence as they all thought of the one death in those thirty that had led them to this point. Mary-Jane blessed herself and exhaled slowly as she tried to avert the inevitable tears that coupled the dull pain in her chest at the thought of her precious Charlie.

Granda James broke the silence with a proposal.

"James, girls, the way I see it, the situation in Belfast is becoming even more dangerous. We already lost Charlie and we don't want to go through this pain again. The ceasefire has held in the South but not here. The new Prime Minister James Craig is trying to create a Protestant state enabling the B Specials to target Catholics, branding all Catholics as terrorists. The IRA are trying to defend Catholic communities and are probably hoping to destabilise the fledgling new state in the vain hope of stopping the partition of Ireland," James shook his head, "I for one don't see any end in sight."

A murmur of agreement went around the room.

"Myself and your grandma would really like you all to stay here for good. Your home in Belfast is gone. You can never go back." Mary held her daughters hand and gave it a squeeze as James talked. "James, I know you have your own home and you have Maria's mother to think about, so I understand that you will not leave Belfast, we all do, but always remember that if your circumstances change, we are here, and you and Maria are always welcome."

James shook his Granda's hand expressing his gratitude for his hospitality.

"Mamie, you need to go ahead with your wedding plans. This family needs a celebration and what better celebration than a wedding. Eddie is a good lad, your Da approved of him and everyone likes him. I know he has a house and work in Belfast but why don't you stay here until the wedding?" Mamie said nothing, but her eyes filled with tears.

"Susie…" Susannah spoke up before her Granda could say anything else.

"Before you say it Granda, I know I am welcome here and I really appreciate it, I do, but I have my job in Belfast, that's where I was born and raised, and I don't want to leave it," Susannah finished what she had to say with a little defiant tilt of her head upwards. "I can't leave it." Susannah's interjection brought a smile to everyone's lips.

"Fair play Susie," James clapped hands in appreciation of his sister's spirit.

Jimmy loved clapping hands and he joined in and started to sing bringing laughter from everyone into the mix. Even Mary-Jane had a smile on her face, Mary noted before getting up from the table to start clearing away. The girls jumped up quickly to help their Grandmother as James sat down beside Mary-Jane.

"And you Mary-Jane, will you stay with us," Mary-Jane looked up into her father's face noting the deep lines and the grey hair,

"Yes, Da, I will stay for a little while."

"Good girl." James patted her hand before turning back to Jimmy who was still clapping and singing much to everyone's amusement.

CHAPTER 48   JAMES AND MARIA

James returned home from Annalong the next day, anxious to get back to Maria, worried about her mother Kathleen and her illness. The doctor had said there was nothing he could do for her, she was going to die soon, and Maria was distraught. An only child Maria and her mother were extremely close, to the extent that James sometimes felt superfluous to their requirements in his house. It was his war service that was responsible for him getting the house in John Street. It was a bit far from his parents, but it was in a good area, a strong Catholic area and he had been moderately happy there. He had worn his British army uniform to get married in and he used to wear his army uniform every time he left the house, back then people used to treat him with respect because of it but those days were gone, gone since the rebellion in Dublin.

He remembered the first time he noticed the change, he and Kathleen had been walking in the Falls Park on a fine summer's evening the year after the war had ended, and a group of kids had started following them, jeering and calling him a traitor to Ireland. He was astounded that evening. He remembered the sun in his face and the beautiful rose beds that they stopped to admire, the scent heavy and sweet in the warm air, the petals perfectly formed in bright crimson and sunny yellow. He remembered how happy and content he had felt just before they spoke, how he saw that happiness reflected back at him in Maria's eyes. Then the ugliness started. A group of boys, children really, came up behind them and started jeering him. He was so shocked he stepped backwards stopped by the prick of a thorn on a crimson rose bush. His mouth fell open as his brain raced frantically to think of some way to chase these urchins away. It was Maria that recovered her composure first, telling the boys off,

"Go home, you little tearaways, get away from us."

The boys just continued to jeer,

"Traitor, traitor, peg leg."

Maria flicked her bag at them, catching one across the ear and they ran off, still shouting and laughing as they ran.

"Don't mind them James, riff-raff, that's all they are."

James agreed with her but inside he was totally disgusted, children calling him a traitor when he had gone to war to fight for Ireland. He remembered the patriotic speeches by John Redmond, the call to war, to fight for the freedom of small nations. He remembered the promises that by going to war Home Rule would be enacted when it was over, and Ireland would have self-determination, okay not independence but as good as.

"I kept my side of the bargain," he said to Maria "it's the British who are the traitors, it's the unionists who have led us down this path, they are the traitors, not me."

He had stayed indoors for several days after that. He had hung his uniform in the back of the wardrobe vowing never to don it again. His own family did not consider him a traitor, he knew that. He used to call to his parents once a week and the boys called into him at least once a week for a bath and bed. Those days were also gone. His father was dead, shot by the B Specials.

"Was he shot because he was married to a Catholic or was he shot because wee Charlie and Ernie were in the IRA?" He asked Maria, "Did my brothers cause our father's death or would he have died anyway because he was a "Fenian lover" Which is it Maria?"

Maria shook her head unable to give him a straight answer.

James remembered the last time the family had been together the day after the funeral. Wee Charlie and Ernie were sitting quietly in Eddie's house preparing to leave again and Susannah had rounded on them.

"Heading back to your unit are ya, with Da's blood on your hands, it was one of you the B specials wanted, not Da, make sure you tell your unit that." Susannah's voice rose to a crescendo as she finished speaking breaking down in hot tears.

Mamie ran to her side, holding her, "Shush now Susie, that's not fair on the boys."

"Not fair," Susannah screamed, "we buried Da, yesterday and it was their fault."

Mary-Jane walked into the room silencing everyone.

"What is whose fault?" she asked, her voice small and broken.

"Nothing, Ma, Nothing, Susie is just upset, that's all."

Mamie, once again the peacemaker led her mother back into the front room away from the discordant family. She settled her mother in a chair pulling a shawl over her to warm her just as Eddie arrived with a cup of tea for her.

"Thanks Eddie, I really appreciate all you have done for us. We have practically taken over your house," Mamie whispered to Eddie.

"No thanks needed Mamie, my house is your house, I told you that and that extends to your whole family."

Mamie reached up her hand and touched his cheek.

"Thank you, Eddie, you are such a gentleman."

The two retreated on tiptoes leaving Mary-Jane to sleep, the cup of tea untouched on the table beside her.

The argument had continued in their absence. James was inclined towards Susannah's view that their father had died because the B Specials were after either wee Charlie or Ernie. Much as he loved his brothers he couldn't help but think that they were partially responsible for their father's death. After all, they had lived in Sherwood Street as a mixed religion family for over thirty years and they had never even been threatened up till then. James said as much to Ernie.

"Do you honestly believe that we would put our family in harm's way, that we would purposely put Ma and Da in danger?" Ernie was incredulous at the opinions proffered by James and Susannah.

"No Ernie, I don't think you purposely put them, or any of us, in danger but the simple fact of the matter is that you did put the family in danger by joining the IRA," James replied.

Ernie jumped to his feet, "No, James, you are so wrong, don't you forget that when our Charlie joined it wasn't called the IRA, it was called the Irish Volunteers, the very same organisation you joined before the war, the same organisation that brought you, and brought Martin, and countless others off to the Great War. You were a member of the very same organisation, did you put Ma and Da in danger?"

Confusion reigned as James struggled to reconcile what Ernie had just said with what had happened since the war, eventually having to agree with him, "yes, I know, Ernie but these are different times."

"Yeah, James, different times but we are not the ones that changed the goalposts. It was the unionists did that with a lot of help from the Brits."

Ernie and Charlie left the house without saying another word. James followed them out the door but could not say anything other than to wave goodbye. Wee Charlie never turned around to see his salute, but Ernie did, hesitating just a few seconds before returning the wave just before they rounded the corner and disappeared out of sight. Susannah remained angry and hurt pacing the floor of the small scullery muttering to herself and to anyone else who would listen. James stopped her pacing holding up his hand,

"Enough, Susie, enough."

Susannah cried harder, flouncing out of the room and upstairs to throw herself on the bed, beating the pillow in temper and grief. James said his goodbyes and left the house returning to his own home in John Street.

Two months passed, and James heard nothing from his brothers. Their mother was catatonic with grief, Susannah was her usual spirited self and Mamie was trying frantically to placate everyone while planning her wedding to Eddie, who had turned out to be the hero of the hour providing accommodation and practical help and advice to everyone.

James entered the house with a smile on his face thinking about what a good sort Eddie was and what a good match he was for Mamie. His smile quickly faded as he heard his wife calling him from the back room. Kathleen had been so poorly that they had cleared out the back room and moved her bed in there so that she was beside the kitchen which made it easier for Maria to look after her. Kathleen had taken a turn for the worse and Kathleen had called the priest who had just anointed her. James blessed himself and knelt beside his wife joining in the prayers. Kathleen never regained consciousness and died later that evening. James had no more time to brood about the situation within his own family as he helped his wife plan her mother's funeral.

CHAPTER 49   MAMIE AND EDDIE

Mamie lay on her bed day-dreaming. The day had finally arrived, her wedding day. It was a beautiful morning with not a cloud in the sky, the type of May morning she had prayed for when she left out the Child of Prague statute on the front step the night before. Mary Bridget had known Eddie McCartney forever, or so it seemed. Everyone had partially guessed they would end up together and now their wedding day was here. Mamie gave a little shiver of excitement. She looked up at the beautiful dress hanging on the back of the door, designed and hand stitched by Susannah, it was quite the most beautiful dress Mamie had ever seen and she could not wait to put it on and walk down the aisle to Eddie. A cloud passed over her face as she remembered her Da and she blessed herself. James had offered to give her away and Mamie had gratefully accepted. James used his stick on his right side, so she would be able to link his left arm and walk with him down the aisle of St. Matthews. She had been christened in St. Matthews, made her First Communion and Confirmation there and it was only fitting that she married there even though she no longer lived in Sherwood Street. Mamie hugged herself in anticipation.

Her Mother and her grandparents had travelled up from Annalong the night before and they were staying in Eddie's house with her. Her mother had stayed in Annalong for the last few months and while she was a shadow of her former self she was in much better form than she had been before she went. Mamie could not help but think about her father and how much she missed him, especially today and a cloak of sadness covered her face.

Susannah walked in with a cup of tea in her hand,

"Now now, no looking back, look forward little sister, today is going to be the best day of your life," and she grinned at Mamie who grinned back, sadness dismissed to the back recesses of her mind. Susannah helped Mamie get ready, doing her hair and makeup and then their mother arrived to help get her into her wedding dress. Susannah stood back to admire her handiwork before swivelling the mirror allowing Mamie to see herself. Mamie gasped as she pirouetted in front of the mirror delighted with her dress and delighted with the way she looked in it.

Her mother smiled at her youngest daughter,

"Mamie you are a beautiful bride, as pretty as a picture," she kissed her lightly on her cheek, "No hugs, no tears, we don't want to spoil that beautiful smile or that beautiful dress."

The death of Mamie's father in such shocking circumstances, and the short illness and death of James's mother in law, only months previously meant they opted for a low-key affair. It had taken a while for them to decide how they were going to spend their wedding day. Belfast was still in turmoil, with shootings and burnings and bombings every day, and the death toll steadily rising. Eddie's parents and his two older sisters and their families were happy to take a day out in Newcastle and all of the O'Brien family in Newcastle and Annalong were delighted to get invited to the Donard. Mamie was torn about wee Charlie and Ernie. She loved them dearly and wanted them at her wedding, but she also loved James and Susannah and she knew that Susannah, in particular, would only get upset and angry and she did not want to hurt her sister. She debated with Eddie on the best course of action. The very mention of her brother's names brought anger to Susannah's voice. She was adamant that wee Charlie and Ernie were responsible for their father's death and she could not be persuaded otherwise. Mamie tried to talk to her, but any conversation ended with Susannah snapping at Mamie and Mamie changing the subject. Eddie offered to talk to Susannah on her behalf, but Mamie would not let him. She didn't want any bad feeling between her precious sister Susie and her beloved husband to be.

It was Ernie who took the decision away from her, telling her that he and Charlie had to go on a mission to the south and would only be able to get to the church for a few minutes before the ceremony. She did not know whether he was being truthful or if he wanted to avoid any possibility of friction on her big day but either way she was grateful. When all the guests had entered St. Matthews Church and it was just her and James standing there waiting to walk down the aisle her brothers popped their heads around the corner. They both hugged her to them taking care to avoid wrinkling her dress or tossing her hair, they gave James an envelope with cash inside to give to Eddie as their wedding present, then ushered her into the church, standing back and watching in secrecy from the eves of the church as their sister walked down the aisle on James's arm.

There was a collective gasp from the congregation at the beauty of the bride and the happiness she radiated. Eddie waited at the altar, beaming from ear to ear as he watched her approach. He gratefully accepted her hand from James and both turned to face the priest and exchange their vows.

The wedding party travelled by train to Newcastle and walked along the promenade to the Donard Hotel for the wedding lunch in the Donard Hotel, where Mamie and Eddie were spending their honeymoon.

Mamie and Eddie returned to Cawnpore Street two days later. They had a wonderful time in Newcastle, walking along the promenade with Mamie telling Eddie stories from her childhood and the wonderful days they had spent in Newcastle. Eddie carried Mamie over the threshold of their little house and Mamie thought she was the happiest woman alive. Susannah continued to live with them and her mother Mary-Jane was considering coming back to Belfast but hadn't decided yet. Eddie had assured her that she was more than welcome, and Mamie had felt a sense of pride in her husband's good and generous nature. She looked forward to a lifetime with this man. Eddie was a quiet man; his mother reckoned the reason he was so quiet was that he couldn't get a word in edgeways with his two older sisters. Eddie's father just laughed and agreed with his wife, telling Eddie that it was always easier to just agree with the wife, no matter what. The McCartney's were fond of Mamie, as she was of them.

Eddie was due back to work the following day, so Mamie lost no time in getting the house organised, preparing the evening meal and a packed lunch for Eddie to bring with him to work in the morning. Susannah was staying with James for a week to give Mamie and Eddie the house to themselves for the first week of their married life. Mamie had blushed when Susannah told her she was leaving them alone for a week, telling her there was no need, but Susannah had insisted. Eddie, always mindful of his father's advice, just smiled and said nothing.

Mamie loved being married, she loved to say the words, my husband, she regularly checked her wedding ring, smiling at the sight of it. Eddie smiled every time he saw his wife, obviously totally smitten by her and he regularly told her so. Mamie secretly loved the way he put her on a pedestal but would never admit to it, smiling shyly every time he pronounced to the world how wonderful she was.

The only blight on Mamie's horizon was the family. Her mother was slowly but surely getting over her grief and for that Mamie was grateful. She had returned to Belfast and was staying with them for a few months until she got a new place. Mary-Jane had insisted that she had to get her own place so that Susannah, wee Charlie and Ernie had a home to go to and Mamie hadn't the heart to tell her that Susannah would not live in the same house as her younger brothers. Mamie decided to leave that discussion for another day.

James and Maria appeared to be doing fine on the face of it, but Mamie knew James still had nightmares that woke him screaming in the dead of night in a cold sweat, crying and clutching his leg. Maria had confided in her, needing to talk to someone about it and knowing that Mamie would listen and never tell another soul. Maria had told her that after the screaming subsided and he was fully awake he would shake violently and rock back and forward oblivious to his surroundings. She could not touch him during that time. She had learnt that, to her cost, on several occasions when she had tried to hold him only for him to lash out at her. On one occasion, she had sustained a black eye and didn't leave the house until it had healed, feigning sickness. Over time she learned that the best way to bring him around was to get out of bed and sit out of arms reach, then speak to him, quietly and gently or hum a lullaby and eventually the obsessive movement would stop, and his eyes would slowly focus as he returned from the twilight world that sprang up around him in his nightmare. By the time he came around, he would be drenched in sweat and utterly exhausted. The nightmares were happening less frequently than before but still occurred every few weeks. Mamie had sympathised with Maria and offered to help in any way she could, and Maria thanked her for that, telling Mamie that she had helped in the best way possible by just listening to her and offering her support. She begged Mamie not to say anything to James as she reckoned that he would view her speaking to his sister as a betrayal of his trust. Mamie reassured Maria that nothing was further from the truth and that anytime she felt overwhelmed or just needed to talk, her door was always open.

Susannah had stayed with James and Maria for the week after the wedding but during that week James was fine, so Susannah was totally unaware of his night terrors. Susannah told Mamie that she had thought that perhaps James and Maria would ask her to stay rather than return to Eddie and Mamie's. "I have always been close to James, I am really surprised they didn't invite me to stay with them," Susannah complained bitterly to Mamie on her return to the house. "After all, you have Ma living here, they have a spare room, I am actually a little hurt." Mamie tried to reassure her sister without betraying Maria's trust, realising that Susannah was unaware of James's affliction.

"Och Susie, they have been on their own for so long it probably never dawned on them to ask you, and anyway are you not happy here?" Susannah assured Mamie that she was happy, worried that her little sister would get offended thinking she didn't want to live with her and her new husband and never mentioned living with James and Maria again.

Susannah had become increasingly bitter over their father's death, putting the blame squarely on wee Charlie and Ernie. Mamie realised that Susannah had always been hot-tempered but since the death of their father she could flare up over the slightest incident. Mamie had decided after the last time she had got a lashing from Susannah's tongue that it was better to say nothing in her presence. She would not listen to reason where her younger brothers were concerned and some months later when the news filtered through to them that wee Charlie had been arrested under the Special Powers Act and interned, she had no sympathy for him.

"Pity they didn't arrest Ernie as well," was all she had to say to Mamie.

Mamie was concerned about both brothers. Charlie had not been charged with any offence, he had just been arrested and interned on the "Argenta," a prison ship moored off Carrickfergus, some ten miles north of Belfast. Mamie had talked to others and had heard the rumours about the terrible conditions on board ship and talked to Eddie about going to visit Charlie hoping that seeing him in the flesh would allay some of her fears. For the first time since she had met him, Eddie put his foot down.

"No Mamie, it would be too upsetting for you and anyway to visit Charlie you have to go out to the prison ship on a row boat, the water is really choppy around there and it could be dangerous."

No matter what Mamie said Eddie was adamant that Mamie should not go but he did volunteer to go visit himself and give her first hand news on how Charlie was coping. Susannah thought they were both wrong,

"Leave him where he is, he doesn't deserve our sympathy."

Mamie despaired of ever talking her sister around but eventually agreed with her husband that he should go and visit Charlie. Eddie came back dejected, Charlie was in a bad way, he had gotten a hiding from the B Specials during his arrest and had the cuts and bruises to prove it. Charlie implored him not to tell his family about the state he was in and to keep his mother and sisters away,

"I don't want them to see me in here, Eddie, don't let them come."

Eddie assured Charlie that he would tell Mamie and Mary-Jane that he was well enough and would be home soon. He kept his word with Mary-Jane but couldn't lie to his wife.

Her other concern was Ernie. She hadn't heard from him since the introduction of internment and was worried about him. The violence in the city was ongoing with more and more shootings, more prosecution of Catholics and thousands fleeing to the south. Mamie hoped that Ernie was one of those who had left for Dublin. She was even more concerned when she read about the outbreak of a civil war in the new Free State. The new state was split down the middle with those who had fought the British for independence now fighting each other over the form that independence would take. The whole country was at war, brother against brother, committing atrocities against each other in a cycle of destruction. The commander in chief of the new Irish army, Michael Collins had been supplying the IRA in Northern Ireland with arms but that supply now dried up as Southern Ireland descended into chaos. The papers were full of the events surrounding the Civil War in the Free State as gradually an uneasy peace settled on Northern Ireland. The death toll petered out as the violence came to an end.

"Probably not an end to violence in Northern Ireland but definitely an end to this particular cycle,"

Eddie told Mamie, as he read the paper in front of the fire one Sunday morning in early winter.

"I hope so Eddie, for I don't want our child to be born into this city if it had continued,"

Mamie answered without looking up from her knitting as she sat in her chair on the other side of the fireplace. It took a minute for her words to sink into Eddie's brain as he read the latest statement from the ruling Unionist James Craig, he dropped the paper.

"What did you say?" he asked.

Mamie grinned back at him.

"I am having a baby, my love."

Eddie jumped out of his chair punching the air in delight. He hugged his wife tenderly.

"Thank you, my love, you have just made me the happiest man alive."

Mamie laughed as Eddie pulled her up and waltzed her around the small room.

"What's all the commotion about?" Mary-Jane asked opening the door when she heard the noise. Mary-Jane had to sit down for a minute when they told her the news. Her first grandchild.

"Oh my sweet Mamie, a baby. I am delighted for you. What wonderful news."

Mary-Jane vowed to meet up with Alice the following week and make a start on a baby layette. Eddie and Mamie went over to Eddie's parents the following evening to tell them the good news and Mary-Jane went with them. She was fond of Eddie's parents and they her. They already had five grandchildren but were delighted to hear they could expect a sixth.

"Just the good news we all need in the run-up to Christmas" Mary-Jane told Mr McCartney, "something to look forward to in the new year."

CHAPTER 50   CHARLIE AND ERNIE

Mary-Jane dreaded Christmas. It would the first Christmas without her beloved Charlie. She had lost her home and was dependent on the goodwill of her son in law for a roof over her head. She had one son interned on the Argenta prison ship and one son on the run. At least there was one bright spark on the horizon with her first grandchild due to come into this world in May. Mary-Jane tried hard to dismiss negative thoughts but sometimes they overwhelmed her and when that happened she tried to keep herself busy and avoided interaction with Mamie for she didn't want to upset or worry the proud mother to be. And Mamie was blooming, she loved being pregnant almost as much as she loved being married. Joy seeped out of every pore and she lifted the spirits of everyone around her. Mary-Jane shook her self visibly, dismissing negativity and pushing herself to get into the Christmas spirit. She hadn't been to church since Charlie's funeral and she had always been so devout, but she now found herself questioning her God.

"Maybe Christmas Day is the right day to go back to Church Ma," Susannah and Mamie had both said to her at different times that day.

"Susie, obviously you two are talking about me and scheming behind my back," Mary-Jane said to Susannah rather crossly when she broached the subject of mass some hours after Mamie had said the exact same thing.

"No, Ma, we are not scheming about anything, we are just agreed that maybe you should try going to mass just once and see how you go, and Christmas day is a good day to go."

Susannah left the room leaving her mother pondering on why she was so reluctant to go to mass. She decided that she would accompany the girls to mass on Christmas Day and take it from there.

"If only the boys could get home and come with us," the thought jumped unbidden into her head along with a wash of despair. She immediately sat up and shook herself again, refusing to let the negative thoughts win. On Christmas morning Mary-Jane woke early, automatically turning as she did every morning to greet Charlie and once again feeling the confusion when she saw Susannah beside her and then the sharp pain in her chest followed by palpations with the realisation that Charlie was dead, and she would never wake up to him lying beside her or smell his distinctive woody scent or hear his deep voice or feel his strong arms around her. Grief once again overwhelmed her as it had every morning for the last ten months and she gulped in air trying to ward off the inevitable tears. She rose, tiptoeing quietly out of the room so as not to wake the sleeping Susannah, grabbing a shawl on the way out to wrap around to ward off the cold. She went downstairs and decided to poke up the fire and get it going after Eddie had damped it down only a few hours previously. She found that keeping herself busy doing menial chores helped keep the deepest dregs of grief at bay and gave the appearance that she was functioning normally.

She pulled back the drapes to reveal a dark sky with dawn still an hour or so away. Its promised to be a bright, cold day and she decided there and then that she would go to mass with her family. She felt a bit brighter after making that decision and after tidying up retired upstairs to wash and dress. The family set off for 8am mass with Susannah linking her mother in front and Mamie and Eddie trailing behind. They met James and Maria on the way exchanging Christmas greetings with friends and neighbours. The mass went quickly, and Mary-Jane was thankful that she had decided to attend as they walked back home together. They had a hearty breakfast on their return then exchanged Christmas gifts. Mary-Jane had a small gift under the tree for wee Charlie and Ernie in the hope that they could get home and they looked forlorn under the tree when everyone else had exchanged theirs. Mary-Jane had just started preparations on the Christmas dinner when she heard a rap on the back door. Cautiously opening the door, just a crack she peered out, then squealed in delight when she saw Ernie standing on the back step. Eddie came running to see what the matter was, stopped abruptly when he saw Ernie, then pulled him into the house, greeting him as a long-lost friend and insisting that he stay. Mamie hugged him tightly wishing him a merry Christmas and turned to Susannah, "oh look, Susie, Ernie is here for Christmas." Susannah just stared at Ernie, a cold hard stare with no smile of welcome,

"Ernie," she nodded curtly.

"Susannah,"

Ernie replied, his smile disappearing in the face of such a cold welcome from his sister. Eddie took matters in hand, taking Ernie's coat and sitting him in front of the fire. Ernie looked tired and bedraggled, his clothes were dirty, his hair unkempt and he looked decidedly haggard. Eddie asked him if he wanted to bathe and set about putting the tin bath in the back room while Mary-Jane boiled water. Ernie gratefully stripped off his old clothes and stepped into the warm water, hidden from view by a large blanket that Eddie had rigged up. Eddie disappeared upstairs and returned within minutes with clean clothes, that he had stored away when they cleared out the house in Sherwood Street, months ago. As Ernie was bathing Mary-Jane called Susannah upstairs and had a quick word with her.

"I know you are still angry Susie, and I know you still blame Ernie for what happened to your Da, but I have missed my boys and I am happy that Ernie is with us today."

Susannah tried to interrupt but Mary-Jane lifted her hand gesturing silence,

"Susie, please, for my sake, no arguments today, please let us have our Christmas Day in peace, I will understand if you don't want to speak to him but please let me."

Mary-Jane's tone dismissed any argument. Susannah hesitated, anguish visible on her face but she loved her mother more than she hated her brother, so she made her mind up there and then to do what her mother asked. She would not argue in front of her mother, she also had no intentions of speaking to Ernie, but she would not stop others from doing so.

It was a fairly happy Christmas dinner that day in McCartney's. Ernie had pride of place beside his mother with Eddie on the other side, Susannah sat next to her mother on the other side so that she wouldn't have to be face to face with Ernie at the table. The meal went by uneventfully, Mary-Jane cautious not to say anything that would infuriate Susannah and Susannah saying nothing. They hadn't seen Ernie since shortly after the funeral some ten months earlier and she was anxious to know how he was.

"I am heading to the Free State to sign up for the National Army, they are crying out for volunteers and let's face we are finished up here. All the volunteers are dead or interned. I went to Dublin for the funeral of Michael Collins. It was unbelievable, it was like the whole country had turned out to honour our hero."

Eddie had loads of questions for he too was an admirer of Collins, "Worst thing that could have happened, his death was a massive loss for this country."

Ernie agreed, "you're right Eddie, time now to put an end to it all, so a few of us are heading to enlist. I will put your name forward for next of kin Ma, but Eddie is it okay to use this address?"

Eddie nodded his agreement, "course it is, Ernie, sure this is where your family live now."

After dinner Ernie asked if he could be excused and nobody objected. He looked exhausted and Eddie brought him upstairs to his own bed and settled him there. Ernie slept straight through until nightfall and woke hungry again but well rested. Mary-Jane made him a feast from the leftovers from dinner which he devoured and then she made him up a parcel to bring with him for he was adamant that he couldn't stay.

"I don't want to bring any trouble on your house Eddie, you have my sisters and my mother to look after, I think you are doing quite enough for our family and my brother and I thank you for that."

James shook Ernie's hand, wishing him luck, "Good luck Ernie, mind yourself. Keep in touch with us and let us know how you are getting on." Susannah left the room as her brothers were shaking hands, reluctant to speak to Ernie but unwilling to make a scene on Christmas night.

Mamie hugged her brother, "And you Mamie, you have a great man there, he will take care of you and that little bundle of yours. I will write as soon as I have a unit, you make sure and let me know when I become an uncle."

Mary-Jane hugged her son to her, "Ernie you mind yourself, write me when you get settled and try and keep out of harm's way, love ya son,"

Ernie kissed his mother on her worn cheek and after hugging her to him one last time, he left, waving to them all, out the back door and down the alleyway.

Eddie took out a bottle of Black Bush whiskey and set up three glasses on the table.

"Mamie, go get Susie, tell her to come down and have a drink with us."

Mamie went upstairs and minutes later returned with a red-eyed Susannah in tow. Eddie handed her a glass, then handed his mother in law a glass before lifting his own "Sliante".

Chapter 51 Ernie joins the National Army

Ernie met his friend at their rendezvous in the park and they set off to the Free State. They travelled at night, keeping away from busy roads and sleeping during the day in safe houses. Sometimes their travel arrangements were compromised and sometimes they had to stay in one place for several days at a time but eventually, they made it across the border and wound up in the recruiting office in Wellington Barracks on the South Circular Road in Dublin. Although he had only turned seventeen the previous month Ernie was a seasoned soldier when he joined the National Army in January 1923, although he used his older brother's date of birth just in case. After training he was assigned to the Railway Maintenance and Protection Corps. The anti-treaty side were raging a campaign against the rail network throughout the Free State and the newly formed unit were charged with protecting the rail network from further attack. Ernie found himself surrounded by young men who had fled the northern counties and flocked to the Free State to support Michael Collins. With their leader Michael Collins, now dead, the civil war was descending into an increasingly violent cycle of atrocities. The IRA that had fought the British in the war for independence was split down the middle with former colleagues, brothers even, who had fought together in a common cause, now fighting against each other with a viciousness that had never been seen before. Ernie wrote home to his mother as soon as he was assigned his unit, joking that at least he was going to get to see a good bit of the country. He wrote to Charlie but didn't expect a reply as Charlie was still interned with no sign of release. He quickly settled into military life. He enjoyed travelling from depot to depot and the hard physical labour that was demanded of them from time to time. He was involved in far fewer skirmishes than he had been in when he served with the IRA in the north and wrote as much to his mother, hoping to assuage her worries. He posted the letter through the internal mail and headed into the town hoping to meet up with Simon, an old pal from Belfast who had moved to Mayo with his family when their home had been destroyed in the riots a few years previously. He had been surprised and pleased to bump into Simon the previous day when his unit had arrived at the station. There was Simon, in his conductor's uniform, just boarding the train to Dublin. The two shook hands and arranged to meet the following evening when

Simon's shift finished. Claremorris was a small town and seemed quiet as Ernie walked the short mile into the town centre. Sure enough, Simon was there waiting for him and the two had a lovely two hours exchanging stories. Simon's family had settled into the area well, his father was working in a local pub and his sister in the library. Simon had heard about Ernie's father and he sympathised with his friend. Ernie found himself opening up to Simon about his secret worry that maybe Susie was right and that he and his brother were at fault, that they were responsible for their father's death.

"Nonsense Ernie, how many people died that year, how many people were shot in their own homes, look at the McMahon family, sure that was only a few weeks after your Da was shot. No, Ernie, it was the B Specials that shot your Da, they are responsible for his death, not you and not Charlie."

Even though Ernie believed that to be true it was still a relief to him to hear someone else say it. Someone who had been through the mayhem and madness of Belfast and understood the sectarian nature of the violence. He made it back to barracks with seconds to spare before curfew. He lay down on his bunk, memories flooding into his brain of his father, days in Belfast flying kites in the park, days in Annalong with Da bringing them for long walks on the Slieve Donard pointing out the flora and fauna, for even though Charlie was Belfast born and bred, he loved nature and he particularly loved the Mourne mountains. Ernie felt a sudden burst of anguish at the realisation that he would never see him again, never hear him talk or laugh. His heart hurt with a physical pain that caught him unawares. Totally engrossed in his own thoughts, he didn't hear the Corporal entering the room, jumping as Corporal Brady put his face up against him roaring to stand to attention. Ernie leapt off the bed, apologising and jumped to attention at the end of his bunk. That wasn't good enough for Corporal Brady, a small man with a large attitude and a loud voice. He berated Ernie in front of the rest of the platoon, calling him an idiot, a northerner, a lazy good for nothing yoke. He walked around Ernie yelling up into his face, "Look, at this good for nothing northerner, gather round men, Private McMullen is the type of soldier you should never aspire to be." He continued to pace, "A lazy good for nothing yokel," he roared, his face red, "and a prod lover to boot."

That was the last straw for Ernie. Corporal Brady knew Ernie's Da had been shot by the B specials and he also knew that he had been a Protestant. Ernie felt his temper rising as the abuse continued, he could feel the anger in his stomach rising up to his chest and then felt his neck and face turning purple before he snapped. In a split second, he lifted his fist and knocked Corporal Brady to the ground with one box. He had completely lost his temper and would have continuing hitting Corporal Brady if the other privates in the room hadn't intervened pulling him away holding his arms behind his back.

"Steady Ernie, steady, you're in enough trouble," Jim whispered in his ear, "Calm it." Ernie's temper dropped as quickly as it had risen, and he hung his head in shame. Corporal Brady jumped to his feet teaming with rage just as Sergeant Murray entered the room.

"Private Hughes, bring Private McMullen to the guard room," he ordered, "Corporal Brady come with me,"

and he marched out of the room and straight over to the company office. Ernie sat in the corner of the guard room totally dejected. How could he have been so stupid, he thought to himself, Corporal Brady was known to be an aggressive, horrible little man and every single one of them had been on the receiving end of his vile tongue at some stage or other, but Ernie had never allowed his hateful words to rile him before, the way he had this evening. Ernie was escorted over to the guard room by Jim Hughes, who had the bunk next to him, a tall ambling man, a good soldier with a placid even temperament who hailed from Armagh. Jim advised Ernie to say as little as possible when he was brought up in front of the commanding officer, instructing him to only give his rank, name and serial number and then to apologise for causing any disruption. Corporal Brady had a reputation for being nasty and Jim reckoned that everyone who had been in that billet would support Ernie, for while he should never have lifted his fist to a higher rank, there had been serious provocation.

Sure enough, when Ernie was called into the company office the next morning to face charges, he was given a telling off by the C.O. and a punishment of seven days detention with loss of pay. Ernie reckoned he got off lightly and was grateful for that. He also reckoned that Corporal Brady got admonished for his behaviour, albeit privately, as he was never at the receiving end of Corporal Brady's tongue again which was something to be thankful for.

The Civil War ground to a halt with the pro-treaty side claiming victory.

"But at what price?" Ernie said to Jim as they bulled their boots that evening in the billet, "the country has been torn apart, the atrocities and the loss of life has been horrendous, there is more damage done to the country in the last ten months than there was for the full two and half years we fought against the British."

Jim agreed, "Sure, my own uncle, me Ma's brother doesn't speak to her or to his own parents, and for what, that story is repeated in every town and village. How can we put all that behind us and start to live together in peace now?" Others agreed, they were a mixed bunch in that billet, representative of every province with Ernie and Jim the only ones from the new Northern Ireland state.

"God knows what I am going home to, I cannot believe that the unionists got their way. A Protestant state, a unionist state more like, God help us. All this fighting and for what, part of the country left in the union and the rest of it divided against each other."

He had a letter the next morning from wee Charlie who had finally been released and was living in Annalong. He couldn't wait to go see him, but he was also anxious to see his mother who was back living in Belfast with Mamie and Eddie. The Civil War was over, and the demobilisation process started. Ernie was discharged in October and he packed up his scant belongings eager to get back to Belfast and to his family. He had his military rail pass to travel home and his spirits were high as he boarded a train in Claremorris bound for Dublin. Ernie admired the changing landscape from the train window as he made the journey from Mayo to Dublin. The wild, rocky west with its stone walls and agile sheep changed to the lush, green fields of the Midlands with cattle munching on the grass and hedgerows bursting with berries. He passed forests full of trees turning russet and gold in the autumn sun and shedding their golden leaves making a carpet of shimmering light under them, sending memories unbidden into his mind of days in the park with his family, kicking through fallen leaves, hiding in the thickest parts of the moving carpet and jumping up roaring to frighten the girls. He felt nostalgic and sad and once again felt the loss of his father. The train from Dublin to the North would take longer than usual. Parts of the railroad were missing so the journey was broken up in stages. Customs officers boarded the train at the newly formed border. Ernie shook his head in disbelief at the idea of a border within a small island like Ireland. The Customs Officer checked his papers and his rail pass, querying where he was going and the purpose of his visit. They finally got underway and it was after dark before Ernie got off the train in Belfast. He made his way to Cawnpore Street hesitating at the back door wondering what type of reception he would get. He gave the door a light knock with his knuckles and was rewarded by his mother opening the door, her inquisitive expression changing to pure joy when she realised who was knocking the door.

"Och Ernie, so good to see ya son, come in, come in."

She shouted back to the front room,

"Mamie, Eddie, it's our Ernie."

Mary-Jane escorted her youngest son into the front room where Mamie and Eddie sat by the wireless, listening to music. Mamie was nursing her three-month-old baby, Gerard, and smiled her welcome to her brother while Eddie jumped up and shook Ernie's hand. Mary-Jane fussed around making food for Ernie and tea for everyone. Ernie was glad of the welcome but also aware that Susannah was not there. After eating his fill and regaling them with stories of his travels around the new Free State, the subject of Charlie came up.

"Why is he in Annalong Ma? I got a letter from him and he said he had argued with Susie, but he didn't say what about."

Mary-Jane took a second to compose herself and then chose her words carefully to her youngest child.

"Ernie, when Charlie got out he decided to go and live in Annalong. Your grandparents are getting on and they need help on the land, Jimmy needs minding too so Charlie decided he would stay for a while."

Ernie looked at his mother thoughtfully,

"What are you not telling me Ma?"

but before Mary-Jane could answer they all heard the back door open and close and Susannah call out.

"Only me," as she walked into the front room shaking her hair out of her headscarf, stopping abruptly when she saw Ernie sitting there.

"What are you doing here?" Susannah's voice rose an octave, "Don't you think you have done enough harm to this family?"

Everyone froze, uncertain what to say or do. Mary-Jane turned to her daughter imploring her,

"Susie, please, Ernie just wants to visit, to see his nephew, to see me."

Susannah continued to stand ramrod straight with her head held high defiantly, "You don't deserve to be part of this family Ernie, it's because of you that Da is dead. You are not wanted here."

Ernie was stunned, he could not believe his sister was saying that to him,

"what on earth are you on about Susie," and he took a step towards her. Susannah put out her hand to stop him,

"Don't you even speak to me Ernie McMullen, I never want to see you or that other traitor Charlie ever again. It was your fault Da was shot, you might as well have pulled the trigger yourselves. It was one of ye that mob wanted, not Da, it is all your fault, that Da is dead, that we have no home, your fault,"

Susannah's voice continued to rise louder and louder until she was shouting at Ernie.

"Now you get out of this house and never come back."

Mary-Jane started to protest but Ernie stood, putting his hand up to his mother,

"Ma, it's okay, I don't want any trouble."

Mary-Jane wrung her hands,

"But where will you go Ernie, it's late, where will you stay?"

Ernie assured her that he had friends he could stay with despite the late hour, so Mary-Jane reluctantly let him leave making him promise that he would come back the next morning after Susannah went to work.

Susannah waited until he left, "Ma, how can you stand to look at him, or Charlie, those two are the reason Da was shot."

Mary-Jane looked tiredly at her daughter,

"Susie, I have told you before, your Da was shot because of all of us, he died because he was a Protestant who married a Catholic, who had Catholic children, he died because of Carson and Craig..."

she got no further as Susannah stomped out of the room crying,

"Stop it, stop it,"

and ran up the stairs to the bedroom she shared with her mother. Mary-Jane shook her head wearily sitting down heavily in her chair. The shouting had woken baby Gerard and he started to cry startled out of his peaceful slumber. Mamie rocked him gently and put him back to sleep while Eddie picked up the cups and plates and carried them through to the scullery, his back ramrod straight and his shoulders tensed. He leaned over the sink, troubled by what had occurred, worried about the effect on his wife and child, worried about his mother-in-law who was only starting to get on with her life and worried about Susannah who was becoming increasingly bitter.

The next morning Ernie knocked on the back door shortly after 9 am. He had watched from the end of the road and had seen Susannah leaving some ten minutes earlier. Mary-Jane welcomed him in and put a hearty breakfast in front of him within minutes. Ernie had decided the night before that he wouldn't bring any more trouble into Eddie's home.

"Ma, I have to go and see Charlie, I haven't seen him since he was arrested, and I want to see granny and grandad, so I am going to head to Annalong and plan what I am going to from there."

Mary-Jane nodded her understanding. She tried to explain away Susannah's outburst and Ernie listened to her but disagreed.

"Ma, Susie should not go on like that, it's not fair on you and it's not fair on Mamie and Eddie. She is living under their roof and if Mamie and Eddie have no problem with me then that should be enough for Susie."

Mamie looked up from where she was sorting out baby clothes,

"Ernie, Susie isn't usually like that, she just can't seem to help herself when you or Charlie appear on the scene."

Ernie looked at his sister's face, concern etched on it,

"Ever the peacemaker, Mamie,"

Ernie smiled at Mamie trying to lighten her concern and change the mood of the room. Mamie lifted her son and put him in Ernie's arms.

"Och he is a fine child, Mamie, you have a good man there and a fine home, don't let anyone spoil it for you."

Ernie left shortly afterwards with a bag of scones and preserves for his journey and the warmth of his mother and sister's goodbyes ringing in his ears.

The house in Annalong was exactly as he remembered it from his last visit which was over two years previous, but his grandparents were not. They had both aged considerably and he was quite shocked when he saw them at first. Grandad appeared to have shrunk, he had always remembered him as a large imposing man but now he towered over his slight, bent frame and what little hair he had left was pure silver.

Granny was just a smaller version of herself but still as feisty as she had always been. Charlie heard his approach first and walked out to the top of the laneway to see who was approaching. When he recognised Ernie, he let out a whoop of delight and ran to meet his brother.

"What about ya, Ernie, the army sure agreed with you, you've filled out, must have been feeding ya right at least."

Charlie led his brother up the garden path shouting out to his grandparents as he walked. James and Mary O'Brien were delighted to see Ernie, still in his uniform he looked handsome and fit and both fussed over him, helping him remove his overcoat and hanging up his cap.

"Granny is just dishing out the dinner, your timing is perfect,"

said Charlie with a smile for his baby brother. They all sat to dinner, eating and talking until well into the night. Ernie slept better that night than he had in years and awoke the next morning feeling refreshed and relaxed. He heard a noise outside and looked out to see Jimmy and Charlie chatting as they worked in the back field. Ernie jumped out of bed and went out to give them a hand. He settled into the routine quickly and was happy to do so. He was surprised at how frail his grandparents had become and realised that they would not be able to cope if Charlie hadn't arrived to help Jimmy. Jimmy did what he could, but he was getting older as well and ageing rapidly.

Charlie and Ernie sat that night over a smoke in the rose garden after their grandparents had retired for the night.

"Jeez Charlie, it's just as well you came here to stay. How were they coping before you arrived?" Ernie quizzed his brother.

Charlie explained how their cousins had been helping out when they could but that was only one day a week and the vegetable plot had suffered. Jimmy could manage the chickens and the sheep, but the dairy cows had been sold off two years ago. Charlie had only been there five months, but he had the place nearly ready for the planting season early next year and had only finished planting the winter vegetables the day before Ernie had arrived. The two brothers worked hard, and their grandparents appreciated the help. Jimmy loved having them there, enjoying the male companionship and so appreciative of their help.

CHAPTER 52   SORROW AT CHRISTMAS

The Christmas of 1923 was Mary-Jane's second Christmas without her beloved Charlie and her first Christmas as a grandmother. She travelled to Annalong to spend Christmas with her parents along with Mamie and Eddie and their baby Gerard. James and Maria were staying in Belfast for Christmas. Their marriage had still not produced any children and Mary-Jane felt their pain although Maria said nothing. Mary-Jane had encouraged them to get a dog knowing from her childhood in Annalong how much love and attention a dog takes and how much love and attention Maria had to give.   They were besotted with their chocolate brown Labrador. He was named Rex and was a lovable character with boundless energy and a penchant for eating shoes. They couldn't bring Rex to Annalong so opted to stay home, which gave Susannah the perfect excuse for staying home too.

"Ah Ma, sure if I go then James and Maria will have no one for Christmas. It wouldn't be fair on him, Ma, and anyway I don't want to stay under the same roof as those other two," Susannah reasoned to her mother.

Mary-Jane reacted sharply,

"Susie I will not tolerate you speaking about your brothers like that, you have to stop this, it has gone on for too long."

But Susannah just walked out of the room, head held high, and ignored her mother's calls for her to come back. The boys appeared quite happy when Susannah didn't arrive to Annalong with the rest of the family, although they didn't say so to their mother. Mary-Jane was tired from the journey but shocked into action when she saw how old and tired her parents were. She immediately took over the kitchen, persuading her mother to sit with her great-grandchild while she made dinner and prepared for the Christmas day feast. She had brought presents of whiskey and tobacco for her father and some pretty lace and wool for her mother. Her mother spent the rest of the evening knitting a cardigan for baby Gerard and Mary-Jane noticed how much slower she was. Her needles used to clatter along like a steam train now barely clicking as she sat chatting to Mamie and cooing over the baby.

They rose early the next morning as was their usual custom to get an early mass before breakfast. Mary-Jane was dressed and ready and wondering what was keeping her parents when she heard a cry from their bedroom. She ran to the room getting there seconds after Ernie who had also heard his Grandfather cry out. Ernie burst open the door and stopped abruptly. James O'Brien was sitting on the side of the bed in his long johns holding his wife's hand in his. Mary O'Brien was dead, she had died in her sleep by her husband's side. Mary-Jane went to her father while Ernie checked his Grandmother. He shook his head at wee Charlie who stood in the doorway, with Jimmy peering over his shoulder.

"What is it, what's wrong Da?"

Charlie turned and put his arms around Jimmy.

"Jimmy, it's your Ma, she's gone,"

a sob escaped Charlie as he looked back into the room. Mary-Jane held her father as he wept, while Charlie held Jimmy. It broke wee Charlie's heart to tell Jimmy that his mother was dead. Poor Jimmy understood what wee Charlie was saying and the rest of the family took comfort from him.

"Mam was gone to heaven to look after Will and when my time is up, Mam and Will are going to have my home ready," Jimmy told them.

The rest of the day passed by in a blur, the priest was called, relatives were notified, and the neighbourhood sprang into action. Susannah, James and Maria arrived just after the neighbouring women laid out Mary's body in the front room of the cottage. All curtains were closed, and mirrors covered, and Mary lay in her best dress with her rosary around her cold fingers. Friends and neighbours filed by paying their respects and bringing food for the immediate family. Musicians arrived, and music was played, and stories were told.

Susannah, James and Maria stood apart from the family keeping their own counsel. When wee Charlie or Ernie walked into a room Susannah walked out, never rudely, always making an excuse that she had something to see to in the kitchen or someone she needed to speak to in the garden. Mary-Jane noticed how her children were behaving but said nothing, too wrapped up in her own sorrow in losing her husband and her mother within two years of each other. She was just about to go into the kitchen to fetch more cups when she overheard Mamie speaking to Susannah and stopped, partially hidden by the open door.

"Susie, stop it, granny's death is enough for Ma to be coping with without you holding grudges against your brothers, have a bit of respect."

"I beg your pardon." Mary-Jane saw the look of surprise on Susannah's face. Mamie was always the peacemaker and had never reprimanded anyone before, or at least not as far as Mary-Jane knew. She sensed Eddie at her side. He had witnessed the exchange and couldn't help the half smile that escaped him as he whispered to Mary-Jane.

"About time someone took that one down a peg or two, never thought it would be my Mamie though."

Mary-Jane smiled at her son-in-law and allowed him to lead her back into the front room. She had no worries about Mamie for Eddie loved his wife and would do anything for her. Mary-Jane knew that Eddie had been completely sincere when he told Mary-Jane that she was welcome to stay with them for good. She wasn't so sure about Susannah though. Eddie may put up with her for Mamie's sake, but Susannah was just too opinionated for Eddie's liking. Mary-Jane could see that and realised she was going to have to have a serious conversation with Susannah about her brothers. Eddie was fond of wee Charlie and Ernie, they had always been friends and he made them welcome in his home. Susannah had no right to throw them out of Eddie's or her grandparent's home. Susannah was becoming more intransigent and arrogant and Mary-Jane didn't like it.

James O'Brien held up well at the funeral but the day after he sunk into a deep depression. Mary-Jane and her sisters held a family conference and it was decided that, providing it was agreeable to wee Charlie and Ernie, that they should stay at least until the summer when the girls would meet again and reassess the situation. Wee Charlie and Ernie were delighted to stay and promised to keep a close eye on their Grandad and on Jimmy.

Mary-Jane headed back to Belfast along with the rest of the family.

"Christmas day will never be the same again,"

she told Mamie as she laid her head against the train window oblivious to the scenery as they sped through the countryside on their way back to the city. Susannah spoke to no one on the journey home. She sat deep in thought, her head held high, occasionally flashing disparaging looks at her sister Mamie. Mamie was oblivious to her sister's black looks as she sat opposite her mother at the window, nursing her baby son and smiling gently as he nestled into her. Eddie sat watching his wife and son, a smile on his gentle face.

Mary-Jane looked out at the dark and dreary day. The sky was low and full of rain, cold rain with patches of sleet that soaked through your hat and scarf and bit into your skin. Mary-Jane was glad to get back, she never thought of Eddie's house as home, it was always Eddie's house. She reminisced about her home in Sherwood Street, "no doubt given out to some loyal Protestant family at this stage," she silently fumed. Mary-Jane often daydreamed about going back, just to see if any of her old neighbours would speak to her, but she couldn't, she couldn't face seeing where her beloved Charlie had been shot that fateful day.

The new year brought no more surprises. Mary-Jane lived a quiet life helping her daughter with her only grandchild. James and Maria spent their time walking their dog Rex, James was unable to find work, but he had his invalidity pension which provided a modest living for them. Mary-Jane called to visit them twice a week. Maria was always pleasant, and the house was always spotlessly clean and a credit to her.

Baby Gerard was walking by the summer and Mary-Jane loved going to the park with her daughter and the baby, letting him walk on the grass, letting the feel of the grass tickle his toes, twirling a buttercup under his chin and making daisy chains. Those days were the best or, so Mary-Jane felt. She still met up with Alice at least once a week and two women enjoyed their weekly catch ups. Alice was still living in Sherwood Street and Mary-Jane couldn't resist asking if anyone had moved into her old home.

"Aye, Mary-Jane, a large family of eight, all boys, good help the poor woman, they moved up from the country when he got a job in the engineering plant, do you know the one near where my Willy works."

Mary-Jane wanted to ask if the family had been told about her beloved Charlie, but she couldn't bring herself to ask the question.

Alice continued, "Ellen, is her name, Ellen said to me that beggars can't be choosers and her with eight mouths to feed had to take what was on offer or live on the streets, so they took number 23 and there they stay."

Mary-Jane decided she didn't want to know any more. She had loved her home when her family had lived there but Charlie had died there, and she could never go back. Although even if she had wanted to, she couldn't have, because they had been told, in no uncertain terms, that they were not welcome back in that street. She was lucky her son-in-law had such a generous nature, or she would have found herself homeless.

CHAPTER 53 SUSANNAH SAILS ON THE BALTIC

Susannah was delighted to wave goodbye to Mary-Jane, Mamie and Eddie at Easter. They were staying for a week and she had the house to herself.

"Charlie and Ernie have settled in well in Annalong. They are enjoying helping your grandad and it seems Jimmy imitates everything they do. He idolises them," Mary-Jane had told her.

"You need to nip that in the bud, Mam. Idolising those two."

"That's enough Susannah, just stop." Mary-Jane's tone was sharp.

Susannah knew she was annoying her mother, but she couldn't help herself. She couldn't forgive her brothers. As far as she was concerned they were responsible for their father's death and she just couldn't put that behind her. She knew she had become bitter and nasty, even to Mamie but she just couldn't help herself. Mamie had asked her to go with them.

"It will be fun Susie. We are going to bring the baby to the beach. Let him feel the sand on his toes. I can't wait to see his reaction to the waves."

"I will never set foot in that house while those two are there, Mamie."

She knew Mamie had been disappointed, but she hadn't meant to hurt her either. She tried to placate her sister,

"Anyway, I have to work, I just can't get time off at the moment and then there's Billy. I don't want to be apart from Billy."

She had met Billy Shiels a few months back at a church social. He had been reluctantly escorting his sister while Susannah had been keeping her friend Jean company. They had hit it off straight away. Billy had been in the British army the same time as James and had returned to Belfast unscathed at the end of the war. He had been working in the shipyard but lost his job the year of the riots when he was ousted out of the yard by unionists along with over seven thousand others and had not been able to find steady work since. Susannah was still working but the initial thrill of the position had dulled somewhat when she discovered that every decision she made on stocking the ladies' department had to be agreed in writing with the male manager before she could proceed. She felt she was being held back and supervised unnecessarily. She had said as much to Billy who was enamoured by his feisty girlfriend who was so sure of herself and her place in the world.

Billy had family who had emigrated to America before the great war and were prospering, working in an engineering plant in Detroit. Billy thought it all sounded rather exciting and was actively researching what he needed to do to get an American visa. Billy was seriously disillusioned with Ireland. He had joined the Irish Volunteers the same time as James and had signed up with the British army at the start of the great war in answer to Redmond's call in support of Home Rule for Ireland. He was a welder by trade and had no trouble finding work when he returned to Belfast but less than two years later he had been run out of the shipyard under threat by a maundering group of unionists, many whom had never served in the British army but were firing missiles at him calling him a traitor. Now he found that instead of the Ireland under Home Rule he had gone to Europe to fight for, his country had been divided with the north west of the country remaining under British rule and the rest of the country declared a Free State. The last few years of violence had left their mark on Billy and others like him. They were living in a state which had no respect for them and treated every Catholic as a terrorist no matter what their background.

"I tell ya Susie, I have had enough, no work and no prospect of it. I am going to head to America, I can make a new life there."

Billy showed Susannah the letter he had received from his cousin. The plant he was working in was crying out for quality welders and he had written to Billy asking him to apply for a job, offering to put him up until he got settled.

"You should come with me Susie, I know its early days for us but ya know I love ya, we could travel to America and build us a good future there."

Susannah thought long and hard about it. She was unhappy living with Mamie and Eddie. Ever since the time Mamie had turned on her at their granny O'Briens funeral, Susannah had a different opinion of Mamie. She had always been so close to her sister and was upset that Mamie should even consider having any sort of communication with Charlie and Ernie when she knew how Susannah felt about them. She had said as much to James and Maria on one of her frequent visits, hoping for understanding from them. While both James and Maria sympathised with her they did not offer her the spare room in their house. Even though Susannah had not asked them outright if she could move in, she felt rejected that they did not offer her a home.

She voiced her feelings to her mother,

"Och Susie, James is different to Eddie, it would never occur to him to offer you a room and to be honest I don't think he would say yes if you asked him. Don't blame him for that, that is just the way he is."

Susannah was even more upset to think that her brother would refuse her a roof over her head. Susannah told her mother about Billy's plan to go to America and that she was considering going with him. Mary-Jane was quite shocked. She had met Billy and liked him, but she considered him asking Susannah to accompany him to America was disgraceful behaviour.

"And as for you even considering going with him without him even asking you to marry him is just so wrong, whatever would your granny have thought."

Susannah argued with her mother,

"but Ma, Billy wants to marry me, I just don't know if I am ready to marry him." She knew she cared deeply about him, but Martin was still in her thoughts and she wondered if she could ever love anyone fully again. Billy had known Martin and he and Susannah had talked about him at length, so he understood, and was willing to wait for her, confident that she would come to love him as much as he loved her. He did not put any pressure on her and Susannah appreciated that.

Mary-Jane had sat down wearily in her fireside chair,

"What on earth is going on with you, you won't speak to your younger brothers, you barely speak to Mamie or Eddie, you argue with James and now you want to run away from us all, with a man you barely know, to a country which is so far away we will never see you again. Susie, please, what about your job, your family."

Mary-Jane felt tears spring to her eyes as she contemplated her life without her Susie and fear gripped her, making her nauseous,

"Susie, you can't go, it is just too far away."

Susannah wrestled with her decision for weeks, one day afraid she was making the biggest mistake of her life if she went with Billy, the next day afraid she was making the biggest mistake of her life if she didn't go. Billy's mother was of the same opinion as Mary-Jane, that if Billy and Susannah were going together to America that they should marry first and told Billy as much. Billy came up with a solution that suited both mothers. It was his mother's family that Billy was going out to, his mother's sister Molly and her husband. Billy wrote to her telling her the dilemma he was in. Molly wrote back inviting Susannah to stay with her and her husband while Billy could stay with her son Brendan and his wife. Both mothers were happier with those arrangements and Susannah finally made her decision, applying for her visa to travel on the ship "The Baltic" which was sailing from Belfast the following May. They would sail to Eilis Island in New York and from there they would travel by rail to Detroit.

Susannah applied for a position in a large department store in Detroit and within weeks had been offered a position as an assistant buyer in the ladies' department. Susannah read her job offer with delight, things were certainly starting to look up and she couldn't wait to make a fresh start. Billy was also looking forward to their new life in America and asked Susannah once again to make him the happiest man alive and marry him, but Susannah declined yet again but with less conviction giving Billy confidence that the next time he asked she would say yes. Susannah was looking forward to her new adventure. She stared down at the piece of paper, her visa, her passport to a new life. Two more weeks until the SS Baltic sailed out of

Belfast Harbour bound for New York. Her and Billy starting a new life together in the United States of America. She hugged herself.

Mary-Jane helped her daughter pack her belongings. Billy had persuaded her that Susannah would do well in America and Susannah was really looking forward to it, to the new opportunity afforded her.

"Ma, when I get settled I will write to you and you never know, when I get some money together I will send for you and you can come and find your fortune in the brave new world."

Susannah chatted as they squeezed Susannah's considerable wardrobe into two large suitcases. James, Maria and Mamie were escorting Susannah to the port along with Mary-Jane and they set off in good time arriving at the port with an hour to spare. Susannah hugged her family one by one and made her way on board. Mary-Jane and her family waited on the quayside watching for Susannah to appear on deck. They met Billy's mother waiting to wave goodbye to Billy. The two mothers nodded at each other, each aware of the others pain at waving goodbye to their child. It was nearly an hour later that they saw Susannah waving at them with Billy by her side. Mary-Jane barely recognised her, she made a handsome figure, a tall, willowy woman in stylish travelling clothes with her fashionable hat tipped to one side of her head and waving her handkerchief, a little square of lace that fluttered in the breeze. Billy was equally fashionably dressed in a handsome suit and trilby hat. They made a handsome couple. They waved until the figures on board were match figures on the horizon before turning for home.

CHAPTER 54   LIFE GOES ON

Mary-Jane was dejected. She kissed her grandchild goodnight when she got into the house and retired upstairs to her room. She got into her nightclothes and climbed into bed, her limbs heavy and her mind racing. She missed her beloved Charlie so much, what would he make of it all. His family scattered, James in Belfast damaged in mind and body, Charlie and Ernie hiding away in Annalong reluctant to come back to Belfast, in reality because they had no home to go to, Susannah on her journey to a foreign land with a man she wasn't married to and probably still holding a torch for a man who had died in a different foreign land so long ago. The only bright spark on the horizon was Mamie, happily married to a lovely man Eddie, with a healthy, happy baby boy, the spit of his mother and a pleasure to them all. Mary-Jane closed her eyes and dreamed of her Charlie, the love of her life and prayed for him to watch down over them all and keep their beloved children safe and happy.

THE END

26371479R00132

Printed in Poland
by Amazon Fulfillment
Poland Sp. z o.o., Wrocław